THE WAILING ANGELS

NENGTHENKIM

INDIA • SINGAPORE • MALAYSIA

ISBN 979-8-88667-580-1

DEDICATION

This book is dedicated to the following three beautiful Souls

1. (L) Lhingkhongah d/o Mr. Semmang Touthang (1973 -1999)

2. (L) Krishan Kumar Sharma s/o Mr. Vidya Dhar Sharma (1988 – 1999)

3. (L) Manoj Kumar s/o Mr. Jagdish Yadav (1979 -1999)

My beloved sister (L) Lhingkhongah died of diabetes on 31st January 1999 at the age of 26. The two innocent boys—Krishan Kumar and Manoj Kumar—were hit by stray bullets in an encounter at Mantop Leikai, Churachandpur on 21st July 1999.

CONTENTS

Contents

FOREWORD

Nengthenkim's book is a deeply emotional work. One chances upon very few literary works in one's entire life that is capable of inducing such a vast sea of emotions in him/her as one traverses through the pages of such an important work. The reader here understands that the book for the writer is a personal journey. Nengthenkim's interpretations of her own world and how the various power hierarchies around her (the colonial history and the role of "mainland" India) engender her own positionality in relation to her own community and different people from "mainland" India is experienced through the characters here as their narratives unfold in the book. The Wailing Angels introduces us to women who take charge of their own narratives. Every woman here has a story and despite all the contradictory conditions that confront them, they derive strength from within themselves.

As religious and indigenous cosmologies get positioned in relation to each other, the characters of this book emerge as people whose experiences are not just shaped by these events but rather people who shape these events back. Nengthenkim's book is indeed a testimony of poetic love, of love that has the power to challenge problematic kin and familial relationships while women here recast power structures, bringing their romantic agencies to the fore. As the newly independent Indian nation comes into existence, people like Esther, Ron, Gloria, Disha, and Jesse too come of age. While falling in love, fighting for their love and protecting their love, these characters rewrite their narratives and come to understand themselves and their subjectivities.

While reading this book I am reminded of Sylvia Wynter's book titled *The hills of Hebron* (1962) where women like Miss Gatha, Rose and Kate navigate the intergenerational trauma of being abused, sexualized and most importantly being denied their own subjectivities by their *own* menfolk. As men in Hebron are seen as possessing the *choice* to be able to leave Hebron and pursue their respective passions and desires, the women here are left behind to clean up the messes created by their menfolk and immerse themselves in a life of enforced motherhood, a life devoid of their own choices. Nonetheless, as Miss Gatha and Kate towards the end of the book come to acknowledge their own positionalities, they reclaim their lives and move towards rewriting their own narratives.

Despite Sylvia Wynter and Nengthenkim writing in completely different and incomparable historical contexts, what is common here is how women themselves come to discover that no matter how difficult the circumstances, no one apart from herself can protect her *own self.* This is evident in how Nengthenkim sketches the character of Dinah and Maria. Women who proclaim that they "are not weak" or women who refuse to be cast as "victims of abuse" by standing up to speak for themselves, once again *rewriting* and *reclaiming* their own narratives. This is a book where women thrive and connive, where women sing, dance, give birth and fight for their rightful share of power but this is also a book where *She* problematizes the family and questions everything around her. Here a woman like Maria surprises everyone else around her, even the men in her own family.

As a woman from the Assamese ethnolinguistic community within the Northeast, the realization that both Nengthenkim and I come from different communities and with differing degrees of privilege has dawned on me.Nonetheless, I also stand alongside Nengthenkim and become inspired by her laborious efforts to pen down her thoughts and share with the world how women from India's peripheral Northeast write their own love stories. May this be the first of many of her works.

Shivangi Baruah, University of Oxford.

ACKNOWLEDGEMENTS

This book would have been a short story of 7,000 words had not Sir Laishram John Meitei, my English Teacher at Bethany Christian College inspired me in time. I wrote some short stories in vernacular and bagged the title 'Super in Literal' in one District-level short story writing competition. I had never dreamt of writing more than 10,000 words. So this book would not have seen the light of the day had not Sir John encouraged me to dream bigger.

I am always grateful to my beloved parents (L) Mr. Semmang Touthang, Hindi Teacher, at Gandhi Memorial High School and (L) Domnem Touthang who had inspired me to write songs and poems from my childhood days. Both of them were good songwriters. My father had been writing all his life but had published only a few books. I had seen that many of his old manuscripts remained unpublished. I used to write at night as long as my father wrote in the next room. He is my role model to sit the whole day writing, an inspiration to sit the long nights writing in solitude. I thank God for giving me good parents, supportive siblings and friends and above all, His blessings for this piece of writing to have materialised.

My special thanks to Mr. Paokholen Hangmi, Income Tax Officer, Hyderabad, who during the 2000s, was an Assistant Teacher in Gandhi Memorial High school, Molnom. He went through every line of my first handwritten manuscript. He corrected grammatical mistakes, suggested word choices and encouraged me a lot. I am thankful to Sri Mangcha Touthang, Assistant Professor, Martin Luther Christian University, Shillong who in 2002 served as a Teacher in Soikholal Ideal High School, Tuibong. He not only went through the lines to proofread my second handwritten manuscript but also gave valuable suggestions to improve the story. I can never repay the debt, only acknowledge it.

I am grateful to my husband Dr. D. Letkhojam Haokip, Asst. Professor, Gauhati University on whose advice I finished my MA in English Literature just to improve my writing skills. He is also a great writer who has been my constant support.

I am thankful to Shivangi Baruah, a scholar from Oxford University for taking her valuable time going through all the details of the book and writing the Foreword. I am grateful to Zamminlun Singson for helping me with the sketches of some pictures. I wish him success in his Studio of Zamminlun Singson Art and Painting.

Last but not the least, this book would not have been possible without Miss Suchitra Shekhar, Publishing Manager, Mr. Vishal Menon, Publishing Consultant and the editing teams of Notion Press Publishing, who, by agreeing to print and publish it, made many corrections and suggestions thereby improving the flow of language which I had written in my own capacity.

—Nengthenkim

PREFACE

This piece of writing came into my mind as a result of an unfortunate incident that happened in my hometown way back in 1999. I had just entered a new stage of my life at Bethany Christian College, Churachandpur, Manipur. That year, I was questioned by some unknown voices every day after the unfortunate incident in which an eleven-year-old boy named Krishan Kumar Sharma along with his neighbour Manoj Kumar, was killed by stray bullets in an encounter. The terrorists ambushed the CRPF convoy at Mantop Leikai, Churachandpur, at around 9 a.m. The gunfire, which happened for about an hour, claimed the lives of many, including the two innocent boys in a school uniform. Some bullets also injured Krishan Kumar's mother and sister.

An innocent soul lost, the only hope of the family. It hurts me when I consider myself in their position. Where will the boy's spirit go? How will God judge human beings? The Angels will be wailing for the innocent souls. One night, unable to ignore the persistent nagging, I scribbled a few lines about the Angels, how, why and where they will weep. Thus, the title "The Wailing Angels" came out, and it guided me on my journey to the unknown world with the Angels by my side till I completed the story.

I prepared for my exams while busy with other affairs. I also wrote poems from time to time. I got married, had two boys, and continued my studies. I typed the novel on my computer and decided to publish it. I had my third child, again, busy with family matters as a mother. My computer crashed and I had to retype all the lines, some paragraphs missing, and some lines were newly added and modified. I lost my typed manuscript when my computer crashed again. After five years, in 2021, I recovered them from my email in bits and pieces and started afresh.

INTRODUCTION

The Wailing Angels is an intergenerational historical novel set against the backdrop of North East India during the British colonial war. The village Broadvale, established in 1850, was one of the oldest and biggest of the time. The role of the tribals of Northeast India in the freedom movement, their struggle against the western culture and religion are the main issues of conflict in the story.

The story begins with Ron and Esther, who were lovers since their childhood. Ron's father, Daadi was the chief of Broadvale. Esther's father was a pastor working under the British Christian Missionaries. Daadi had tortured and burnt alive Esther's parents. Daadi also killed many early Christian missionaries including the British. Esther was the only daughter of Pastor Gina. She had five brothers who were dead against their relationship. So the duo eloped in 1943 and settled in a far away place called Sinai.

Ron and Esther were called back after India got Independence. Benjamin and his brothers forcibly took Esther to Israel in 1950. In 1953, Ron went to Israel but sadly returned to India after meeting Esther with her new husband. Esther died in the same week when Ron left Israel.

Benjamin went to Broadvale to fulfil the obsequies of Esther. He reconciled with the Broadvale family somehow. Ron remarried in 1957 and begot three sons from his second wife, Disha. His eldest son, Jesse suffered a lot when his father became handicapped. Ron was retired from the Indian Army after the Indo-Pak War in 1966.

Disha had an extramarital affair with a man named Doon. They had a daughter named Maria. Maria was raped at the age of 13. She left home and spent her years in the nunnery with Catholic Sisters.

Jesse married a girl Dinah from the Khasi tribe in 1970. Disha hated Jesse and Dinah. On the day Maria was raped, there was a terrible fight in the royal house. Jesse would have been killed by his stepbrothers had not his trusted friends rescued him in time. Jesse and Dinah left Broadvale and settled in Sunray village with their only son Levi.

The gifted child, Levi grew up in Sunray. He was obedient, good looking and a brilliant boy. He was awaiting the result of his B.Sc. Exam. He was killed by stray bullets in an encounter in his hometown. His spirit is guided by the Angels. The theme of the story is about the life after the death of Levi, how and where his spirit encountered the wailing Angels. The Wailing Angels reincarnated the spirit of Levi in 1997, two years after his death.

CHAPTER – 1

1942 – A MEMORABLE YEAR

There stood a pillar number 143, the tallest of the entire boundary post, quite attractive and the courting place for dozens of young soul mates. It was the same for Ron and Esther whose souls were true mates, made for each other. The pillar was leaning against the adjacent branch of a eucalyptus tree beside the main road of the old village school near Gaitlane, the town that was recently torn down by the British Indian soldiers. Esther sat on a log smoothened and tidied like a feather by dozens of butts all-day long, in the corner of the campus with her back to a fenced area of green grasses, harvested chilly plants and ginger garden, poorly maintained by the school caretaker. The golden lips of the Sun had just kissed the horizon: Cool, lively breeze blew gently cuddling, then more excitedly playing with the loose silky hair on Esther's head as if going crazy to see a maiden in her youthful age, perky breast and full lips sitting alone at that unusual time. The place looked empty although a few last-trip pedestrians were passing by that way returning from the field after a daylong work. Esther's imagination pictured various things, mostly about her family and felt sad to go far away from them. There was no certainty if she would ever come back the way she was before; everything is temporary in this world and she decided to flow with the time and enjoy life with her love by nature's will. Everything had changed, people had changed and the world had changed for her the moment she touched her belly and felt the fruit of love growing inside her womb. Very soon she heard the Church bell ringing and became panicky when it was dusk. She looked around to check if anyone noticed her. She then moved a little to the pillar to hide in case the British Indian soldiers on patrolling happened to pass by before her lover arrived to take her. The wind became livelier and played with the log of hair on both sides of her rosy cheeks. She knew from the music of the wind that her soul mate was coming nearer, his soul thinking about her. She closed her eyes, smiled and took a repeated deep breath. She enjoyed the fun playing with the wind, which was carefree like her: again, indulging in her carefree way as ever, drunk with the wine of her youth, the naughty mind not caring what other people would think about her.

That was the year 1942, a memorable year, a moment to remember for the lovers. Ron was 16 while Esther was 15 summers. In that year, they had promised to fulfil their love no matter what came in their way. They promised in that ever-courting place and wrote their names on the pillar 143. In fact, women are quite more thoughtful than men when it comes to making a promise or taking responsibilities. Esther recollected her days the lovers spent their time filling their lungs with a deep laugh, their popularity, laughing off the rumours created about them. They had been used to it that way from their childhood, had hardened their minds, thickened their skin, saying no sorry to the game of love. Too early the confidence with which they dared to explore the forbidden things until they felt the great wind of change shattering their dreams, blowing their spirits open. They had to take the risk of their sin too early, their love no longer was a child's play, they could not run away from it as the devil in society kept an eye on them; moreover, it was a decision between life and death for Esther while now or never for Ron. They started life too early, yet had to live a dead life with no worries, no future, and no second thought but only love and romance. Ron used to call her *Pinky* while she called him *Redy*. The reason behind being Esther, a feminine naughty girl who got scared to depict her promise with her blood and used a pink colour ink, the day they had the unrecognized betrothal, the unaccepted commitment yet selfless sacrifice and unfathomable love. Besides opposition from both their families, society condemned the unlawful acts they committed at school. Amid all these adversaries, their love blinded their vision and they indulged in playing the game of fire, loved the pleasure of losing innocence without any regrets. Esther smiled when she remembered those lovely moments the lovers spent sitting near a bonfire on cold winter days. The amber was as hot and bright as their minds while the night just passed as they talked about their dreams. Esther was bewildered by the time it became dark. She spoke to herself saying, *"My God, has Ron forgotten the dating, what shall I do if he does not turn up or has he known my secret?"* Sitting in the dark alone, she soon became busy with the flies and mosquitoes who also liked to join with the wind in teasing the young lady sitting alone there at the wrong time. The pale moonlight gave her little comfort, she looked at the Moon and said, *"Oh silvery crescent queen of the night, have you seen my beloved Ron? Oh! How will you see with one eye closed and half of your face veiled?"* She looked at the front then the back gate of the school campus; there was complete silence except for the croaking of frogs in the nearby pond. *"Oh, he has to come all the way from Broadvale,"* she was saying as her love for Ron never dwindled. She hesitated to retreat and go back home. She rested her head on the canvas bag on her lap and slowly wiped her face with her handkerchief. She took out a piece of the smoked beef piece from the bag and smelt it once. She smacked her lips and started chewing the meat little by little to ward off boredom. She said to herself, *"I will enjoy my time: it's my rule never to waste it."* She closed her eyes to fully enjoy the taste of the smoked meat. When she opened her eyes, she saw two men like a shadow carrying something resembling a bag. They hurried towards pillar 143. One man spoke up, *"Okay pal, take my torchlight too and have a safe journey."*

Esther looked more closely, blinking her eyes when saw the man hurry back as if he had an urgent appointment at the same time. When the man crossed the front gate which was about 50 metres from pillar 143, he turned back and waved his hands. He mounted his horse soon disappeared from their sight.

"*Who is he, why is he in such a hurry? Oh, Ron, I have been waiting for you, you take a long time, you know how I feel,*" Esther said hugging her sweetheart, rubbing her soft cheeks with his rough chin. Ron hugged her, kissed her forehead, smiled and smell her neck, her hair, then to her lips saying, "*I love you. I made you wait so long; I am sorry.*" Esther sweetly moaned and gently pushed him back saying, "*Let's not waste a second; what if my brothers come to know of it; I locked the door inside and escaped through the back window. Let's move out of here. The soldiers may come for patrolling; where is the chariot?*" Ron held her hand and they went towards the back gate where Ron's friend waited with a chariot. They boarded the chariot and very soon they disappeared towards the Zumbo forest. Zumbo forest was famous for wild animals like elephants and leopards. Ron fired his gun now and then when they suspected any danger. They travelled throughout the night on the rugged road under the pale moonlight. They crossed the Zumbo forest at midday. They had their tiffin pack of maize, meat, bread and wine. The three made plans as to which direction would be the safest. If they followed the roads, they might end up in the hands of the British Indian soldiers, who during those times, forcibly recruited young men as soldiers or slaves to carry heavy loads.

They decided to follow the river Tuivai. They all took bath in the Tuivai River. The river was rich in water animals. One could easily catch fishes as big as a jackfruit. In the afternoon, Ron separated the ropes binding the three horses of the chariot. He gave the oldest to his friend for his return journey. The three friends hugged each other as they parted in the opposite directions. Ron and Esther travelled during the day and rested at night following the Tuivai River.

Ron and Esther were overjoyed in their new world of happiness like a bird freed from the cage: They enjoyed life like a bird that soars high up the sky, flying freely in the air not bothered by anything. They ate, sang, danced and made love all-day and all-night long. They had always dreamt of living far away from the rules of their families. They had been fed up with the rules of life and the laws of society. They had always dreamt of a place where no one would disturb them. They both loved adventure and sport; so, for the young lovers, the whole week was spent like climbing a stairway to heaven. They reached a beautiful place near a hillock after five days of their lively journey. The beauty of the place was breathtaking with waterfalls on the next hills, the enchanting beautiful scenery of blue hills and green meadows. The sounds of cattle braying and the sweet lovely songs of the cuckoo caught their mind. They reported their arrival to the village chief by presenting him with the best wine and a shawl. The villagers welcomed the newly-wed couple after they did all the formalities, like the usual interrogation of an intruder into their territory. Ron and Esther also gave some silver coins to the chief of Sinai. However, they did not disclose their true identity to them. The villagers arranged the hall to celebrate their wedding after the village priest declare no objection. They built a small temporary house for them. They donated a few earthen pots and utensils for them. The couple enjoyed the love and affection of the people in that village. Ron would go out daily with the village men for hunting and fishing. Whenever Esther was alone, she remembered her brothers and felt sorry for leaving them that way. Esther used to do household chores and never stepped out of her house till her delivery. The village girls were all crazy about Ron who was friendly with all of them. Esther worried if her brothers would come and take her back. She also worried about why they did not come to take her back. She again worried if Ron would come to know the secret of their family's enmity. She loved Ron very much and did not want to tell him the truth but also felt guilty for not revealing the truth about her identity. She had loved him since her childhood so much so that she didn't possess anything untouched by Ron. They shared all their sorrows and happiness as husband and wife, except for the top secret in the heart of the woman as against the saying "*Women cannot keep a secret.*" That secret gave her sleepless nights in the warm bosom of her eternal love. Esther said to herself, *"When will my families call me back, I am not safe here. When will this dilemma end? Is this written along the lines of my destiny or am I on the wrong path in life? Will the dilemma never end?"*

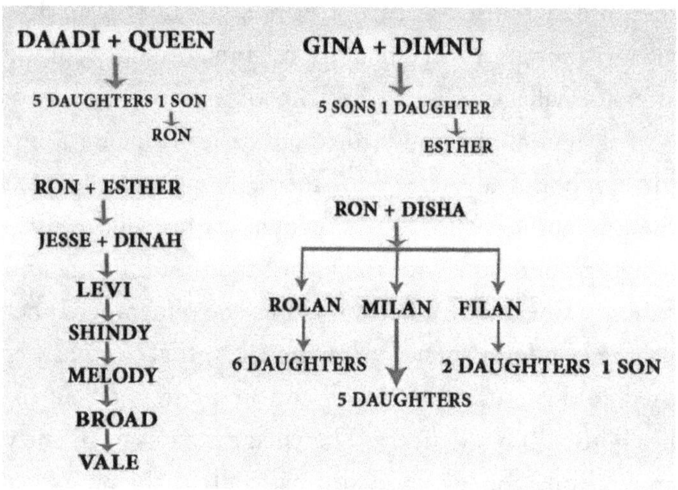

CHAPTER – 2

THE NEVER-ENDING DILEMMA

Ron was the only son of the Broadvale chief called Daadi. He was popularly known as Daadi—The Great, by people for his bravery. Daadi was a powerful and wicked chief whom even the British respected for his power. The British made many attempts to capture him but they could not capture or conquer his territory. He was well-trained in martial arts and black magic and was well-known for his super magical powers. He had bodyguards: a strong army ever ready to fight with any intruder into his territory. He had scars all over his body which made him look like a hollow man. He had killed a tiger single-handed. He survived an attack from many wild animals. People called him the *immortal man*. He had killed many wild animals, celebrated his achievement with great pomp and show several times. He was the leader among the tribes of the southern part of the state who plundered the British when they tried to rule over them. He had five daughters and a son. Ron, his only son, was the fourth child. He was brave, handsome, had a well-built body like his father.

Esther was a beautiful teenager, living with her five brothers at Gaitlane. She was the youngest of the siblings. Her boyfriend, Ron, compared her beauty to the beautiful princess of Panchala—*Draupadi or Panchali,* the wife of the *Pandavas* in the Hindu epic, the Mahabharata, because of her dark, glossy skin and her silky, lustrous hair reaching up to her ankles. She was the only daughter of Pastor Ginna. Her parents were burnt alive at Broadvale when she was barely one and half years old. Her brother Benjamin and Tintin worked in the Church, while the younger siblings were given free education in a Mission School fully sponsored by the British Christian Missionaries. Benjamin was given his father's job. He served in the City Christian Church as Pastor while his brother Tintin assisted the priests in the village Church at Gaitlane.

Ron and Esther studied together in the same Mission School in the city. They both stayed in the boarding run by the British Christian Missionaries. They become best friends and fell in love with each other since their childhood. As they grew up, people began to doubt their friendship. When Esther was a little girl, everyone loved her due to her bad luck in losing her parents untimely, before she even recognized their loving faces. Now that she was grown up with everyone favouring her, she became a spoilt and wild child. The childhood friendship had lost its innocence too soon; they discovered the bliss too early and very soon the love affair between Ron and Esther took a wrong turn even before they learnt the definition of what love is. Both of them were suspended from the school as well as from the boarding when they were caught red-handed in the sinful act. There were lots of mockery and Esther was blamed thrice as much as Ron. Benjamin gave a strict warning to her that if she ever met Ron again, he would kill both of them. Benjamin was very ashamed of his sister so he confined her in the house. The more she was under control, the more her love became uncontrollable, and the more she became wild. She became pale and sick. She cried day and night longing for her love, Ron. She became frightened when her sickness was doubled up with something that she never dreamt of. The fruit of their friendship, the seed of their love had sprouted inside her. She was on pins and needles as the baby in her grew bigger day by day. Ron too could not live without Esther and wanted to meet her. He knew that his lover was in trouble even though they could not meet each other. He always knew, felt her worried mind. He too felt her sickness, he knew her mood, and he knew her love because they were already one soul in two bodies. He attempted many times to meet his lover, but the religious fanatic brother, Benjamin would not let them meet each other. Ron was warned many times not to meet Esther, and when he did not pay heed to their warning, at last, he got thrashed by Tintin and his friends. Esther could not tell her condition to her brothers. She loved Ron, and she knew he too loved her as much as she did. When she was distanced from her lover, she became as mad as a hornet. She began to find ways to figure out a way to lighten her burden. She experienced a new sickness, lovesickness, a kind of love different from the one she had experienced. She called it the true self of true love that she had never realized earlier. Her love was now too strong to hold back anymore; love became wonderful, it was wrapping with fire in her breath from her heart through her lungs, ran in through her pulse, pushing out the sweetest tears of love in her eyes, running down her cheeks in the wonderland. She said to herself, *"I am sorry, brother Benjamin: I have to break my word. I know you love and care for your sister. I cannot live without Ron. I am defeated in the face of love. Please understand me."* She was tired of waiting for Ron to come and take her out from the wonderland to her dreamland, far away from the tyrannical society, where there were no rules of life. She became restless. She wrote a letter for Ron, in the form of a poem.

How will I escape these four walls?

Prisoner of love, captive of war

In the dark world guarded by demons

Will you not come to me like a Prince?

Will you not be a soldier strong enough?

Break this wall of the enmity of duo foes

How do you think your love will sleep?

Close your eyes then see the look in my eyes

The fruit of our love in me growing

Day by day, don't you ever dream about it?

I cried to the Sun, I ask the Moon

If they could stand still and cover me

Exposed to the light or take my life back

What is love that made me cry today?

No, this is not love mean to be, my love

Love is true, it's wrapping in my breath

Love is beautiful, it's gushing out like a spring

Love is real: it's the fire that burns in me

So painful without the lover yet love is divine

Love is not a sin, love is divine

Come, my love, touch my heart and feel the beat

Take it in my name, enjoy it, love is divine bliss,

Rise from your dream and claim your love

I am like the withering lily, need thy Sunshine

Love gives me new hope to live, to smile

Come on, my love, take me to our dreamland

From wonderland wondering about these beautiful changes

I want to show you the reason for my tears

If we are to start again from the beginning

I will give you the same all that I have for you

There is no regret and no choice in love

It's not a give and take; it's a give and gift

My love is selfless, my love is sacrifice

It's your turn to shoulder the responsibilities.

The fruit of our love, of the sweetest moment

I want to show you my eyes and make you wild

Take me in your arms and lead me

To the garden of love among the roses

I lay my life for you: give me yours.

She sent the letter to Ron while he was hospitalized after being beaten by Tintin. Esther had no idea about the critical condition of Ron. Ron had been beaten black and blue but he did not disclose it to anyone, not even to his mother. Ron replied to Esther's letter after a month.

As long as you see the Sun, my love

Remember pillar 143 and the promise

I'm always with you, my love

The moment you think of me

I send my love in the wind

I will be there in your breath,

My sweet name is there in your pulse,

In your sweet name will draw out

The sweetest tears, I will kiss and lick it

Never let it cross thy rosy cheeks.

I will bite those love looks, and make you dance

Love made me a drunk and I am lost in the dream

Love drives me crazy and I'm filled with music

Tell me the day and the time, I will be counting

Every minute counting the day for your call

You will touch and reach the core of this heart

Yours and yours alone, mine and mine alone

I am always there wherever you go

Say your time I am waiting for you, my love

To take you to your dreamland, it's a promise.

To the garden of love among the roses

Where there is just you and me

Breathing the same air, laughing in the fire

Get drunk in love and run wild ways

Love is not a sin, love is a sacrifice

Love is not a game, love is understanding,

Love never lies, love never dies

Love is not a choice, love is a commitment

Love is not a wound that heals with time

Love does not cease with distance

I want to say your name and hear you say mine

I want to see your smile and listen to your sweet voice

I want to touch your lips: I want to whisper to your ears

My lung longs for your smell, my soul long for your songs

I love you, Pinky; I love you, baby.

Esther received Ron's letter and resolved that she was not guilty of marrying her love, Ron. She made plans to leave her brother Benjamin as soon as possible. She said to herself, "*Love will not separate two people on any basis: religion, status, distance. It's between two hearts, two souls. Love is divine, love is selfless sacrifice.*" She touched her belly, felt the baby inside her womb. She again said to herself, "*Love is a dangerous game, take the risk. There is no decision or second thought in the face of true love.*" She wrote a letter and requested her friend to deliver it urgently. Ron opened the letter and reads the lines.

My love, tell me what is love?

It's between two people, two hearts, and two souls

Together into one forever, my love

You are my love, my path, my strength

You came to me as waves: you came to me as the breeze

You came to me as rain: you came to me as fire

Now come in your true self, my love

Saturday, Sabbath day, seventh day

I am there at our promised pillar 143

At dusk, alone I will wait there

Let us fulfil our heart's desire

Begin our journey into the new world

Come well prepared with your wits

It's now or never, let's not miss the chance

I love you, Ron.

Benjamin knew very well what and how Esther had been through when she was expelled from the boarding. She did not look like a normal girl: She no longer appeared to be his lovely sister whom he knew from her childhood. Her lovely face had lost its moisture, her eyes were sunken and her beauty had lost its innocence. He was worried about how to revive her life back to normal. But Esther would shut her door and lie on the bed the whole day. She never talked to Benjamin and hardly ate anything. She had been a spoilt brat,alas! the time was late to mould her life. Benjamin was ashamed as well as sorry to ever promise over the Broadvale family. He didn't want to break the heart of his only sister. He thought of ways to solve the problem.

Meanwhile, Ron's family also kept an eye on their only son, Ron. They knew that the time was not ripe for him to get married. They wanted Ron to continue his education in another institution and undergo pieces of training and life skills that the son of a chief ought to have. His father, Mr. Daadi was helpless when his son did not cooperate with whatever plan he initiated for him. He turned down all the offers and became drunk day and night. He could not concentrate on anything and became like a mad man. The family had to arrange his marriage with another girl from their clan. They criticized Esther and her family so much that it was hard for Ron to live with his family. It hurt him more to hear the disgrace of Esther. He blamed his sisters for gossiping about their affair.

Ron's five sisters played with rumours. They spread everywhere that Esther and her brothers wanted Ron because of his fame and property. They said Esther was following Judaism while they were Christians. They couldn't accept such a poor Jewish girl to be the Queen of Broadvale. When Benjamin came to know of the wicked plan of Daadi and his daughters, he got very angry and said, *"After knowing Esther is in trouble, how can they arrange a marriage for Ron, I will never give my sister's hand or her child to Broadvale. They have ruined my sister, my only sister's life and played with my name."* He remembered the vow he had taken on Broadvale 15 years ago. The reason behind Benjamin denying Ron to give his sister's hand was rather pitiful than furious.

When Benjamin was 14 years old, the family settled peacefully in Broadvale. Broadvale was a very prosperous land where many famous, brave men hailed from. It was a land where many beautiful, as well as skilful women, hail from. The village was a large province with 500 families living as one family under the dictatorship of their brave chief, Daadi. The place was one of the most developed of their time. Across the village was a small irregular-shaped hill, resembling a monster, with clouds overshadowing all the year-round, where people derived occult and practised rituals. They believed it to be a sacred place and called it the Giant Prayer Hill. On top of the hill was a viewpoint where one could have an astonishing look at the scenic beauty of the village. The breathtaking ambience of the mist below the hanging silvery clouds, the rich, varied flora and fauna of the blue mountains, one ultimately praised the founders of the village in that spot. One of the oldest villages of the time, the jungle-dweller forefathers who established the village in 1850, left behind a legacy to stand for the cause of their motherland. The village was bounded by the Giant Prayer Hill in the east and a brook called Tuivai that flows from west to east marking the boundary with the rest of the neighbouring villages. Every year, the Tuivai River would be loaded with resources and dumped its load in Broadvale. Tuivai brings those stones and sand, quite sufficient for an economy for the people. They use it in developing the construction of houses, fencing,besides it also fetches livelihood for the people of Broadvale. The village had a thick jungle in the north where the British once settled and built their camp. To defend from enemy attacks, the villagers built a huge wall with a gate called the military gate. The entire households built big houses of pine and oak wood. They had proper fencing with an underground tunnel all leading to the middle of the village. They built the underground tunnel to escape from enemy attacks. All the household tunnels were leading to the playground, which was located in the middle of the village. The tunnels were made with mortar and stone. The playground was like a stadium with a front and a back gate. Each household had sufficient livestock with chariots. They had big farms and fields. Every household was self-sufficient in its needs: they ate, drank and celebrated festivals all the year-round. Each household owned a single-barrel gun, country-made gun, bow sets and sufficient gun powder. They were very advanced, compared with the neighbouring villages. They had proper drainage, rainwater harvest, excellent handloom and handicraft. Every boy who attained the age of 15 was given a sword, dagger, spear, shield and gun if he passed the test done by the village army. All the boys had to undergo four months of vigorous training, on the use of the traditional weapons and warfare tactics which was mandatory for every son of Broadvale soil. The villagers paid an annual tax of ten percent of what they produced to the royal family of Broadvale.

Throughout the village, there was not a single family that fulfilled the norms of the village except one and that was Benjamin's family. His father was a pioneer Christian missionary among all the tribes of the time. The chief of Broadvale, Daadi had warned him to stop polluting the minds of his people with his nonsense religion brought by the white western people. They imposed laws to heavily fine whosoever went against the norms of the customs, traditions and religion of their forefathers. They seized the land, all the livestock and farms of Mr. Ginna for going against the law. Ginna suffered a lot but continued preaching the word of God and toiled hard to feed his family of six small children. They lived hand-to-mouth, asking help from one neighbour to another now and then, to make both ends meet. When the British Missionaries came to know of their condition, they immediately contacted him. Ginna accepted the invitation and left Broadvale for one year. The British Missionary Trust trained him in their Ministry, taught the English language, anointed him. After a year they conferred him the Pastor title with a monthly salary which was quite sufficient to support his family. Pastor Ginna secretly used to bring the British Missionaries into Broadvale. Together they preached the living word of God. Pastor Ginna worked as the translator of the English language to the native tribes. They distributed religious books, clothes, other items which were valued by the tribal people. He baptized and converted some people to Christianity. They distributed thousands of Holy Bible and other storybooks, free of cost to the people whether they were converted or not. Ginna became popular, was loved by his people for his kindness. As much love and respect he had earned, so much he was also hated, mostly for spreading the western culture and religion which greatly affected the integrity of the tribes, who were constantly fighting with the British Indian government. He endured the pain and travelled the rugged roads barefoot for miles and miles of his journey. He never gave up despite whatever troubles and obstacles stood in his way. He prayed, sang, undoubtedly continued his mission. Slowly and steadily, he won the hearts of thousands of blessed souls. He conducted vocational training, camps and crusades in collaboration with the British Missionaries. They distributed pencils, notebooks, clothes, books and the Holy Bible. This made the chief Mr. Daadi infuriated.

Meanwhile, a war started when the British Indian Army killed many chiefs and burnt down many houses in the neighbouring villages. The British looked on to Broadvale with envy. They built a camp across the hill at the back of the village military gate. When the tension was high in the air, the innocent Pastor Ginna kept preaching the word of God despite repeated warnings from the higher authority of the Tribal Chiefs Association, mastermind by Mr. Daadi. He repeatedly countered with Daadi, and on many occasions, he had proved himself victorious over the orthodox culture, by converting many people of the village to Christianity, and showed him that his God was the living one. When all the appeasement policies were turned down by Mr. Ginna, Mr. Daadi hatched a plan to kill Ginna to teach his people a lesson. He collected the Holy books of the Christians and burnt them down to ashes. They made propaganda to bluff the people that Mr. Ginna was a spy working in the British Indian Army. He blamed him for all the defeats of the tribal people. The British soldiers had burnt down some houses in the nearby villages. The atrocities of the British soldiers had been known by all. The first World War was going on, many young tribal men were forced to join the British Indian Army. The first world war had ended but not the Colonial British rule in India. There were internal conflicts in the tribal areas with the progress of the British Missionaries.

In 1930, the tribal chiefs announced that Ginna was a traitor and declared him a "Wanted" person. Broadvale village soldiers decided that such a traitor in their village was a shame to the nation and should be burnt alive in public. Daadi sent his army to look for Ginna but they could not find him. They again sent some of the village men, who were good friends of Ginna, to enquire about the traitor but they also came back in the same manner. After threatening his wife and children, they learnt that Ginna had gone out that very day with three of his white friends for their usual preaching. The day was Good Friday for the Christians. He was expected to return home after Easter Sunday. The village soldiers prepared everything and waited for Ginna's arrival.

Unaware of the wicked plans of his kinsmen, Pastor Ginna preached the word of God unceasingly, through the incessant rain and storm. He was scolded, lectured and humiliated by people in some places, while in some other places, they spat on his face and called him "A fiend, mercenary, traitor!" Ginna knew that his end was near and wished to do his best wherever he preached the gospel. He knew that he was being targeted by his kinsmen but he was not afraid to die in the name of God. He, instead, continued preaching as far as he could and speaking the Holy words of God as much as he could—thirsty, hungry, tired and wounded. The people had been warned by the higher authority not to welcome the traitor but to treat him the way that he deserved. However, God heard the prayer of this humble man, and did not want him to die far away from home, without meeting his family; no one dared raise his hands against the Holy man.

When Ginna's wife, Dimnu, heard of the news that her husband would be prosecuted, she immediately approached Mr. Daadi. Instead of listening to her, he humiliated her by saying, "After I kill your headstrong husband, you will be my servant in the daytime and the second queen at night time." Daadi's wife, popularly known as the Queen, was a strong and wise woman. The Queen, as her name implied, was truly a queen in her beauty, words, thoughts and deeds. She was full of love and devoted her time to the service of her people irrespective of their status, clan and religion. She immediately met Ginna's wife and told her to flee with her children to a safe place. She also told her never to show her face again to people of their tribe. Benjamin's mother went home in tears and people who met her on the way followed her to her house. They asked her the reason but Dimnu, being perturbed, had become deaf and dumb. She could not communicate with her husband. Slowly she became normal when she breastfed her daughter, Esther who was one year and 11 months old. She told her friends and relatives what she heard from Daadi and Queen. Her friends told her to beg forgiveness from Daadi and the village soldiers. Some of them suggested to convince her husband to quit his job. Dimnu knew that her time was limited; she also knew that Daadi would never forgive her husband and they would never beg to them in the name of God. She had no hope for impunity from Mr Daadi. She sent out the visitors and packed some food for her children. She did not know where to flee or how to save her family. She asked for help from her friends and relatives to drop them somewhere but they all gave her a cold shoulder fearing the higher authority. The day was Sunday, she knew her husband would return the next day or the following day. She ran from pillar to post carrying her baby on her back weeping for help. In the evening, she sent her second son, Tintin to bring back his brother Benjamin who was working on the farm in a nearby village when Daadi seized their farms and fields. Tintin was 12 years old. He ran as fast as his legs could carry him, heading towards the field where Benjamin was working. The helpless woman cried and prayed to God the whole night when both the sons did not return home in time, "*What shall I do now? My love, I am sorry. I have to flee and leave you to die for the sake of our innocent small children.*" Saying so, she woke up early in the morning. She cooked food and fed her children; she packed tiffin for the day and secretly left the house before the villagers could get up. She climbed the Giant Prayer Hill and hid her kids in the dark cave. She knelt and prayed with her children for their safety. Her children ask her many questions, endless questions one after another. She simply pretended to smile at them while secretly wiping her tears saying, "Ah!

A speck of dust stuck in my eyes." She just replied what came to her mind as the best. She entrusted her third son who was ten years old to take care of his siblings till she returned. She went back to look for Benjamin and Tintin.

On the way, she saw her husband from distance with three white men. She walked faster as her mind too thought faster about how to save them. Before she even made up a solution, she realized her husband was already a captive in their hands. Pastor Ginna was followed by the village army in great numbers. They met face-to-face within minutes: She looked at her weary, wounded husband and wiped her tears not knowing where to start or what to say. Pastor Ginna hugged her and said, "*My dear, we suffer too much. God wants us to take rest now. Please don't cry.*" The village soldiers and authorities together asked pastor Gina to take an oath by biting the tiger's tooth that he would not repeat his preaching. Pastor Gina boldly told them that he chose to be a martyr in the highest degree than betray God. Nothing abated his zeal for missionary work. The villagers tied their hands at their backs and stripped them. They paraded them up to the playground. They collected the Holy books from his house and burnt them along with their clothes. The five martyrs closed their eyes and prayed to God, weeping at His feet. The mob poured out litres and litres from a can, sprinkling kerosene over them. They held each other's hands and still prayed, weeping at the feet of the Almighty. As soon as they were beaten and pushed into the blazing fire, the four of them died instantly while

Pastor Ginna struggled, and could not die as easily as his friends. He cried in the fire for some time and shouted at the top of his voice saying, *"Anyone who destroys and sets fire to the Church shall meet with my curse. Praise the Lord!"* Alas! At last, he breathed his last of suffocation.

Many people cried out while some were shocked by the punishment. Some people said a silent prayer for the safety of Benjamin and his siblings. The barbaric mob went towards the Pastor's house and burns it down. They looked for the small children and resolved to enrol them either as village soldiers or take them as slaves for the royal house.

The Queen of Broadvale and some women rode on horses looking for the missing children while another team of soldiers demolished some houses in search of the children. The Queen divided the village women into three groups. She sent them in different directions. She ordered them to rescue the children and drop them in a safe place. When the Queen was alone riding her horse towards the cemetery, she saw Benjamin and his friends carrying Tintin on his back tied with a cloth. She quickly rode towards them, told Benjamin to flee. She took Tintin on her horse and dropped him to the village magician deep in the forest and said, *"This boy is bitten by a snake. Save him and I will pay you double. Just make sure he recovers soon, and then secretly drop him off to his uncle at Gaitlane village. If you disclose to anyone, our relationship will end."* Benjamin escaped from Broadvale according to the Queen's instruction. He went to his maternal uncle at Gaitlane. When he reached Gaitlane, it was already midnight. He knocked at the door of his uncle but no one opened the door in the dead of night. He went to the back of the house. He was hungry, thirsty, and weary. Suddenly he heard the sound of galloping from a distance. He then happened to slip on fresh cow dung in the dark. He hit his head on a pole and was unconscious the whole night.

After some time, the village soldiers of Broadvale raided his uncle's house. They searched for the children of Pastor Ginna. When they could not find the kids, they left for Broadvale. The poor man was told by the villagers that Pastor Ginna and his wife were burnt alive and they were looking for the missing children. The poor uncle could not go back to sleep, so waited for the dawn. The whole family worried about where the small kids would be if the village soldiers could not locate them. In the morning, the poor uncle heard an unusual noise of his cattle at the back of his house. When he went and checked, he saw a young boy lying unconscious in the cowshed. When he turned the body to look at his face, he saw the face of his sister Dimnu, and called out, "Benjamin, Benjamin, hey! Do you hear me, children? Bring water, Jessica, bring water, Johnny, hurry up!" They carried him near the fireplace and sprinkled drops of water on his face and called his name many times. Benjamin opened his eyes and was shocked. His uncle nursed him as he was a priest. He went out, took some herbs, ground them and gave a few drops to him.

Soon Benjamin sat up and said, "Uncle, I am hungry, give me something to eat." They gave him chicken soup, some bread and fruits. Benjamin narrated what happened to him and his brother Tintin and how he had reached his uncle's house. His uncle also narrated the raid, about the midnight incident to Benjamin. They were both worried for the kids. His uncle thought of taking help from his friends. He at once drove out his chariot and was about to leave his house. He saw from a distance three boys, one of them carrying a baby on his back while another boy was carrying a bag load on his head. Benjamin was going behind his uncle holding a rifle, trying to give it to him. He gave the rifle to his uncle, who sat like a statue on his chariot looking straight towards the road. Benjamin looked at his uncle's eyes for a few seconds, then turned his head right. He too stood still with his mouth wide open. The children came nearer and called out, *"Brother, I know you are here."* They were unaware of what cruel fate had befallen their parents. They looked as fresh as the petals of a lotus in full bloom. Their happy face made Benjamin and his uncle speechless. They stood still until the kids touched the feet of their maternal uncle. The uncle took the two small brothers in both arms, while Benjamin took his sister, Esther, who cheerfully smiled at him. Benjamin rubbed the soft skin of her face with his and kissed her. They ask the kids how they managed to find them and where they had been the whole night.

The kids took their turn, said rather excitedly, "*Mummy dropped us at the hill and left us. She came in the evening with daddy and his friends. They brought food and drinks and they took us to one big house where there were dutiful servants to take care of us. We spent the night eating meat and rice. Baby Esther ate bread, milk and honey. There were many people too. Mummy told us Bible stories. In the morning they took us in a chariot and left us near our uncle's house. Father told us to wait for them here, at our uncle's house. They said that they will go and look for brother Tintin.*" Their poor uncle's hair and brows stood straight. He had stopped breathing for a moment. Their strange story had taken away their breath. The other members of the family had also held their breath for a moment, dumbfounded about how to tell the poor kids about their parents' death. Their maternal uncle and aunty quickly lit up the lamps and made a bonfire all around his house. They filled the campus with smoke to protect the kids from the next visit of their dead parents. He quickly arranged for the burial ceremony of the five martyrs. He took help from one Pastor, who was a good friend of Pastor Ginna and along with 30 other young men; together they all left Gaitlane at dusk. They secretly entered the cemetery gate and search the location of a new graveyard in the cemetery at midnight. They unearthed the precious remains of the burnt skeletons of the martyrs and buried the bodies altogether in one pit, under a bridge beside the river Tuivai. There was neither the singing of sad songs nor the lamentations from mourners for the dear martyrs' burial ceremony. They were laid to rest in complete silence in the dead of the silent night. Some verses from the book of Hebrews were read out by the Pastor after a short prayer; the wind blew around them, hovered around the silent waters and shook the suspension bridge. They all stood still for some time until the wind became calm. They buried the remains of the bones in haste. They put a cross made of oak wood on the graveyard which they brought from Gaitlane. Benjamin wrote their names and the cause of their death in the small diary of his father. He kept the diary near the cross. They put a huge stone over it. Benjamin clutched the cross and wept bitterly while the others took bath in the river. Before they left the place Benjamin promised that he would take revenge on Broadvale someday. They consoled the young boy; they felt the pain while worried for the siblings. His maternal uncle said to him, "Benja, we have no time to cry. God has taken their lives because He wants them back for some reason that is incomprehensible to us. God will open the right door at the right time; so, leave everything to God. Don't worry dear, I am here. Come, a man must be a soldier, what cannot be changed must be endured, we should not weep in front of the kids, they are too young to know the truth. You are the eldest of the siblings, your greatest responsibility now is to endure the pain however hard it is or how much it hurts you. You should show your smiling face to your brothers, especially to your only infant sister. God understand the pain, leave all your worries to Him, come, let us go back home." They dragged Benjamin up to his chariot and left the place at twilight.

No one chooses to be an orphan, no parents choose to die and leave their children untimely. However, God always watches over His children and opens new doors far beneficial for them in the long run. The Christian Missionaries took Benjamin and his siblings and gave them protection for a few months in the City Children's Home for Christ. They anointed Benjamin to be a true servant of God, to follow in his father's footsteps and fulfil his unfulfilled dreams of spreading the gospel in the dark world. He was conferred a Pastor title at the age of 15 years. Tintin worked in a missionary institution helping the priests. The small children were sent to an Orphanage Home and given education free of cost by the Missionaries. The youngest of the siblings, Esther was with Benjamin until she was seven years old. Benjamin loved her so much that he let her have all that she wanted. He would do anything to make his sister happy. Everyone loved Esther as she was deprived of a mother's care. She suffered from tuberculosis along with all sorts of childhood diseases. She was dark, pale and skinny. Nobody believed she would grow up like her friends and lead a normal life or marry a handsome man. When she was seven years old, her brother sent her to the best school in the city. From there, she became good friends with Ron, the only son of the Broadvale chief, the son of Mr. Daadi who was the mastermind in the burning of many more martyrs. Alas! her best friend was the loving son of the wicked man, responsible for all her misfortunes, ill-fated, who had stolen or ruined the childhood of the siblings' happy family. Ron and Esther fell in love from their childhood before they bothered to know who they actually were. Since then, all her diseases and ailments slowly healed by themselves and she quickly grew up into a voluptuous charming girl.

The lovers eloped on a Saturday so that Benjamin and his men would not be able to chase them. Benjamin was a religious man and observes the Sabbath strictly, meditating the whole day. There was chaos on the Broadvale family's side. They had been arranging a marriage for Ron but when Ron eloped with Esther, the bride's family charged the Broadvale family with defamation and betrayal. Together they looked for Ron and Esther. The chief of Broadvale was also very angry, Ron being his only son. Benjamin and his brothers also searched for Esther everywhere. The search party could not go out far due to the British troops who occupied all the roads connecting the places and jungles where they were likely to escape. Again, it was wartime between British troops and the Japanese. Many people fled from their homes to villages and jungles when their city was attacked by bombs. People panicked to see Japanese troops with their planes. The sound of the planes shook the land, soon people dug bunkers for protection from enemies. The people had never been attacked by bombs before. British troops had taken many men for labour corps and deported them to distant unknown places during World War 2. Mr. Daadi worried about his son. He blamed Benjamin's family for all the misfortunes right from Pastor Ginna. Benjamin countercased Mr. Daadi that his sister was taken away by Ron. He charged them with kidnapping his only sister. According to the custom of the tribes, Daadi sent his men to Benjamin for negotiation. Benjamin demanded they first return his sister safely. The second time Daadi's men went to Benjamin, the latter said sternly, "If you don't return my sister within a week, we will show you our strength and power. I will slay Ron wherever I find him."

Broadvale's family did not cancel the proposed marriage of their son. They keep searching for the lovers and wanted to kill Esther. Many months passed but none got a clue about the lovers.

CHAPTER - 3

THE HONEYMOON

The lovers eloped with some of their valuable possessions. They lived in that small village, Sinai. The place was far from development and the people were uncivilized. There was no proper water supply, no medical facility, no educational institution or a Church. The people were ignorant and worshipped stones and trees. They also believed in black magic, witchcraft and Spirits. The couple enjoyed fooling the villagers: they called it their honeymoon and spent their best time in Sinai. However, their happiness was as short-lived as the silvery dewdrops that vanish as soon as the mighty Sun rises. The village was raided by the British Indian soldiers when the chief did not comply with his order to send his men to them. The British Indian armies had issued an order that all the men from the village must come for the labour corps. Such a small village like Sinai could not protect itself. They captured the chief of Sinai who was in his late fifties. The brave man shouted in his language, alerting his men to flee from the village. The soldiers knew his plan and tortured him to call out to all his men. Many of the villagers escaped and hid in a cave at the back of the waterfall across the village. The couple too ran away from the village and hid in the jungle. Ron and Esther could not climb up to the cave when Esther cried all through the way in the pangs of her childbirth. The jungle was full of snakes, leeches and caterpillars. It was the time India fought for independence from British rule. The British soldiers used to take away valuables and livestock along with young men for the labour corps. When the chief did not disclose the hideouts of his men, they burnt down his house along with some other houses in the village. The British soldiers had taken 10 men who surrendered to the soldiers, to defend their chief, when the soldiers tried to kill him for not obeying the order. The soldiers made them carry loads of grain from their granaries and walk up to a distance of 25 miles carrying the heavy loads, crossing the Tuivai River. They were beaten up by the soldiers if they stopped for a while or happened to fall on the slippery road. They made them walk up hills and down hills, where even horses could not travel. They were hungry and thirsty; their feet were bleeding due to the rugged road but the soldiers whipped them like animals. The British camp was situated at the top of a hill. When they reached there, they became unconscious and fell at the feet of a white British officer, who was shocked to see the inhuman treatment done by the soldiers. The white man at once ordered the soldiers to give them food and water, and also gave first aid to the wounded villagers. He punished those barbaric soldiers who played with the lives of the ignorant tribes.

In the jungle full of leeches and worms, Esther gave birth to a baby boy at midnight. The baby died the next day. The couple wept bitterly and wanted to return home. The British soldiers had occupied the jungle areas. They controlled the roads and highways connecting the villages. After three days in the jungle, the villagers returned home and mourned for days and nights. They all wanted to flee from the place but there was no place that was safer than theirs. They learnt that the British Indian soldiers were recruiting young men from every village and torturing those who disobeyed their orders. They made strategies as to how they could protect themselves from their enemies in future. There were only 15 men left in the village. They decided to leave the village and sojourn in a bigger village so that they could fight together with them against the foreigners. They prepared to give information to the neighbouring villages by burning the king chilly in a fire, which by sending out the smoke in the air, served as a sign of alarm or SOS, but instead, many people came to Sinai even before the information was dispatched. They gave information to the remaining villages, who all agreed to merge with Sinai. So, they all settled anew in Sinai. There were now 77 men and 107 families. Later the other far-flung villages too joined them and then they formed a group called Sinai Soldiers. They had no more grains in stock. To feed their family, the womenfolk climbed hills searching for food like bananas, fruits, banana stem, elephant yam, taro, cassava and sweet potato. The menfolk would catch fish, prawns, starfish and snails from the Tuivai River. They could not move further into the jungle for hunting because of the British soldiers. Life was difficult but they loved one another, struggled together against their common enemy.

Ron was made the commander of the village soldiers. Soon their figure rose to150 in number. They underwent strict training every morning. Ron taught them first, how to make gunpowder and within a day they could make gunpowder. They made it by mixing charcoal, sulphur and potassium nitrate. Ron taught them the basic English language for communication. He also taught them how to look at the map in case they get lost in the jungle. He taught them how to watch the times of the day. He made a big wooden clock for the village and mounted it on the roof of his house. The villagers shared their knowledge in different fields. They made bows and arrows, practised shooting every morning while the womenfolk worked hard to maintain and feed the village soldiers. Some taught martial arts, some taught herbal medicine while some taught how to make poison from herbs. They made bunkers, laid traps in the jungle. They all learnt how to rear livestock like poultry, cows, goats, sheep, ducks, swans and pigs. They reared bees and used honey for medicines. They made curd and cream from milk. They trained their dogs, birds like doves and eagles. They invented their sign language and code words. They also made a pledge which they said like a prayer every morning:

Sinai Soldier

I am the true son of my brave father

Never surrender or step back

Ready with my sword and gun

I will march forward, never step back

In truth and love, we march forward

To protect the land of our forefathers

I will spare none who comes my way

I will cut with my sword

I will fire with my gun,

I will stab with my dagger

The blood of my father runs in my veins

A true soldier of my brave forefathers

I fear none for the freedom of my motherland.

After three months, they selected the best seven boys out of the soldiers. They named the section **"Sinai black cats"**. They sent them on a mission to spy and enquire about their men in the Indian soldiers' camp. They applied charcoal masks on their faces, and dressed in black, like real black cats. They took their guns, swords, daggers, then headed for the British Indian soldiers' camp. They tiptoed at night into the camp and searched for their men. They found them in the last barrack, five in number who slept on the ground like cattle, ropes tied on their necks. They quickly freed their men. They poisoned the water in the tank before they left the camp. They escaped and travelled the whole night. Wearily they reached Sinai the next day. The people were happy to meet their men alive after many days; on the other hand, they also worried for the other captives. The five men looked pale and malnourished. They had cuts, bruises and wounds all over them. They narrated the ordeals and the ill-treatment they had to bear in the British Indian camp. They also said that many of the young tribe boys were already deported to far places, places unknown to them. They were left behind because they were rejected for some reason that they didn't know. The villagers celebrated their freedom with a feast. They celebrated their first victory by killing five cows and five Mithuns. The British soldiers could not chase them back. They all suffered from diarrhoea for days. They saw them in rows carrying their bodies like a bride in a palanquin. They watched from a distance how the British Indian soldiers suffered because of the poisoned water.

Esther was very sad about losing her first child. She wrote a letter to her in-laws at Broadvale, telling them about their misfortune. She begged them to accept their marriage and requested to take them home. She kept the letter on the back of her horse tied with a cloth although she was not sure whether it would be delivered or not. She told her horse to go to Broadvale and give the message to the Queen. After some months of a hectic life, Esther found time to mingle with the village folk who came from different places, far and wide. Soon after, she was shocked to learn about their way of life. She wondered how she and her husband would live with those uncivilized people. She saw them eating red meat that was not properly cooked. Some of the village folk ate leeches, maggots and worms. She also realized that not even a single woman was able to read and write. She wondered about their perception of life. Men and women had sex freely, anytime, anywhere with anyone. The women were cheap, and there was no law enforced upon men who committed adultery. Some of the men had three wives living together. The wives and their children fought among themselves now and then. There was no true love and no respect for women. They were gluttons, sloppy and so uncivilized. The women used to take bath only once or twice a month. Their houses were a mess and the surroundings were filthy. The menfolk seem to have an evil eye on Esther and the woman folk were all crazy for Ron, who was smart, kind and very handsome. Esther devoted her time to educating the womenfolk. She taught them how to take care of themselves and their household. First, she taught them about personal hygiene. She taught them how to groom and tie their hair in different styles. Gradually, she taught them the values of a woman, her role and responsibilities and inspired them to stand for a cause, so that their men would respect them. She taught them cooking, food processing, and fermentation. The villagers benefited a lot from her teachings. They started preserving different food items like soya bean, bamboo shoot, meat, mustard, fish and prawn through the fermentation process. They preserved dry fruits, seeds of different kinds in their seasons. They also baked food for themselves. The villagers were so happy to have Ron and Esther with them that they worshipped them like God. Teaching them good lessons and changing their lives made them believe that Esther must be a Goddess. They were so grateful to Esther and loved her so much that they began to worship her like a Goddess. Again, Esther taught them about the existence of God. She convinced them to believe in the Almighty, The creator of all things. She taught them the word of God, stories of prophets as she was taught by her brother Benjamin, who was a Pastor. She also had learnt many Bible stories besides other moral stories in the mission boarding. Later, the situation of the people made them become true missionaries. Esther said to herself, *"I must help these people and serve humanity. They may have evil eyes on me and my husband, yet I will serve God even to these undeserving people. I will show them who I am, follow the path of my parents and brother, and be a light in this dark world."* They built a synagogue and Esther taught them the word of God, starting from the book of Genesis, and slowly and steadily convinced the people to follow the laws of the Ten Commandments strictly. Ron and Esther become the pioneers and a lamp in the dark world. They had been compelled to do all these and in doing so they were eventually touched by their noble job thereby making themselves discover the true joy of life. They loved and enjoyed their work. They missed their families at Broadvale yet they both felt deep peace at once. They had been changed in the process of changing the ignorant folk at Sinai. They gained joy, an inner peace, a kind of satisfaction and glory that they had never dreamt of in their life. They taught about what clean and unclean animals are, according to the Holy Book, about the holiness of the Sabbath day and tithe.

CHAPTER – 4

THE SUN FESTIVAL

After one and half years, Ron and Esther saw a drastic change in the whole village of Sinai. At the same time, they were overjoyed to welcome the new member of their family. Esther gave birth to a son. The couple attributed it all to their fate when they were not called back by their parents. They circumcised the baby on the seventh day. They performed a baby shower on the tenth day, by inviting all the villagers for a grand feast. They named their baby JESSE. However, Ron didn't forget his Broadvale traditions. With the coming of the Sun festival, which was one of the most important festivals of Broadvale, he told Esther not to enter the house till the sunset. He went to the Tuivai River, bathed in the morning to welcome the sunrise, just as his people used to do at Broadvale. They bathed the baby with milk, massaged him with virgin olive oil and laid him outside the house to get the blessings from the mighty Sun. Ron and Esther prayed together, sang, danced and ate the whole day under the Sun. The villagers watched them in wonder. Some of the neighbours asked them the reason why they celebrated the Sun festival. Ron called them to join dancing with him. He taught them how to do the Sun festival dance. They looked up at the sky, slowly closing the eyes, released all their worries by breathing deeply, then slowly raised their hands, closing their eyes. Slowly they turned clockwise, then anti-clockwise seven times. Then they formed a circle, clutched each other's hands with smiles on their faces. They became enlightened, free from fear and frustrations. Their faces glowed, ready to dance. They moved sideways from right to left singing folk songs and started dancing, jumping, smiling, and laughing out aloud. After the dancing, they poured wine for one another. They ate and drank together happily. Ron looked at their happy faces and said, "Brothers and sisters, we human beings are social animals. We all live together with our family and relatives and we all have our valuable traditions. We may or may not live together under one roof as one family, but we do have certain things in common that help form the structure and foundation of our families and our society. Every tradition contributes a sense of comfort and belonging to the family and society. It brings families together and enables us to reconnect with our dear ones. We are bound by cultural social norms and traditions, customs, languages and religion. We need to know our roots; we need to know our forefathers, to build a strong family relationship. We need to know how our forefathers lived, married and died, their beliefs and practices, their successes and failures. We need to compare with our generation to start counting the blessings from

God. The Sun festival is not related to religion. I am not worshipping the Sun, but through the Sun festival, we remember our forefathers and know our roots. We meditate and count the blessings of God, the Almighty. We sacrifice one day, once in a year, to sing and praise God through the mighty Sun, which was regarded as a father figure by our forefathers. This festival had been part of the Broadvale tradition since time immemorial. As the saying goes, at the heart of every family tradition is a meaningful experience. It is indeed very meaningful to count the blessings together with our dear ones and be thankful to God. We should preserve, promote and love our traditions, cultures, language and religion." The curious villagers again asked him how Broadvale used to celebrate the Sun festival. Ron again explained to them and said, "First we went to the nearest river, took the Holy bath by dipping our full body into the water three times. We stood in the water to welcome the rising Sun with a prayer to God, not to the Sun. Then we wore white clothes and meditated in front of our house. We wrote down the new names of our family members in a family book. We started reading out the genealogy tree of our family starting from the Sun, then the descendants, all the names of our forefathers to our generation, the present family members. We read out all the names of our brothers, sisters, cousins, nieces, including the maternal families right from our forefathers down to the present generation. Then we meditated, connected with God through prayer until we were touched by the blessings of

God. Once we saw the blessings, we started singing and dancing. After that, we could eat and drink together with our family members, outside the house, in the divine Sun. We made confessions under the Sun. We forgave each other's faults. We hugged our brothers and sisters and our parents too. Our forefathers believed that the Spirits of the departed family members used to come and visit us on that special day. So, they used to invite the Spirits of our dearest dead by performing some rituals, and together they enjoyed drinking, eating, singing and dancing. However, all those were superstitions. We celebrate the Sun festival to remember our family tree and preserve the traditions. The main theme of the festival is, to connect with God for one day and count his blessings in our lives."

Jesse was a healthy, cool, and friendly child. His eyes were bright and one could have solace seeing the face of the baby. It seemed as if he knew all the good things his mother said or did when he was inside the womb. He had been well-fed with the Holy words of God right from his mother's womb: He was different from the other children of the village. With the birth of Jesse, there was peace in the land. World War II came to an end and India too got independence from the colonial rule of the British. The British soldiers began retreating from their camps. Roads and highways had gradually become safe once again. People once again led a normal life. Yet there could not be true peace between Broadvale and Benjamin. There was none to douse the fire of enmity between them.

The Queen of Broadvale was handed a letter by a stranger. The man told the Queen that he found the letter tied to the back of a white horse somewhere in the Zumbo forest. The Queen read the letter and at once went to meet the couple along with her young daughter. They travelled for five days and nights and reached Sinai. The Queen was given a warm welcome at Sinai. When the Queen learnt the role taken by Ron and Esther in the village, she was overjoyed. She touched the face of Ron with her trembling hands saying, "My son has become the true son of Broadvale; how happy your father will be to hear the good news! You were a drunk, mad and naughty spoilt child of mine. I understand your love and did my best for you. But why did you leave behind your mother and go far away from me? I am happy to see you grownup and admire your maturity. My son, you had taken the right decision. Don't you ever imagine how much we miss you? Your elder sisters had married in your absence. How much they wished you were there to bless them! Come back, my child; I live for you." Ron and Esther were surprised to see them. The Queen loved them and blessed them. She took Jesse in her arms and blessed him. However, she could not convince them to go back with her for fear of Benjamin. She stayed with them for a week and returned to Broadvale.

CHAPTER - 5

GLORIA AND THE BRITISH COMMANDANT MR. RICHARD

On their way back, they met with some Indian soldiers. The soldiers told them there was a landslide ahead of them. They requested them to spend the night in the camp with other travellers. The Queen looked around she saw men, women, children tired and hungry, halted by the landslide. She also saw the British soldiers nursing the victims of the landslide in the tent. She went around, inspected the victims of the disaster. She was glad of the generosity of the soldiers who were taking care of the victims besides saving many lives. Now and then, she saw the soldiers come in carrying the victims, who were muddied and filthy and going out of the tents. The Queen was given full respect by the white commanding officer of the army. The soldiers prepared food as well as arranged accommodation for the weary travellers. The Queen and her daughter slept in a separate tent with many other travellers who came from different places, speaking different languages.

At night, while they were all asleep, the young daughter was woken up by a strange sound. At first, she thought that it was just the wind playing with her head. Soon after, she realized it was not her imagination; she heard the scream of a lady and sensed something was wrong. As she went out of the tent, she saw three tall men in the dark, near a bush beside the main entrance of the army camp. She took a few more steps when she saw a lady struggling from their arms. As she went nearer to help her, the three men became nervous and the lady managed to escape from their clutches. They caught hold of the unlucky girl, in the blink of an eye, dragged her away closing her mouth with their big hairy hands. As they dragged the young girl, they suddenly released her at the sight of a man who stood in their way. They quickly released their captive and saluted their officer who stood in their way pointing his revolver at them with both hands. The young girl was surprised at being saved by a white soldier. The white men scolded them in their language and brought back the girl to her mother. Before she entered her tent, the white soldier asked her name to which she replied, "I am Gloria. Thank you, sir." The white soldier slowly said to himself, "*Gloria, Gloria.*" The very name '*Gloria*' struck her mind, pierced like an arrow sweetly bleeding with honey, in the heart of the young girl. She wanted to hear again her name spoken from the very mouth of the white man again. She immediately turned back to look at him. She saw the face of a man that gave her peace of mind for the first time in her life.

The Queen woke up and found her daughter missing. She called out her name but got no reply. Soon, her daughter came inside the tent telling her mother that she had gone out to pass her needs and everything was fine. The next morning, Gloria secretly looked for the white soldier here and there. She saw him from a distance punishing the three black beasts. As she looked at them from a distance, a young lady came to her and flung her arms around her neck. First, she introduced herself, then thanked her for saving her life the previous night. While the two were talking, the white soldier saw them and rushed towards them. But the girls got scared and walked faster to avoid meeting him. Gloria ran to her mother who was busy packing their things, preparing to start their journey on another route. The white soldier came and said a few words but the travellers didn't understand his language. There was no translator right that moment. Just before the travellers departed from the camp, the white man came and gave Gloria a bunch of morning glory flowers saying, "This place is full of wild morning glory plants and I love to see them every morning. Have a safe journey. Take care."

After he casually smiled at them, he went his way straight, never turning back at them. Gloria watched him till he disappeared from her sight. She said to herself all along her journey, *"Oh! What a man, am I dreaming? I am told that the whites are like the devil. They said that they came in the name of God, conquered our land, changed our minds, took away our peace, and took away our pride. They divided us, tortured us, plundered us, and tore us into pieces, but I see with my own eyes, who a white man is, a different one from the rest. What the white men are, yeah, all white men are not bad, some of them are good. Or am I becoming soft? Yeah, I am becoming so soft, I like the white soldier. He is a true soldier. How he respects women, oh, the way he smiles and talked, wish I dared talk to him or at least ask his name. Will I ever meet him again?"*

Gloria smiled, unconsciously smiled, laughed at silly things all through the way without any reason. The Queen asked her again and again suspecting her of hiding something. Before they reached Broadvale, Gloria told her mother that three unknown soldiers tried to rape her for saving another girl outside the army camp and that she was saved by a kind-hearted soldier. At first, the Queen was impressed to hear the incident; she also smiled and admired the soldier. But when she learnt that the soldier was a Britisher, she scolded her daughter. All the way home, she told her daughter who the British were and what they had done to the Indians, especially to the ignorant tribes. They reached home the next week, exhausted. The girl had fallen in love with the white Unknown Soldier while her mother was dead against him. The name 'White Man' gave her an allergy and she worried if her husband would come to know of Gloria's love for the white soldier. Gloria wanted to go to Sinai for the sake of meeting the white soldier. The Queen took it as a punishment for them for all the things they had done upon innocent Esther. She blamed her daughter for going out of the tent alone at night. The Queen took everything as a bad omen and planned to take Esther into her family. She tried to convince her husband to accept his daughter-in-law. She convinced her daughters to accept their marriage and call back the couple. The Queen's mind was restless. She decided to marry off Gloria as soon as possible before her shameless daughter fell prey to the trap of that white soldier without any condition.

Gloria visited her brother's family at Sinai. She met the white British soldier on the way. They smiled at each other but didn't talk. She was on pins and needles when her parents asked her to marry her cousin, her father's sister's son. While she helped babysit Jesse, everyday dreamt of her lover, the white soldier. Sinai and its neighbouring villages in collaboration with the Indian Army stationed in the area organized a 30-days'-training course for the youths. One hundred youths, including girls, registered from different villages to participate in the training. Ron and Esther enrolled Gloria to undergo the self-defence training. They were given training in shooting guns, bows and arrows. They underwent training in rock climbing, rope climbing, horse riding, pole climbing and many more. They were taught special life skills on how to survive in the jungle and basic English language every night. Gloria overheard her brother and the organizing committee arranging a big function and they proposed a white British Commandant to be the chief guest. Ron was surprised to see the name of Gloria thrice, on the list of trainees who were selected to receive prizes. Gloria bagged the first prize in the 1000-metre race, bamboo climbing and English language.

On the big day, Gloria received her prizes from the hands of her dream man. On that day, she was overjoyed to hear her sweetest name again from the very mouth of her dream man, Richard. Richard told her that he had known everything about her after the day she left the army camp with her mother. He said that he had secretly followed her up to her village, Broadvale. Gloria left Sinai with a big relief that she had met her lover who also loved her. She always felt a kind of warm suspicion that her lover was behind her back watching over every step of hers secretly. She always felt someone like a shadow was following and protecting her soul.

Broadvale's family sent a man as a mediator, requesting Benjamin to accept the marriage of Ron and Esther. Benjamin accepted them to perform the customs to begin the negotiation. When both the family councils met face-to-face, the old feud crept into every sentence of their conversation. They did not trust each other. The bitter negotiation from the very beginning could not calm down both the family councils easily. Soon they began to argue over the bride price. Benjamin, at last, told them to divorce his sister. The other party immediately pressured indirectly Benjamin to demand anything he wished if they were going to divorce Esther. Both the family councils showed off their pride as prestige. Benjamin's side demanded Broadvale, the whole of Broadvale saying it was the land where his parents were buried. From the side of the public, some leaned on the side of Benjamin and some praised the Broadvale family. The two families became a hot topic of debate in public places. The opposite factions spread rumours far and wide, added a fuel to the fire that worsened the bitter relationship.

Meanwhile, Second World War ended and the Israel state came into being. Jews all over the globe praised their Lord: God of Abraham, Isaac and Jacob for answering their prayers. The wailing wall of Jerusalem called the Israelites to praise God for answering their prayers. They had been tortured enough for ages by the Nazis. They suffered a lot in World War II. Jews who had been scattered in different parts of the world called for their brothers to come back to the land of their forefathers. The scattered Jews started moving to the land of their forefathers, the Promised Land in the Bible. They had suffered much, so much in the hands of the Pharaohs and then the Nazis. They called all the descendants of Jacob, the 12 tribes of Israel who had scattered far and wide. Benjamin, the pioneer of the Jewish movement or the Sabbaths in India, and his brothers too prepared to move to the Holy home. They were anxious to meet with their brothers after thousands of years and eager to tread on the land to be with their people and be called the Israelites—God-chosen Nation. Benjamin took it as a golden opportunity to defeat the villain Broadvale family. He would also save his sister, being defiled by the cursed gentiles. He was sure that Esther's happiness wouldn't last long, living in Broadvale. He knew his sister would, however, regret someday, when all her brothers left her behind. He did not want to leave behind his dear sister to suffer in the hell of Broadvale. He forethought the plan so that each of his acts remained undetected and unidentified by Ron and Esther. He waited for the ripe opportunity and arranged their passport and visa for Israel. When he thought the time was ripe, he informed the chief of Broadvale to call back the couple. He also informed them that he would not take any bride price for his sister saying, "I cannot compare my sister with anything in this world, she is more precious, more valuable than the Kohinoor. Please love her as I love her. Do not ever hurt her. Even if you don't love her, don't let her know." The couple left Sinai unwillingly: they had fallen in love with the place and the people. On the other hand, their joy knew no bounds when their families accepted them at last. They came home to Broadvale with their three-year-old boy, Jesse. The two families did and fulfilled all the customary laws of marriage from both sides. However, their relationship was like the clouds that gather for days ready to pour down heavily and create havoc where they fall on the earth.

Gloria heard of people saying that matriculation exam toppers would be feted by the British officers and the chiefs' association. She studied hard and become the topper among the tribal girls in her matriculation. On the day of the felicitation, she dressed in her best gown despite her mother's advice to put on Broadvale's traditional dress. She was accompanied by her parents along with her younger sister Breza to the town hall. She was excited to reach the town hall and ordered the servant to drive the royal chariot as fast as he could. She became more and more nervous as they approached the town. She requested her mother to drive back to Broadvale. She became embarrassed to have dressed like the British when everyone attended the function in traditional dresses. Her mother and sister laughed at her and said, *"You look pretty in your gown, he will hold your hand and dance in the British style."* Just as they said, they were welcomed by British young soldiers. Gloria's parents were surprised by their warm reception. Since they could not communicate with the English people, they felt odd to be among them. They left the platform and look for a seat on the back benches. However, the ushers requested them to go to the front stage and let them be seated on the dais.

After the felicitation function, they were even surprised to see the white soldier propose to Gloria in front of the audience. The white Captain knelt in front of Gloria, held the microphone in his hand saying, "I love you, Gloria; I declare my love to you and these people are the witnesses. Please accept my love. Gloria, my morning glory, my love, please give me your left hand, I want to put this gold ring on your lovely finger." Gloria smiled and happily accepted the proposal of the white Captain. She gave her both hands when the man asked for her left hand to put the gold ring on her ring finger. They shamelessly hugged each other and danced on the platform like a couple. While the soldiers clapped their hands and cheered up the two, Daadi and Queen left the hall shamefully, waited for their daughter outside. They were ashamed of their daughter and hid their faces from their kinsmen. The white soldier and Gloria came out from the hall cheerfully. People were congratulating as well as blessing them. Gloria introduced the white soldier to her parents saying, "Father, mummy, he is Captain Richard of the British Indian Army." Gloria put her left hand on Richard's shoulder trying to rest her head on his arms. As Daadi looked at her, Richard flicked her hands and put them down slowly, he then bowed down to greet them in the Indian style. Daadi tried to turn away from them pretending he didn't see him bow down; the Queen raised her face to Richard smiling, and then shook hands with him. Richard said a few words in the tribal language to impress them but Daadi looked straight into his eyes and left the spot. Richard was handsome, kind, brave and polite but Daadi and the Queen were strictly against their love. They never liked a white man to be their son-in-law.

Daadi went home leaving his wife and daughters. He was furious, too much ashamed of his daughter. The innocent girl, whom he had trusted most, among his children and the most brilliant of all, had betrayed her father. He realized why his daughter loved to plant morning glory flowers all around their house. Daadi uprooted the morning glory flower plants all around his house. He blamed Ron and Esther as responsible for ruining the character of Gloria. He realized that Gloria visited Sinai only just to meet Richard. From their intimacy, he realized that the two had been meeting secretly many times.

The Queen came home late in the evening and calmed him down. They made plans on how to deal with them. Gloria and Breza stayed back in the town. The next day, they went straight to the city seeking admissions to the prestigious colleges. They were accompanied by Richard and his guards. After one week, Richard dropped them back at Broadvale. The Queen welcomed them along with some of the family elders. They told Richard to send his family elders to Broadvale to fulfil all the customary laws of marriage if he loved Gloria. Richard promised Gloria that he would come back with his parents to Broadvale to ask her hand in marriage.

CHAPTER - 6

PASSOVER FEAST

The Jews observed the Passover celebrating the exodus of the Israelites from slavery in Egypt. They celebrated the Passover with great joy with the passing of the 'The Law of Return' by the Israeli parliament in 1950. After seven days of celebration, the Jews strengthened their faith and devotion to God. Benjamin and his family, his four brothers and their family along with other Judaist brothers had a special feast before they departed for Israel. Benjamin summoned the Broadvale family too, for a feast after the Passover. He slaughtered for the feast five cows, and they enjoyed singing and preaching the word of God. They requested Esther and Jesse to stay back for some more days. Ron and his friend, Jensta, decided to stay along with Esther and Jesse. Benjamin blessed Jesse and the two families ate and drank, and played different kinds of games. They made merry eating grilled beef and mutton. The guests were rather hysterically tamed by the host, eating and drinking, talking so confidently it made the host execute his plan without much effort. On the third day after the Passover, Benjamin's brothers and the party had a drinking wine competition. They poured wine into the goblet after mixing it with sleeping pills. Ron and Jensta were not aware of their plan and they drank obediently so long as they were given. Soon they became like swans, they did not know what they were talking about or where they had been. Benjamin came home with some men in five jeeps. They parked the jeeps outside the gate. The men rushed in, took the pack of the things and drove away. Esther was feeding Jesse, unaware of her brother's evil plan. Soon another group of jeeps arrived again and they talked in private with Benjamin outside the house. Esther peeped through the window and saw five men wearing white caps. She carried her baby on her back with a loincloth and checked out the rooms. She saw her sister-in-law looking very nervous. Esther asked about the whereabouts of Ron and his cousin, Jensta. Benjamin called Esther into his room and told her how their parents were killed, and how much Broadvale had tortured their lives. He revealed to her how much Ron's family had disliked her to be their bride. He disclosed his plans and showed her name written on the tickets for the Holy home. Esther pressed her head with her palm and stooped down for a long time, lost for words. She listened to her brother dumbfounded. She was afraid to talk back to Benjamin. However, when Benjamin told her to board the jeep and leave her husband and son, she could no longer control her emotions and burst into tears. She said to Benjamin, "I respect you not as my brother alone but with all the love and care you shower upon us like a mother figure, like a father figure, and yes… you are my parents, brother and also my Spiritual teacher. This does not mean that you can do anything and come in between me and Ron. If you love me, you need to respect my decision too. I am a married woman with a child. You have no right to separate a mother from loving her infant son. I cannot leave my child and husband and also my family. They love and respect me. I cannot leave them. Yes, we will never meet again, after all, I will miss you all, but I will not come to Israel. I belong to Broadvale, and I am a Christian." The word Broadvale did not appeal much to the ears of Benjamin, he felt so uneasy with the very name Broadvale that he did not know when he had slapped his sister on her face. Without saying anything, he took her hand and dragged her outside where his men were waiting in the jeep. As the saying goes, *"When a woman is aroused by a sudden emotion beyond her control, she exhibits her inner potential, becomes stronger. Push by her veins, her spirit helps her guts by overturning the things that seem impossible in the mind of other human beings."* Esther being nimble, struggled and quickly grasped Jesse from the wooden bench beside her; she acted like lightning and Benjamin and his family were dumbfounded, watching her in action. Esther took her baby, kicked the door open and ran outside. She then jumped through the front gate holding her baby in her arms like a ghost. Again, there is a saying, *"When a man prepares to fulfil his utmost desire right from his childhood, there is nothing that can stop him from, how merciful he ought to be to the victims."* Benjamin ran out and started the engine. They followed Esther in a jeep, caught hold of her and pulled her into the jeep. Benjamin told the men to drive hurriedly to the city. He snatched the crying child, Jesse, from the hands of his mother and got down from the jeep. The other brothers held Esther by her hands and overpowered her. So diabolically did they treat her, that Esther, at last, begged her brothers, "At least, give me my child, he needs me. He cannot live without me."The brothers slapped her several times and she lost consciousness.

Benjamin sent the maid to lay the baby on the couch in the guest room. His maid reluctantly held the baby in her arms and proceeded towards the bedroom. Benjamin requested his wife to lock the door from outside. His wife, moved by Esther's faint voice calling her child, stood helpless holding the bunch of keys in her hand. Benjamin looked straight into their eyes: the maid quickly went into the bedroom; she stood at the threshold for a while as if waiting for another order from her mistress. Benjamin's wife said, "If Jesse is asleep, it would have been good." She then went and held the crying baby, patting him softly on his back trying to calm him down. The maid who was also a mother thought it best to feed Jesse. Soon she somehow calmed down the baby. She changed his soiled clothes and patted the baby lovingly. When Benjamin's wife called her, she left the baby quietly covering him with her scarf. That very night, the whole family of Benjamin bequeathed their house and hurried for the city. All along the way, Esther grumbled and unceasingly called for her rescue. Benjamin swallowed hard her curses and retorted saying, "Suicide, if you wish. That would be better for all of us. You must die in Israel only." Benjamin mixed sleeping pills in her water. Esther slept for the whole journey. She woke up from the pain in her breast. She held her breast and wept bitterly. Milk flowed out from her breast and soaked her top. She tried to escape from them while they were asleep. But the moving vehicle was locked from the outside.

At dawn, Ron opened his eyes, turned his head left and right, surprised to find himself sleeping alone, he jumped out of the bed in wonder. He looked around and saw Jensta sleeping on the wooden floor beside his bed in the filthy room. He heard the chirping of birds that flew up and down around the thatched hut. He turned his eyes and already sensed the danger. Jensta got up quickly and tried to find an escape. He found that the door was locked from the outside. They got very angry and tried to force the door open. Soon the door was flung open and a tall masculine man entered who warned them to return home as early as possible. The man turned back and returned with his gang. Then Benjamin's maid came with her friend and handed them the baby who was sleeping peacefully unaware of what misfortune had befallen him. Ron took his baby and enquired about the whereabouts of Esther. The maid did not tell him anything because she did not know anything about the plan. She told them what she did to calm the baby throughout the night. Ron and Jensta hurried home in their chariot. On the way, he told Jensta to drop the baby home while he would approach his other friends. He took his friend's chariot and hurried towards the police station. Unfortunately, he met with an accident on the way just after crossing the suspension bridge of the Tuivai River where Benjamin's parents were buried. Ron regained his consciousness only to find himself on the lap of his loving mother. He slowly opened his eyes and was taken aback at the sight of the hospital roof. His mother kissed him and asked him many things but he did not listen to anybody. He did not talk or cooperate with anyone helping him to recover. He stayed in the hospital for three days and nights. The doctor discharged him on the third day. On the sixth day, a beautiful lady nurse came to ask him about his condition. She gave him advice as part of her duty. Ron looked at her pretty face as the lady touched his head. Both fixed their eyes on each other, then the lady turned back smiling at the voice calling her "Sister Boria Lhungdim?" As she left the room, Ron glimpsed her figure, "*How perfectly slim and fair she is,*" he thought. Then a faint choked voice replied from inside and echoed simultaneously in his heart from the deepest layer "*No, Esther is fairer.*"

The next day Ron practised standing and walking in his house without the help of a walking stick. All his sisters and family members comforted him. His parents were busy with master Jesse. They all tried to hide the absence of Esther in the family. One evening, Ron looked at his hands and reads the lines on his palm. His elder sister gave him water and talked about their childhood, those days they played together in the big courtyard with cousins and nieces. Ron smiled at his sister who soon left him when he did not say anything. He drank the water and bit his lower lips to think more deeply and questioned himself, *"What does love mean to me now? How can I live without Esther? I am weaker day by day. Shall I trust my family? Am I not worthy to be Esther's husband when my parents are so proud of me? Did Benjamin hate my father? How can Benjamin, such a kind man do this thing to me and Esther? What will happen to Jesse if Esther does not return? Will they go to Israel now? From which planet does Benjamin hail? What will happen to my innocent child if I die? Can I forget Esther when many men get remarried and move on in life?"*

He looks at his wounded leg and touched the scars on his skin gently. His wounded heart saw the wounds on his body; suddenly he wondered how he got into an accident. He tried recollecting the scene, from the very beginning at Benjamin's house, his thoughts and steps; yet he could not figure out how he got into an accident. He said to himself, *"Maybe this is all God's plan. I cannot go against the Almighty's plan. I must try to move on with life and find the purpose of life that Almighty wanted to show me, and the reason I have been in this state."* He closed his eyes and the wind carried the sweet smell of love flower, forget-me-not, spread sweetly in the air. He breathed in the sweet smell of forget-me-not flower deep into his lungs: His blood gushed from his heart rendering him to breathe heavily. Longing for his love, his heart spoke to his soul saying, *"I love the sweet smell of your forget-me-not. My love, wherever you are. I send you my love through the wind again. My soul wails when this poor heart bleeds."* He wanted to hold the hands of his ladylove. He wanted to touch the soft lips and caress her lovingly. The soft hand of the kind nurse woke him up from his dreamland. His mother stood beside them and then left the room after the usual greetings. The nurse bathed him and dressed the wounds. The lady did not talk much but touched him lovingly. Ron asked her when she would come for the next dressing. The lady smiled and said, "If you call me, I will come, though my place is a little bit far from here."

CHAPTER - 7

THE MYSTERIOUS GRAVEYARD

Three more days passed but Ron did not want to call the nurse to dress his wounds for no reason. He liked the way she talked; her touches were soft and her presence was a thrill to all his family members, but he remembered his promise to Esther. He chose to stay away from all those who came into the way that distanced him and Esther. He felt empty and lonely. He called his sister Gloria to do the dressing. After the dressing, he decided to visit the place where he met the accident. He went to the river Tuivai in the evening with his friends in a chariot. He looks at the waters and thought of the day he had the accident there. There was no reason for anyone to meet with an accident in that plane area. He found no explanation for the mysterious accident. He remembered he crossed the bridge hurriedly, and in a wink, he knew he got an accident and become unconscious. He looked at the distant bamboo groves in the Giant Mountain. His friends invited him to bathe and play in the water.

He looked around in curiosity if there was something strange about that place. Then he saw something besides the bridge. To his surprise, he saw some faded flowers as if someone had put flowers in a graveyard a week ago. He went near to inspect them. He found a graveyard on which a flat stone bore the names of five persons. Some words were written in Hebrew script and he tried to decipher them right away. He tried to ask for help from someone. His friends came to him and told him that those names might belong to the early Christian Missionaries. They exaggerated as they told Ron some incidents, ghost stories of that place which villagers said to be haunted. Ron went back home with curiosity as to how he did not know about the graveyard that was right within his territory. He did not tell his family members. The next morning, he went again but this time alone and at a quiet hour. He stood on the suspension bridge and shouted at the top of his voice to hear his voice echo from hills to valleys. He looked at the grasses and flowers which, despite Ron's tragedy, seemed to smile and dance gayly with the serene flow of the river water. He went to the graveyard and tried to read the names. He saw a bamboo pole nearby and with that; he tried with all his might to lift the stone. He tried, again and again, to take out the small diary that was underneath the stone. When he could lift a little, he pushed the bamboo pole into the space between the stone and soil. He took a small long stick and dragged out the diary. It took a few minutes for Ron to pull out the diary himself. He opened the small diary and saw something written in capital letters. He cleaned the pages to read the lines "*Pastor Ginna, his wife Mrs. Dimnu and three British Missionaries—Rev. Richard, Rev. David and Rev. Lisa. They are martyrs, stripped and paraded in broad daylight and burnt alive by the village soldiers in front of a mob in the playground of Broadvale.*" He was taken aback when he saw the name written in the last line as "*Written by: Benjamin and brothers.*" He saw the same line written in Hebrew script. He wondered what that line would mean. He took the diary and kept it in his locker secretly. That night he had a bad dream. He saw the five martyrs walk around his bed while he was sleeping. Ron woke up from his bed and looked around his room. He did not take it seriously, thought it to be a dream that followed his mind.

Ron's family had secretly arranged a marriage proposal for him. His mother told him that the nurse, Miss Boria, was the daughter of the village midwife. Boria's mother was known far and wide for her special skill as a midwife. They were kind to them and when they proposed to her for him, they got a positive reply from her as well as her family. Boria told her family to arrange the wedding if and only when Ron gave her his consent. When Ron was informed of the marriage proposal, he instead questioned his father, who Pastor Ginna and the three British Missionaries were. Since then, the father and son never talked again about his marriage or any other issue/ matter relating to administration. Ron had the same dream again while he was sleeping on his bed, five people walked around his bed. Their conversation was like the buzzing of thousands of bees. He asked his friends what the repeated dream would mean. None of them could give him a satisfactory answer. Ron went straight to the Zumbo forest to meet the magician. The magician told him that he must have taken something that was being protected by some unseen beings, something which showed the identity of some very important thing or event. Ron at once remembered the small diary that he had taken from the riverbank under the bridge. He said to the magician, "Uncle, I did not know that it belonged to the invisible beings: I just took it, out of curiosity, that too with great effort, from under a stone at the river bank. I had no idea of a graveyard until I read the diary. People talk about the strange things that happen near the bridge. I got an accident at that spot, and… the accident was a mystery, hmm. The coincidence made me restless. When I checked that place, I saw some withered flowers, thereafter I got suspicious and could not hold back unfolding the mystery. I have no intention of doing any harm to the diary. I just want to know the truth."

The magician told him, "If you had not met with that accident, you would not have come to me, and if you had delayed meeting with me, perhaps, my story would die along with me, oh, this bony old body. It was an incident, which happened, hmm, some 20 years ago. That day, oh, how much I regret having visited Broadvale! I have regretted it my whole life, till now, oh young man. Five Christian Missionaries were stripped in public and paraded before the villagers. We all closed our eyes and prayed to God; even though I was a magician, I too prayed to God, for my magical powers do not work in the face of the Almighty: I felt the pain of humiliation done to the Christian Missionaries. The village soldiers burnt down the house of Pastor Ginna and scattered his utensils. They burnt the Missionaries alive, with the fire ignited from the torn pages of the Holy Bible. Oh my God! I am cursed to have ever seen that scene: unfortunately, we human beings cannot unsee what we have seen or clean our minds as we want, like a slate. Whenever I remember that day, I cannot breathe properly. That night, I was lying on my bed, still praying for the children of Ginna. I wish I could be of some help to the children of that pious man, oh Pastor Ginna! Just then, the Queen entered my room without knocking on the door. She told me to save the life of a boy who was bitten by a snake. She left my cottage leaving the lifeless body of a young boy of around 12 years after asking me to give him new life through my powers. The Queen told me the whole story again. She left my room with a warning not to disclose it to anyone. What happened next will blow your mind away. Till today I never told anybody. hmm... I will not tell you either. Just go back home and return the thing that you had taken from the graveyard of the martyrs. These things are not meant to be taken away from their place. Whosoever takes and possesses anything from dead bodies, will meet with the curse of Spirits, if it is kept with the dead body for some reason. Do you know why?

The invisible beings are watching over their things and follow wherever it is taken."

Ron asked the magician many questions about what the Queen had warned him of that he should not disclose to anyone. The magician again said to him, "I respect a promise and friendship with the Queen. I cannot break the trust of a woman who is my close friend. I cannot deny her request to use my power, for the good of man, even though I wanted to stop right that moment when the martyrs died in the flame. You can ask your mother if you want to know about it. Go back now before it gets dark, this jungle is also haunted."

Ron quickly returned to Broadvale and prepared to return the diary to its proper place. He had many friends visiting him that night, so he thought of going to the bridge early morning alone. His friends told him to choose a girl from the photographs of many beautiful ladies. They mentioned the names of all the beautiful ladies in their area. They tried their best to help him move on in life and forget about Esther. They blamed Esther as unfaithful and Benjamin for his selfish overnight decision.

That night Ron heard a painful cry of his boy, Jesse. He rushed to the room and saw his sisters and Lily, the babysitter trying to calm down Jesse. They told Ron that the baby was running a temperature. They could not calm him down even after giving him medicine. Ron remembered Benjamin's maid who was experienced in calming the baby. He sent for that maid at once. He took

Jesse in his arms and tried his best to calm him down by singing the same lullabies that Esther used to sing. He went outside and called his mother to help him. They could not bring down the temperature and were all worried for Jesse. Ron kissed him, hugged him and said, "Please stop crying, my child, I can't bear it, daddy can't bear it."At midnight the baby had convulsions and became unconscious. Ron at once drove his horse carrying the baby and went towards the graveyard. When he crossed the bridge, his horse neighed and became frightened. He got down from the horse carrying Jesse on his back with a loincloth. He went to the graveyard, then put the diary back in its exact place under the stone and prayed, *"I met with an accident, that's enough. This boy is innocent, spare him, he's born of your blood and the seed of your tree. We are sorry, please heal him, God of Abraham-Isaac-Jacob, heal this innocent child, forgive me, and forgive us. "*Instantly, the baby regained consciousness, cried out calling "Mama." He came back quickly trembling with fear.

Everyone was amazed, dumbfounded about where he had gone or why was he shaking to his knees. He did not tell anyone what happened. The baby slept peacefully throughout the night. Ron looked at Jesse and said, "My son, you are not borne to suffer this way, where is your mum?" He remembered the day, he went for his daily preaching in the synagogue at Sinai. He recalled that lovely evening when he was welcomed by his newborn son. He remembered his happiness, the moment he touched the tender hands, kissed his son for the first time. How he sweetly christened his name as, "By the grace of God, today, I beget this flesh of mine: let's name him Jesse, what do you say?" Esther replied, "Yes, Jesse, I like it. If our family had accepted us, how beautiful this moment would be. I think we should not wait for them to call back to us. We should instead go back and beg forgiveness from our elders. I want my son to grow up in the arms of his loving grandparents, I want to see him play with his cousins in that big royal house, roam with his friends on the broad roads of Broadvale, see the beauty of his people, get the blessing of his aunties: I want him to grow up in that big family like Broadvale so that his worldview will be broader. He will have many friends, servants, bodyguards. He will enjoy his childhood, besides learning from his royal teachers, well-trained to become brave and broadminded." But he kissed Esther on her head and said, "No dear, we cannot go back until they call us: I don't want to lose you, dear. Neither brother Benjamin nor father will accept us, I know they will not change their mind so easily, it will take time. We are still happy. God is with us. Why do you cry? See, our son is like you, he's got a mole on the temple and a dimple on his cheeks, aren't you happy?" Ron's tears rolled down when he remembered what Esther had said to him, "Ron, he is like both of us. I'm sorry I have fallen in love with someone else other than you, I have broken my word. He is so lovely: I will love him the most. This innocent baby gives me the realization that I am the luckiest woman to have you as my husband. The greatest gift and blessing in a woman's life is being a mother, and it is possible because of God and you, I love you."

Ron wiped his tears and kisses Jesse on his dimples and bade him a good night. He looks at the mole on his temple, when he heard Jesse calling his mother in his dreams, he turned away from him and said to himself, *"Esther, your dream of raising Jesse at Broadvale has come; see, your child is sick, calling your name in his dreams, longing the divine love and warm bosom of his mother; dear, come see your little darling. Let us watch together our little Angel take his tiny steps, come and see his beautiful changes, his amazing milestone, he has everything as you had wished for him except you, the love and care of his mother. Come back, I miss you, dear."*

CHAPTER - 8

MAMI, FIDDA AND JESSE

The next day Benjamin's maid, Mami, rushed in and enquired about the matter. Mami was in her mid-twenties. Her husband left home and had not returned for two years. Her in-laws hated her and blamed her for all the misfortunes in their family. Some people spread rumours that the British government recruited many native young men as soldiers who were deported to another country to fight in the Second World War against the Axis forces. People believed that he must have lost his life in the war. No one knew if he was dead or alive. She had two daughters from her first husband and a two-year-old son from her second husband. Her in-laws treated her dreadfully and separated her from her daughters. They defamed her of infidelity. Her second husband too divorced her with her unborn child. She had no one in this world when she was in need. The saddest thing for a woman is when she is separated from her children for no fault of hers, she looks around for help and realizes that there is no shoulder for her to lean on. She had no brother to rely on: no sister to cry on her shoulder, for during that time a divorced woman was treated cruelly, considered a taboo in the society. People would not let a divorced woman live in the village. They would even change their path if they happened to meet her on the way. She was the target of the evil men. She became the topic of gossip among the womenfolk. Benjamin had taken care of her when she was thrown out of her in-laws' house. Ron requested Mami to breastfeed her child along with Jesse. Ron gave Mami the job of a babysitter in the royal house. She was given a house and property on the condition that she would breastfeed Jesse and give a motherly love until he attained five years. In those days, usually, a child was breastfed by the mother till he or she was five years old. Jesse loved Mami and her son, Fidda, very much. Ron's three elder sisters had married and settled in distant places. The youngest of the five and the most beautiful called Breza, whom Ron loved the most, too, got married. Ron did not approve of the relationship but he also did not want to ruin their love marriage. Breza advised Ron to take good care of Jesse and wait for Esther's return. The other sisters were busy choosing a bride for their brother. After all, Ron was a handsome young man, educated, and from a well-to-do family. He was still admired by many girls. The sisters didn't care much about the momentary suffering. They talked about the beautiful ladies of the area. They even introduced their girlfriends to Ron. When Ron turned a deaf ear to them, they said, "We have all got married, except Gloria, who will also get married sooner or later.

Who will take care of the family and Jesse? Mami too will get remarried: She will never sacrifice her youth for Jesse. It is good that you married while Jesse is innocent. Brother, strike while the iron is hot."The sisters made a plan to send away Mami so that Ron would realize the role of a mother. They rebuked Mami and blamed her for every silly matter, cruelly treated her like a slave. They left no stone unturned to insult her and make her cry. Mami had to bear endless torture everywhere she stayed. She trusted Ron who treated her like his own sister, but alas! Broadvale too turned out to be no exception. Yet her bitter experiences in life made her a strong woman. She loved Jesse and Fidda equally. She looked after them who were like siblings, both of them born in the same year of 1947. She connected with God every Sunday at midnight, weeping at the feet of God, unceasingly praying in her meditation, *"God of Abraham-Isaac-Jacob, I know You hear the prayers of this humble widow. Lord, forgive me for losing my mind. Sometimes I forget that these are the things I am born to face. Forgive me, Father, for my jealousy and short temper: You know how cruel is the fate of Thy helpless widow, You only understand the life of this poor widow. Father, bless this motherless boy, Jesse. Bless my fatherless daughters, and this poor boy, Fidda. A mother's dream is to see her children grow up healthy, happy, and successful and above all, fear God. They are under the care of a husbandless woman. I pray that they become good friends, like brothers and good men. May they never feel lonely and fall sick. Father, I also pray for this Broadvale family whose minds are covered by oil and sealed in darkness. May these innocent sisters of Broadvale never experience the life of a widow! God, I believe that You hear the prayers of innocent honest people. I pray for my brother Ron, please give him new life to move on his life. Give him a new wife and help him forget Esther. I am happy that at least these kids are happy just because of me. Lord, let Your light shines upon me so that I may be able to show the world, Your glory through my light. Lord, I pray, please, shine on me the divine light."*

Ron waited for Esther though there was no news of her return. He only heard that she was safe and sound in Israel. He waited for days and months and now it was almost a year. On the other hand, Mami's life was renewed when her first husband returned home in 1952. Her husband had been deported to France to fight in the war against the Axis forces. God heard the prayers of His humble and honest child, and the seeming misfortune of Mami became a blessing in disguise as her husband came home with a great fortune. They remarried happily after 13 years, in 1953. Ron requested Mami and her husband to leave Fidda with him. But her husband did not agree. He took his wife along with the little boy, Fidda and proclaimed him as his son. Jesse and Fidda loved each other, more like friends than a brother. All the four married sisters were busy with their families while the unmarried sister, Miss Gloria was busy madly in a love affair with the white British soldier. So, Jesse was looked after by his grandparents. Ron also adjusted to his daily schedule and mingled with his friends. He was busy in his state affairs so, could spare little time for Jesse. He became more sociable to forget the past. He took a great role in the election of the Panchayat and was also greatly involved in the first Lok Sabha elections. He was given the job of an accountant but he rejected the offer from his MLA. Instead, he asked the man to give sanctions for a community hall and a stadium and repair the suspension bridge at Broadvale. He planned to make the statues of the five martyrs at Broadvale but his father did not like his idea. He had not talked with his father for many days and weeks because of his project. At last, he decided to fulfil his dream of erecting the statues of the martyrs after his father's death. He had always dreamt of becoming an army officer. He passed a written test as well as viva for the post of Military officer in the Indian Army.

One fine day, Ron's father called him and said, "Ron, let's talk today. If you had no important appointment today, can we just talk plainly about life?"

"Go on, father, I have no appointment as important as your call," said Ron.

Ron's mother gave them coffee and said, "Sometimes we need to talk and sort out all our problems. We need to express our heart's desire rather than keep the burden hidden within us. Life is short and moments are precious, Ron. I will take care of Jesse and the guests." Saying this, she left the room. The room was used whenever important discussions were held in the family. It was a cosy room with white curtains. There were ten single wickers and a long square table in the middle. There were decorations of birds' feathers, displayed heads of animals killed by Daadi, his father and grandfather. It had a round mirror hanging on the wall and guns displayed on the side walls. One could see swords and shields, spears and bows with arrows that truly marked the royal family in their warfare and hunting skills.

Ron's father was a strong and healthy man. They had just celebrated his golden jubilee birthday. He had a square face with hairs all over his body. He wore a red shawl and cream colour traditional lungi. He put a red turban on his head, with a few birds' feathers attached to the turban. He had scars all over his body, and his face had deep lines cut from wild animals' attacks that showed that he was a brave and great hunter. He had dark skin, keen sunken eyes. His voice was harsh and commanding. He looked straight into Ron's eyes and said, "From your childhood, we have a special love for you because you are our only son. I have spoilt you enough and I hope so, your childhood life would be an awesome one, unlike ours, we struggle and toil using our muscles, and physical strength to earn fame and title. We learn different skills which are basic for every man like hiking, rock climbing, tree climbing, how to build a house, shooting, warfare, killing, fighting, swimming and learn to live, have mastered to live by our own feet. I sent you to Mission School so that you will learn how to excel from your forefathers. I should say I have been successful in my mission. Now you have become an independent man. I am happy to see you leading the people and I appreciate your social-mindedness, your attitude, your patience; I appreciate your tolerance power too. These are all the things that I had expected the son of Broadvale should be."

He paused for a moment when Ron seemed to be uneasy. Ron said in a calm voice, "Father, what are the things you want me to do? You can tell me straight as I'm not worthy of being praised by you; I realize how important your advice is to me."

Ron sat more comfortably, relaxed on the chair. His father nodded, thought for some more time as he reclined in his chair, then turned towards Ron and continued, "I want to tell you something. Even though I am your father, I want you to forgive me for not telling you the truth about the graveyard. I did it as a duty, and as a worthy son of my father; customs and traditions are to be respected. I have to stand in integrity with my people, avoid western culture and traditions. I have committed a grave mistake by taking the law into my hand by burning alive the Christian Missionaries. I have killed more than one hundred Christian missionaries in my life. You know I have prospered and earned fame all my life, but I'm no longer a happy man when I see your broken face. Son, I want you to move on in life; sometimes we happen to lose the moon in no time while counting the stars. I'm old now. You need a woman who will stand by you, help you and encourage you; you know, we, men are nothing without our women. Besides, I want to see you settle down peacefully before I die. In life, every one of us falls down no matter how carefully we lead our life; you have to rise and stand up again. Broadvale is in your hand, it's solely your responsibility, to make this land prosper and famous." Ron thought for a while, feeling awkward talking about his love tohis father. His father told him to say whatever he liked. After sometime Ron asked, "Father I will do anything for your name. First, let me know what's going on in Israel. Esther's life will be miserable leaving behind Jesse. I trust her. She will come back to us. I will decide whether to remarry or not after I confirm with Esther. I respect promises and I don't want Jesse to have a stepmother."

CHAPTER - 9

THE MEETING OF RON AND RICHARD

One day Gloria requested Ron to accompany him to the town. They went and attended an auction of government goods and properties. The British soldiers auctioned their bulky goods when they were to leave India. Gloria was looking for Richard who once saved her life. The moment she saw Richard, she ran towards him. Richard tried to hug and kiss her, but suddenly stopped when Ron was behind them. Gloria called Ron and introduced each other. Ron asked his name knowingly to see if the other still remembered him. The white man said, "I am Richard of the British army. It's my pleasure to meet you, Sir. I think I have seen you somewhere. You look like the commander of the Sinai Soldiers." Ron also introduced himself and they became friends. They drank coffee in a hotel. From their looks, Ron understood that Gloria and Richard were in love. He left them and attended the auction programme. Ron had already learnt from the villagers about the good deeds of the British Captain and was happy to meet such a great man. On the other hand, he did not like the mindset of his sister Gloria who, instead of the white man, easily obeyed him and tried to impress him. Gloria became mad when she met Richard. He did not like the way his sister looked at the man, who was by nature possessing a good heart. Even if the white man truly loved Gloria, he did not want to have ties with the western people, their culture and tradition.

Ron bought a piano in the auction. The piano was branded, not found in India. He tested the condition of the instrument and was very satisfied with the sound. Gloria and Richard came to him after some time. Richard said to Ron, "I came to know about your family and your broken heart. If you can please accompany me, I am going to Israel shortly. We can travel the journey together; I would be glad to help you provide a tourist visa to Israel." Ron replied to Richard, "No thanks. I will manage to visit Israel some other time, not in a hurry. You go ahead: I will go when the time is ripe." When Ron reached home, he was shocked to learn that Gloria and Richard had been in love for the past three years. He also learnt that both the families were strictly against their love. Richard gave pressure on his parents that he would not return to Britain without marrying Gloria. The lovers had been eagerly waiting for approval from both the families.

Ron was in a daydream, dreaming about Esther. He held a knife in his hand trying to sharpen it. He sat down on a stone in the courtyard staring at the knives. He thought about what his father had told him the other day. He knew that their advice was far better for him. "*I'm a man, son of my father, I need a woman. How long I will wait for something or someone and there is no certainty of her coming.*" Just then a man in a khaki uniform approached who handed him a parcel. The village postman knew very well the parcel was sent by none other than Esther, so he handed Ron the parcel personally. The two talked about current affairs and when Ron's father came out, the postman left. He headed towards the next destination of his address book. Ron's father saw the parcel but turned in another direction pretending to have seen nothing. Ron took the parcel inside his room. He met his sister Gloria near the doorway. He hid the parcel and hurried to his room. Gloria followed him from behind, peeped through the window, carefully watching her brother. Ron tore open the parcel in haste, first took out the letter, for he knew Esther would surely care for them and come back. He held the letter in one hand and touched the parcel with his curious right hand. His sister quickly informed her mother about the parcel. They both entered Ron's room in a minute. When Ron heard their footsteps, he hid the letter which he had just tried to read. Ron lay on his bed flat just after he kept the letter under his pillow. His mother looked around and saw the parcel. She happily asked Ron," Whose parcel would come at this time, I hope it's from my lovely daughter-in-law Esther. I hope she's fine." When no words of encouragement come from Ron, his mother opened the parcel and his sister exclaimed, "Hey, a beautiful scarf!" They unfolded the neatly-wrapped scarf, found a very beautiful embroidery on a satin cloth. Just then the maid came who told them they had unknown visitors. The two left Ron who heaved a heavy sigh as they moved out of the room. Ron looked at the scarf, touched with his fingers the beautiful red roses all around the border of the scarf and a more beautiful heart shape in the centre. Inside the heart was written, '*REJ*'. He took the other smaller scarf, saw the lines beautifully embroidered "*I love Jesse.*" He again unfolded the third scarf excitedly, saw the phrase embroidered in red shining thread "*p 143*". Ron was reminded of the promise which they had on pillar 143. As he touched the lines with his fingers as if by instinct, his breath became heavy, his nose turned reddish by the impulse. Then he quickly took out the envelope and read the letter. The letter was lengthy. It took him about an hour to read all. Yet he remembered all the lines, those beautiful lines specially chosen from one's soul mate, how Esther described her days and life. He believed Esther would never tell a lie. He got angry with Benjamin for torturing his beloved wife, after forcibly separating her from her child without any mercy. He pitied Esther so much that he hit the table with his fist repeatedly when she told him how she spent her days living in a dark room and was fed like a war prisoner. How he wished he could save her from the cruel hands of her demon brothers! He read all the pages from 1 to 10. He held his hand tightly and wanted to beat those who tortured Esther. At that moment, many of his friends came who disturbed him from dreaming more. He hid the letter in his locker. He moved out with them to attend a marriage ceremony of one of his friends at Gaitlane.

The next day Ron went to visit pillar 143 only to find that the pillar had been cut down for the renovation of the school. He was sad that nothing about the promise could be seen. The fencing was replaced by an aluminium wire. He was very sad at the co-incidences in his life. He looked around, felt lonely that every place had changed. The eucalyptus tree was torn down and uprooted by the last cruel monsoon wind. He asked himself, *"Esther, what is love? What do all these changes mean: Do I have to move ahead of my dreams or rebuild another promise? Is a promise made to be broken? No, no, my dear, lets us not break our promise for the sake of our fruit, let's stand against the storm and the wind; life without adversities is not worth living, we have to create history for the next generations through our seeds."* Then he remembered what Esther wrote on one of the pages of her letter, *"Ron, when I was a little girl, I learnt that God is love, I took love as the way to Godliness. When I grew bigger, I learnt that love is blind. I took love as humbleness to the person we love. When we love each other, we say love is understanding. We understood each other: you defined love to me as the light of life. When I was forcibly forsaken by my loved ones, love meant to me, differently from what I had known earlier. I'm now a slave of love. Love becomes a feeling of sorrow and disgrace; love is no longer a waterfall but a spring of tears. Love no longer brings joy to the mind but a restless mind, like longing for the rain in the dreary desert. This forbidden love will mean the end of my life. I will die for my love. But before I die, I want to kiss Jesse and hug you then close my eyes in your warm bosom."*

"I will wait for you, my dear, please come back soon. I need you so much, I call only your name, I hear your sweet whispers right through my ear to my heart, I'm drunk in the wine of your love, I want to tell you once again how much I love you." He wrote and put it inside an envelope to be sent to Esther. He was filled with love and one thing that kept scaring his waking hours was if Esther would give up her life, how much he would repent for not rescuing her from the dark cell of demons. He decided to go to Israel. He made the necessary documents for the tourist visa for Israel. He then got a call letter from the Indian Army headquarters, his dream job to serve his motherland. Yet he had spent much time and money on his visa and at last, he was granted the tourist visa. So, he withdrew from reporting to his service.

CHAPTER - 10

RON GOES TO ISRAEL

Ron's life was filled with happiness and love. One could see his face glow after many months like the new leaves in the spring season. He became more active, talkative, jolly and friendly. He underwent three weeks of training for his journey. He learnt the geography, history, culture and language of the Israelites. He could not wait to trod his feet on the Holy land and meet his soul mate and wife, Esther.

A devil's hand from nowhere came to destroy his love and happiness. He received a letter in the name of Esther. He thoroughly checked the handwriting, could not believe himself his love was telling him to forget her for good. However, he wanted to meet personally and say a few words to her. The following month, he headed to Israel. Gloria and Richard took him to Kolkata. Richard gave him the name and address of his friend who was a journalist. Ron also had a few names of some Indian friends who recently moved to Israel. He boarded the plane bound for Tel Aviv. He knew from his friends that the Bnei Manasseh from Northeast India who moved to

Israel had settled in Beersheba state. Inside the plane, he also met some Indian friends who were visiting Israel on a tourist visa. Mostly they were from south Indian states like Kerala and Mumbai. When he reached Tel Aviv airport, just as Richard and Gloria had planned, he was received by Richard's friend, the journalist, Mr. Thomas. Thomas took him to his hotel in the city. Thomas introduced Ron to one of his co-workers whose name was Mr Dingo. Unfortunately, Thomas met with an accident and was hospitalized in the intensive care unit. Ron was left with Mr. Dingo, a cold serious-looking person, who talks-less-but-works-more type of man. He never spared his time or gave freedom to Ron. Ron's first four days in Tel Aviv had passed between Dingo's house and the hospital, visiting Thomas who met an accident because of him. Thomas got discharged from the hospital after four days. Ron paid the hospital bills, it was the least he could do for his friend. He left Mr. Dingo's house and met one of his Indian friends who served in the Israel Army. They went back and gave the journalist, Dingo, some money to guide him during his stay until Ron met with his love. Very soon the three became good friends. Ron wrote a letter to be published in the **"heart to heart"** column in Dingo weekly journal, *"Home is not too far when love is deeply rooted. Fate has not been fair to us, love is love. I, Redy, your Ron, comes to the Holy land, travelling thousands of miles to take you home."* It'd been a week again since he reached Be'ersheva, but he could not locate Benjamin's house to meet his love. The journalist interviewed Ron in his hotel. He then flashed the news on his weekly Television channel again. Many people felt pity for Ron. Immigrants from India were informed of the news. Two Israeli army personnel, of Indian origin, came out to help them. They promised him that they would do their best to find out Esther. It was not difficult to trace immigrants from India as they were only a few hundred in number and Benjamin being a Rabbi, was well-known in his locality. Within two weeks, with the help of his friends, they went to Benjamin's house.

Benjamin's family and friends were astonished to see Ron coming all the way just to meet his wife, Esther. It moved Benjamin's heart and he regretted sending away his sister for marriage to another man. They welcomed Ron, the two Israel soldiers along with the journalist to stay in his house. Benjamin invited Esther to come home alone. He arranged a dinner for them. They did not inform Esther about Ron's arrival. They also warned Ron not to disclose his identity. Ron agreed to their condition. The next day, Esther came home not knowing Ron had come to Israel. She came along with her husband and family. Before dinner when all the guests were seated, Benjamin introduced his guests as his relatives from India. Esther was seated behind Ron. She could not recognize Ron as he wore a mask and the costume of a pressman to hide his identity. No one told Esther that the man with the mask was Ron. They had dinner together. Ron wore a sunglass and looked at Esther to his heart's content. He knew from her face that she was not happy in her marriage. He could see her eyes empty; her face was sunken: The moisture and the shining of her skin had gone; there was no smile on her face. She did not talk or say anything to anyone. Her glow had gone: her dimple had given her a hollower face. How much his heart bled and how much he loved her, it was unfathomable to see the more tortured heart of Esther who looked like an undernourished orphan or the uncared flower plant potted inside a room devoid of rain and sunlight. After dinner, they lit lanterns and kept them in the middle as well as in the corners of the living room. There were shadows on the walls as well as on the floor. Before they all went to sleep, they had a prayer together. Ron did not pray but listened to Esther's prayer with his ears fully open. He heard Esther weeping and praying to God for her husband and child. He immediately opened his eyes, looked at her praying. Esther prayed in her mother tongue so that her new husband and in-laws would not be in disgrace. Ron saw Esther stretching out her hands, kneeling and praying to God as if weeping at the feet of the Almighty. It pierced his heart which was already bleeding to hear his name in her prayer and wanted to reveal his identity. He slowly stood up, tried to go to Esther but was quickly thwarted by his friends. He thought of deciding on his instinct gut but then his conscience instantly forbade him from going further. He squeezed his hands hard, somehow reluctantly controlled his feelings in front of his friends. Everyone shookhands bade goodnight after the prayer but Ron did not shake a hand with Esther.

Throughout the night, Ron could not sleep, he became restless when Esther and her husband entered the bedroom. He was on pins and needles, didn't know what to do. He did not want to create trouble, agreed to himself not to lose the trust of his friends. Suddenly they heard a scream from the next room: they all got nervous to open the door. When Benjamin opened the door, they saw Esther shaking like in a state of epilepsy. Her husband cried for help. They sprinkled water on her face but she was still shaking and then cried out saying, "The wind is changing, the wind is changing, where does this wind come from, is it the west wind or the south wind, why is this wind blowing?" Her husband told Ron and his team that they were married just a month ago. For the last two weeks, she used to behave that way. She would sit brooding the whole day, with no stamina to work. Esther was immediately rushed to the hospital by her husband and family. Benjamin and his family were conscience-stricken and requested Ron if he would leave the place in peace. Ron and his team prepared to leave Benjamin's house that very night. Ron was seething but did not say anything; he remembered Jesse and decided to live for him. He parted with his friends in the city.

The next day he went to the city hospital to find out about Esther who was hospitalized in the critical unit. He met the doctors, inquisitively asked about her condition. The doctor disclosed to him that Esther was having a large brain tumour in the parietal lobe which was fatal. The doctor told Ron that she would not survive for long. Ron secretly entered her room in the hospital. He believed that if Esther saw him, she would be completely healed. He went near her bed, touched her cloth with his trembling hands, He tried to kiss her forehead when all of a sudden, the eyes of the night owl old nurse intervened. The nurse at once alerted the hospital attendant, who in turn called for the security guards. They called the security and told them to arrest Ron. Ron was being charged with attempting to murder a woman out of jealousy, and also trying to touch another man's wife. The hospital authority called Esther's in-laws and asks them if they knew Ron. Esther's in-laws told everyone that they had never seen Ron and had no relation with him. Ron insisted they ask Esther who he was to her. They woke up Esther to asked her if she had known Ron. When Esther opened her eyes, she was so shocked to see Ron that she fainted and lost consciousness. The guards beat him up even though he said he was her husband. Esther's in-laws thought him to be a mad man, so they called up the police. The police soon reached the spot, checked his identity card, visa and passport. They found out that Ron's tourist visa had only a few days left. Ron was put in the lockup. Tintin and his brothers rushed to the police station. They bailed him out after some days but with a stern warning never to show his face to them again. They, along with some Indian friends from the Israeli Police Force, immediately dropped Ron at the airport. They sent him back to India without mercy. As the saying goes, *'Every pain gives a lesson and every lesson changes a person.'*

Esther woke up from the coma and shouted calling "Ron, come back, Ron, I love you," in front of her husband and in-laws. But her husband sadly told her that Ron had left her, would never return to her like him. Ron had to return home with a broken heart, but with a decision to marry the most beautiful woman, give all his love to that woman to show off to Benjamin. He prayed for Esther for her recovery and her happy married life. From the city hospital, it took two days to reach the airport. When Tintin returned home, he was shocked to learn that Esther was no more. She had left a letter for Ron and Jesse. Benjamin repented for what he had done to his only sister, Esther. He used to scold her sister saying, "If Ron loves you, he will come and get you. One year has passed but did he turn up? Do you believe his father will allow him to wait for you? Do not trust the Broadvale family: they will never come for you. They are happy that you left them; if only you know how much they hate you! You must marry a man of our religion, live near me, forget about Ron with that Daadi, the devilish chief of Broadvale. They burnt alive our parents mercilessly, how can you live with those people who persecuted your parents, who took away your childhood and youth, who ruined your life and embarrassed your brothers, oh heartless woman." He regretted, cursed himself saying, *"Oh God! What have I done! I cared for my sister too much, and now she has left me with tears in her eyes. I am sorry, dear sister, what curse had shielded my mind from noticing my sister's condition? Whom shall I love, counsel and scold?*

You must have wished to see the face of your Ron, but this wicked heart has veiled the face of your lover." Benjamin blamed not only himself but also Tintin for sending away Ron to India. He at once prepared to send the letter and wish left by Esther. His wife advised him saying, "We cannot simply send the wish of Esther like a coward. We are defeated, the whole world will blame us, we will not be able to hide the truth. We have sinned against God for separating two soul mates. We should go to India and beg Ron to forgive us. Let us forget what they had done to our parents, our parents are martyrs. Everything is God's plan. God has a plan; see, He moves us to his Holy land and blesses us, if only we had the forgiving minds, our beloved sister would not leave us so soon, and we may not face this shame in society. Alas, we cannot hide the truth. Let us no longer raise our fists in the face of the Almighty. We did all possible and tried our best to save Esther, but our seed is growing in Broadvale, little Jesse; the anger of man cannot thwart the plan of God. If we have followed God's desire, these problems could have been averted. Now divorcing a dead woman from her husband is the greatest shame for us. Esther belongs to the Broadvale family. We had not performed any custom of marriage or divorce on our sister, so it is best that we personally go to Broadvale and finish the bond of marriage. Let us go to India, let us go with a good mission this time, to bless Jesse, free Ron of the promise they had; otherwise, Jesse might become an orphan."

CHAPTER - 11

BENJAMIN GOES TO INDIA

Benjamin and his wife went to Broadvale and begged forgiveness from Ron. They apologized to Jesse too. They handed Ron the wishes left by Esther. However, the Broadvale family didn't give them a warm reception. Their family elders tried their best to bring peace between the two parties. Daadi blamed everything on Benjamin, right from his father, Ginna, to Esther for rendering little Jesse, his beloved grandson, deprived of his mother's care. Ron too did not like to listen to Benjamin. He instead blamed them of taking the trouble only to bring the bad news that they could have kept to themselves if they cared for their sister. He also told them straight to beg the forgiveness from Esther's new husband whom they had bluffed or blackmailed by giving the wife of someone else in marriage to him. Ron also pointed at Benjamin, told him that he would marry a virgin girl, that too far more beautiful than Esther.

The irony of Ron's words made Benjamin speechless, for he knew he had gone to Broadvale after 21 years to beg forgiveness. If he spoke more, his mission would not be a success. He had gone to Broadvale with a different mission that time, to help them, bless them keeping aside the past stories that still haunted him. When the Queen, who had been away from home that day, heard the matter, she called them back and consoled them instead. She made peace between Daadi and Benjamin by permitting Benjamin to lay a foundation stone on the spot where he had buried the dead bodies of the five martyrs. She also made peace between Ron and Benjamin by convincing her son to accept the wish left behind by Esther. Ron accepted the remains of Esther at last. He and his family members mourned for days. After the customs were completed, Esther's remains were buried in a manner fitting of a Queen in the Broadvale royal reserve. They buried Esther next to the grave of their grandma. Benjamin thanked the Queen and said, "You are truly a queen, brave and intelligent. You have once saved my life, and, also my siblings. You gave new life to my brother Tintin when he was bitten by a poisonous snake. As the Holy Book says an angry man stirs up conflict and a bad-tempered man commits many sins, but a wise woman is like water that douses the fire. I have lost my precious sister, have sinned against God for separating her from her family. Let us forgive one another. God's purpose cannot be altered by our anger, or due to men's meanness, and insanity. Thank you for everything. Broadvale will be broader and broader and the valley will expand in all directions, just because of you. You have been a blessing to your people, and, me in particular; I am grateful to you, Aunty. Thank you once again, for giving me the land to construct a tomb for the martyrs. I will inform my people and begin the work shortly."

CHAPTER - 12

RON FALLS IN LOVE THE SECOND TIME

One fine winter morning, as Ron was playing the piano on the balcony, he was surprised to see the damsel whom he had dreamt of. He had seen her in his dreams for two consecutive nights. The lady was tall and slim with a shapely figure and fair skin. Her eyes were bright and lovely which seduced Ron in his dream. She walked in grace: there was confidence in her look and modesty in her gesture. The lady was in her early twenties. Ron had been thinking about his dream and wondered who the lady would be. He wanted to search for the lady who hypnotized him from his dream to his days. And she suddenly appeared to him that morning. It was a dream come true, a lucky day for Ron. She had come to Broadvale to offer her prayers in the Giant Prayer Mountain. Ron was playing a lovely tune on his piano, and as he saw the lady from distance, the music came to a halt. The woman slowed down her stride when she did not hear the music. Ron stood from the balcony and looked at her graceful walk, his eyes following the marvellous lady of his dreams. He said to himself, *"She must be a music lover, just like me."* The lady turned around to identify where the sweet music came from. Ron went back and continued playing his piano to impress her. He played the piano with his fingers while he stretched his neck as long as he could to look at the pretty lady who seemed to dance and walk to the rhythm of the music. She knew a man was trying to impress her. She was filled with joy, yet she did not turn around or glance at the man. Ron was happy and at once started singing, doing his best with the music. His family members came and looked at him in wonder. Everyone who heard the song and the music appreciated it. His father came, sat beside him listening to the music. When Ron opened his eyes, he felt embarrassed to see his father. His father stood up, patted him on his shoulder saying,"Go on, your music pleases everyone. But you should also be concerned about your career. You are still very young. This coming Sunday there will be an exam in the Indian Army. You were interested to serve in the defence force. Your last exam result might be declared by now. I will go to town afterwards, will you accompany me?" Ron replied, "Father, you check the result of my last exam. I will play music the whole day, ok?" His father smiled and left him nodding his head. Daadi was on cloud nine to see his son's happy face, for the father knew well that Ron was falling in love once again. Daadi made a plan and told the other family members how time healed the wounds of

Ron. He sent away the servants to check the farm while he and his wife took Jesse out to the town.

Ron waited for the return of the lady from the prayer mountain. He sent his maid, Joyi, to enquire about the woman. He informed one of his men to ride his chariot and help the woman return early. In the evening, Joyi and the man brought the woman in the royal chariot. Joyi was an extrovert girl of 12 years, a very naughty and carefree girl. She told the lady all about Ron, his ups as well as downs and called out to Ron saying, "Brother Ron, your lady is coming, come and meet her." Ron responded from his balcony dressing up and shouted, "Come upstairs, you both, come, nobody's home today." He then started playing his piano as sweetly as he could to impress the lady and slowly sang a melancholic song that he had composed the same day,

"Oh charming lady, night queen of my dream,

You are the one, whom I saw in dreams.

The pretty face I have been searching for,

You are the one, you are the one,

Come and hold my hands,

Touch me, test my strength, taste my wine,

Tease me like your boy and take me to your heart.

This winter is sweetly colder for me

This morning's Sun rays are seemingly warmer

This mind is secretly getting younger

Maybe it is time to sing and dance."

When the woman heard his song, she listened attentively, leaning against the pole at the border of the veranda, and folding her hands at her back: She looked at Ron from head to foot without a wink. When Ron opened his eyes, she went near to him, and said, "You have a beautiful voice, I mean a manly voice. I want to listen again." Ron asked her name looking straight into her eyes; she smiled and said "I am Disha, the singer from Gaitlane town." When Ron tried to introduce himself, she interrupted him and said, "I know you are Ron, I had heard your story a few years back though I had not met you. I also heard about your misfortune, and I felt sorry for you." "Anyway, do you like my music?" asked Ron. Disha raised her thick eyebrow, smiled and nodded her head. Then she said, "I'm a music lover. Music is my life. I started learning music from my teacher when I was ten. Can I play your piano once because this piano sounds special and it appeals to my ears; where did you buy it?" Ron gave her his seat and said, "Sure, sure. Try it. I bought it a few years ago in an auction; heard, it was left by a British army officer. I too want to hear your voice." Disha thanked him and started playing the piano moving her long fingers excitedly. Her face started to glow as she smiled, she sang attentively, giving her heart and soul to her song. Ron could not just believe his eyes, he stood in front of his dream lady, winked his eyes, watched

Disha. Disha closed her eyes, sang slowly but sweetly, the popular romantic song of the time that she had composed herself. He wondered how her face changed from pale cream to pink rose, the moment she started singing. He could not resist his mind from his instinctive thoughts. Disha sang one verse and one chorus, then played the music in different tunes moving her head gently from left to right, gradually increasing the speed, then playing a heavier metal, swinging her head to and fro. Ron smiled and exclaimed, "Wow! You are bestowed not only with rare beauty but also with a sweet voice and great skills. I wish you would stay near me so that I can learn more about music from you."

Joyi clapped her hands, laughing hysterically as she always was, trying to crack a joke at them. Ron requested Disha to have the best coffee prepared by Joyi. Joyi immediately went to the kitchen, soon brought two cups of strong coffee saying "Come on, have the best coffee, it's from our coffee farm." Ron looked at Disha and said to himself, *"My God! How sweet and friendly and beautiful she is! What will I do to impress her, and to convince her to stay with me, what will she think about me?"* Disha asked quickly, "Oh, did you say something?" "No, have your coffee, please," he too replied quickly. He looked at her lovingly as if he was in a dream. Disha wore a blue silk frock; her pleated golden hair was coiled behind her head, with a gold thread fringe at the tail. Her beauty shone with the evening golden sunrays. Her smile gently passed like a wave in the ocean into her surroundings, especially to Ron, the waves of her youth made his heart restless, burning hot inside. The trees and flowers seemed to dance with the evening breeze with her smile. A wisp of hair was rebelliously playing about her face, blowing about in the air, entirely unconcerned with the havoc it caused to Ron's state of mind.

Ron finished his coffee in no time. He kept the mug on the table beside him. He then stood up and moved a few steps back. He looked around and then said to Disha, "I wish my dream may come true." Disha too finished the last mouth of her coffee in one gulp and stood up. She licked her lips and said, "What a nice coffee!" Her bangles jingled as she giggled watching the innocence of Joyi. She made Ron's heart soft as cotton; he looked at her soft, long fingers and her lips that were wet and stained by the coffee. She went near Ron and asked, "What is your dream?" Ron suddenly shook his head a little and said, "I mean I wish I got my dream job in the Indian Army." Disha knew well that Ron was hiding something from her. She knew and it was obvious that Ron had fallen in love with her.

Just then Ron's father came back from the town. Other family members also returned home as usual. Ron introduced Disha to his family members. They all loved Disha and insisted on her spending the night. Disha had to spend the night there as it was getting late to return home. Ron invited Disha to go and visit his park before it was dark. Ron took his horse, mounted it after he helped

Disha on another horse. They went for a long ride and reached the garden. There were beautiful flowers that bloomed happily on the hill slopes. They stood at the breathtaking viewpoint, looked at the waterfall from a distance. They walked around the garden that was filled with the sweet fragrance of roses and marigolds. Next to the flower garden was a coffee farm. Disha was happy to see the green hills filled with the fragrance of flowers. She talked about the beauty of Broadvale and the kindness of its people. Disha asked Ron if she could take some rose stems for her garden. Ron answered her straight, "They are all yours, you don't have to ask." Disha got nervous as she was utterly shocked, absolutely unprepared for that scene when Ron looked straight at her lips, then moved down his eyes to her two big breasts saying, "Disha, you look very charming, I think I have fallen in love with you." Disha moved back and ran towards the horses. Ron came behind her, helped her mount the horse. They looked at each other without saying anything. When they reached home, his friends came to visit him. They spent the evening singing romantic songs on the balcony. Disha spent the rest of the evening with Ron's family. The next morning Disha left Broadvale before Ron get up from bed.

CHAPTER - 13

OBSEQUIES OF A DEAD MOTHER

Ron's family knew that Ron was in love with Disha. Ron's mother asked if she could go and ask her hand in marriage. Ron did not want to go to Disha's place, for he knew she did not love him as he did. He used to go to Disha's house but she did not give him her time. Disha was a popular artist. She had to go to parties to present a special number; she was not finding excuses. She had heard the story of Ron, pitied him as a friend, but did not love him. Since many young men were after her, she was proud. Her ego made her hate Ron, who was then recognized as a widower with a son.

In the meantime, Ron got a call letter from the Indian Army intelligence department. He turned 26 years though his academic age was 21. He spent maximum time with Jesse before he joined his service. Ron's family requested Disha again and again, to marry Ron. She, at last, told them, "I have wanted to marry a virgin man since my childhood." Ron underwent six months of training in the lovely hill station called Dehradun. Ron loved Disha so much that he would go and stay at her house for days and nights. He could not eat or drink without seeing Disha. On the other hand, Disha did not return to her home. She stayed in different places to avoid Ron. Disha's family told Ron to forget her. Ron requested Disha to tell him something to do and he would stop torturing her. Disha told him to look after his son Jesse if he truly loved his wife, Esther. Ron went back to Dehradun after his holiday. He wrote lyrics for Disha to sing. He also sponsored the band so that they included his lyrics in their next album. The same year, the band released the song wherein Disha was the singer. Mr. Doon was the guitarist, and they both made the song very popular. However, they didn't pay much heed to the meaning of the lyrics.

If you think the world belongs just to you

If you think your youth will never fade away

If you think your love will never leave you

If you think your love will stand still with time

You may be right if you have not trod on the second path

Where you realize classic footprints and classy imprint

No longer define you, you just cannot move ahead

But you have to move on in life, you have to live for some reason

The star will never fall down but always shines above you

Destiny holds your hand, oh! the lover is far beyond the blue

You are wrong, for men are mortal though love is immortal.

2. Love is divine though life is often unfair

Beauty is not only for the eyes of youth,

It's more beautiful on the second path

Though the path is trodden only by a few

3. Smile to make millions smile back, you'll then brag

Take no pride: life is not a bed of roses

The zigzag path welcomes you, you'll feel the nag

You only knew the pain, say, this is life.

Ron decided to remain single his whole life if Disha did not become his wife. He wanted to give up the struggle when Disha never gave him her time. He bought flowers and gifts and sent letters weekly, but she never reciprocated them. He looked after his son, Jesse, played with him and taught him music. He appointed one of the best teacher. Ron told him to teach Jesse songs and poems along with his school subjects. He encouraged Jesse to face the challenges in life in his absence. Days rolled on and it was difficult for Ron to remain single. He sent his friends to Disha seeking her favour but she never agreed to marry Ron. Before he went back to his posting, he met Disha just to tell her how much he loved her. When Disha told him that she would rather remain unwed than become his wife, Ron threatened her that he would make her his wife whether she agreed or not. He said to her, "I will stop nagging you from now onward. You will become my wife for sure, hold your tongue you lady, even if you get married to another man, I will kill him and take you as my wife. I will not easily let you go as I did to my wife Esther."

Jesse was very advanced in every way. He used to raise critical questions to his grandparents. He used to question life after death, how dreams were coming or how big heaven is. At school he was the Captain and admired by his teachers; even though he was pampered at home, he was very mature and bold in taking decisions. On his seventh birthday, Ron asked Jesse what his birthday gift would be. Ron handed him a parcel that he had kept buried under the earth for years. It was a wish left by Esther. Benjamin had personally delivered the parcel and handed it to Ron four years ago. Jesse took the parcel excitedly forgetting to answer his father about the birthday gift. Jesse ran to his grandparents and showed them the parcel happily. They tore off the plastic cover with great excitement. Everyone was curious about what was inside a square embroidered copper box. They did not know how to open the lock. Jesse ran to his daddy for the password. Soon he came back with the password shouting "*1942p143!*" The family members looked at each other in wonder and opened the box. To their surprise, they found one photograph of Esther on the top. They took out the photograph and were all shocked to see Esther after so many years. Then they took the envelope covered by a white velvet cloth. The velvet cloth had lines of lip kiss marks by Esther with red lipstick. Under the envelope was a small diary of brown colour. Every face in the family became gloomy as they left the room one after another. Jesse was curious about their faces and the birthday gift. He took the photograph and looked more closely. He called back his grandmother who was just a few steps from him and asked, "Is this the photograph of my mother that you told me about? When will she come to us? How far is Israel from our place? If she cannot come, then why can't we go to her?" His grandmother told him that they would go and visit Jerusalem one day. She then took him in her arms, wiped her tears secretly.

Ron came to Jesse and took him from his mother's arms. He went upstairs and told his son about Esther's life, like a story in an interesting way. Jesse listened to his father's story with an open mouth and then saw his father's tears coming. Ron wiped his tears turning away from Jesse. He told him that his mother would not come back. He told him to read the letter with his grandma. He took Jesse's hand that held the letter in his little hands. They proceeded towards the living room. Ron saw his sister Miss Gloria looking at them. He beckoned, signalled her to help Jesse. Ron kissed Jesse on his cheek and said, "I will go to the town and come back in the evening; what I shall bring for you?" Jesse thought for a while and replied, "Father, I have everything. I don't have anything to ask for this time."

Jesse and his aunty Gloria went inside the room and started playing like crazy kids, throwing pillows one on one. While they ran around laughing, suddenly Jesse asked her to read the letter for him. Aunty Gloria took the rather thick envelope. She shook it for a few seconds, quickly put her fingers at the bottom of the envelope. She took out a gold ring unexpectedly. They gazed together in excitement and exclaimed, "It's a gold ring!" They laughed together and Miss Gloria at once tried it on her ring finger. She smiled and looked at Jesse raising her brow in excitement. She then took out the ring tossing it once, tried it on Jesse's fingers. She said laughing, "You can't wear it now; it's too big for you. Besides, it's for a lady, beautiful like me." Jesse gave the ring to aunty Gloria and again requested her to read the letter. When Miss Gloria opened the letter, her fingers started to shake to see a letter written in blood rather in bad handwriting. Just then the maid came running and called Miss Gloria urgently. The maid told Miss Gloria that their mother had become unconscious. Miss Gloria told Jesse to wait for her to read the letter and left the room. Jesse waited for some time playing around in the room. Then he took the letter and tried to read it for himself. His instinct gut gave him the sense that the letter was important to him, so he put all his efforts to read it out word by word.

"Dear Jesse,

Happy birthday to you, dear! These are my obsequies for you. Before that, I beg your forgiveness for denying your rights. Your mother is the lady who dared to raise you, who dared to love your father, so, call her lovingly— Mummy. Work hard, struggle, obey your father and respect your elders. This gold ring must be inherited by the eldest sons of Broadvale. Neither shall you sell nor lose it. One day we will all meet in heaven in the blessed kingdom where there are no sorrows and disease.

Your loving mother

Esther

Jesse read word by word struggling to finish all the lines. He was startled by the time he finished reading the letter. He perused the letter repeatedly until he digested it all. All-day long he was filled with grief. Sometimes he was afraid to put on the golden ring. He waited for Gloria and soon fell asleep on the bed. He woke up in the evening to find himself beside Gloria. He told Gloria that he saw his mother in his dreams. Gloria hugged him and said, "Dear, it is not good to see the dead people. She is living happily in heaven, she always looks at us, and even now also she listens to our conversations. We all will go to her when we die. What did your mother do in your dream?" Jesse turned his eyeballs around looking at every corner, squeezing his lips for some time, and then said, "My mother brought home one lady and told me to take her to my father. She was dressed in white while the other lady was dressed in blue. My mother hugged me, I felt so warm."

Gloria thought for a while how to interpret the boy's dream. She told Jesse about Ron's life and his love for Disha. She advised Jesse to support his father to win the heart of Disha. Jesse took a bath, went out with Miss Gloria to invite his friends and neighbours to the birthday party. At dusk, he enjoyed a birthday feast with dear and near ones. They arranged a birthday party with the brown cake cut. They had arranged the gathering in the courtyard. Ron played his music and when all the invitees had arrived, the chief of Broadvale prayed and blessed Jesse with all his love. The children enjoyed the brown birthday cake and sweets while the rest enjoyed the drinks. Ron's friends took their turns to make the moment fun-filled, and they give humorous, short speeches one after another, and everyone enjoyed the party. Gloria called out to Jesse to take his time as the birthday boy. Jesse boldly stood up and said, "Thank you one and all for coming to my birthday party. Today I turn seven years old. I have learnt many poems from my father. I shall recite one poem." He cleared his throat and recited the poem *"Home they brought her warrior dead"* written by Lord Alfred Tennyson. He recited clearly in the beginning lines, slowly with emotions in the last line. There was pin-drop silence when he said the concluding lines *"sweet my child, I live for thee."* Everyone clapped and appreciated him. Ron went to Jesse clapping his hands loudly and said, *"Sweet my child, I live for thee, what shall I give you, my son?"* Jesse jumped on the back of his father and said, "Father, I want a mother. Give me a mother." Suddenly Ron put him down, hugged him in his bosom tightly and kissed him on his forehead saying "Who is the mastermind for this time, is it Aunty Gloria or Grandma?" He looked at Jesse's eyes sharply to read his mind. Jesse sadly replied to his father, "Father, no one told me. My mother came to me in my dream a few hours back, gave me a new mother. I want that woman to call her lovingly mummy. My mother wants us to grow and shine. I want this much for my birthday gift and will ask no more, father." Everyone present there was amazed, seconded what little Jesse said. They all gave pressure on Ron saying, "Your son is like an Angel, God chooses to use innocent children, otherwise your son is too wise for his age. Maybe, Esther's Spirit wants you to be a happy father." Ron assured Jesse that he would fulfil his dreams shortly. When all the children had gone after the party, Ron's friends and relatives stayed back a while and insisted Ron marry as early as possible. They assured him that they would go to Disha, and if she still disagreed with their proposal, they would kidnap her. His friends assured him that he could get married in a week.

CHAPTER - 14

RON KIDNAPS DISHA

The next day, Ron and his friend went straight to Disha's house. She had gone out for her usual programme, as a famous artist. They stayed the night at Gaitlane in the house of one of his friends. He waited for her return. The next day, the two friends roamed about the town and came back in the evening towards Disha's house. On the way, they halted for a while when they saw a beautiful woman fetching water from a pond. They become thirsty and also wanted to feed their horses. They asked for water from the woman who invited them to drink from an earthen pot at her house. As they followed to her cottage, they were impressed by her physical appearance and sweet voice. The woman who lived alone with her daughter was in her mid-twenties. The woman gave them cold water from an earthen pot. They quenched their thirst to their hearts' content. They fed their horses in the nearby meadow. They rested for a while more to know more about the woman. They asked her many questions about the place and its people. Ron's friend asked if the woman had wine, for that place was famous for the tastiest local wine. She poured some wine and as she bent, they saw her bulging breasts that looked very voluptuous with her round, sexy eyes that were very appealing. The woman entered her room, attended to her daughter who was two years old. The two friends drank the wine and became refreshed after their tiresome daylong travelling. Ron's friend became fully controlled by the wine and he made advances on the charming woman who in his eyes, seemed to wait for the aggressive attack. But she was, in fact, a kind-hearted woman, a cousin sister of Disha. Ron's friend went to the woman and attempted to touch her, saying, "I like you as much as the wine you offer." The woman shouted at them and screamed to alert the neighbours, throwing her sandals at them. Ron's subconscious state of mind knew that a married woman, however carefree, is irrevocably tied down by custom, society, and religion. It was his duty to lead his friend on the right path. Ron got up from his seat, pulled his friend away from the woman. The woman shouted at them, angrily threw sandals and utensils at them. As Ron picked up the woman's sandals and begged forgiveness, he saw Disha looking at them from distance. Disha instigated the neighbours and a few women came forward who scolded the drunk men. Disha also helped her cousin sister to slap them on their face in front of the neighbours. The two became ashamed though they were drunk. They left the place and followed Disha up to her house.

Disha closed her gate behind and scolded them saying, "How dare you come to me, you who try to outrage the modesty of my sister. Don't even think about me. Go and look after your son. If you are truly a man, you would not have let your beloved wife die in the hospital. If you truly love your wife, you should keep your promise. I hate you, drunkard and beast." Ron felt very ashamed as many people saw them; as he advanced to calm down Disha, her family members warned him not to visit them again. That very night, Ron climbed up the gate of Disha's house and entered her room through the window. It was around 2 o'clock when everyone had their best time of sleep. He forcibly kidnapped Disha from her bedroom without noise, and single-handed. He and his friend took her in their chariot to the Giant Mountain. They locked her in a restroom inside a cave on top of the hill. Ron narrated his life to her and the reason for his kidnap. He gave her his diary where he had written how the love story began and ended between him and his wife, Esther. He told Disha to apologize for her wrong allegations after which he would free her. Gloria and Joyi used to drop their food secretly for them.

Everyone was surprised when the news of Disha's disappearance become far and wide, spreading like wildfire. Disha's family complained to the police that Disha was kidnapped by the Broadvale family. Disha's family, friends and the police searched everywhere for three days but could not find her. Jesse promised Disha that he would do whatever she told him if he married his father. Ron's family members were arrested by the police and tortured daily, interrogating them with the same annoying questions which they could not answer.

Five days had passed, yet they could not locate Ron and Disha. Gloria and Joyi were also detained at the police station. Disha and Ron stayed in a small room where Ron guarded her with a sword. On the seventh day, they both were tired of fighting and arguing. Hungry and thirsty, they no longer talked or fought anymore. In the evening, Disha said to Ron, "Okay Ron, kill me with your sword instead of harassing me, I prefer to die." Ron said to her, "You cannot die like this. You must first apologize for what you have said. Esther is my wife, my love and my soul mate. I did not leave her to die. After you apologize, I will free you forever and you will never see my face again."

Just then the two heard some strange sound near the door. Ron opened the door and saw Jesse weeping beside the door. Jesse hid his face with his hands weeping bitterly. Ron called him to enter the room. Jesse slowly entered the room, gave them a tiffin containing eatables and two bottles of water. Ron asked him what had happened and how he happened to come there alone. Jesse said, "Father, all of them are taken by the police. I am all alone in the house with only my uncle taking care of me. I miss you, Father, do not die." Jesse turns to Disha and said, "Mummy, don't die again, live for me, live for my father he is very unlucky. I love you, Mama. I will always obey you and care for you." Disha was moved by Jesse's words and like any woman, she loved sweet children. Jesse gave her water, eatables and fed Disha lovingly.

Ron got up from his seat, tried to leave them when Jesse called him again saying, "Father, do not leave us. Take Mummy's hand, hold her hand and let us go home." Ron looked at Disha, who also looked at him with her eyes glistening with tears, and they both stared at each other for some time. Ron took a few steps towards Disha, who also stood up slowly, with folded hands apologized to Ron. Disha changed her mind and married Ron at last. Jesse reported to his aunty Gloria about their success. They summoned Ron and Disha to the police station to confirm their marriage. After Disha told everyone that she was happy with her marriage and that she was not kidnapped by Ron. The case was dismissed. Broadvale prepared to welcome the lovely couple. They went to Ron's house on the eighth day. They were welcomed all through the way to their room, up to the royal king-size bed with fresh rose petals spread on the bed and golden marigold string garlands decorations. The following day, Ron's family went to Disha's house for the formalities of their customs. Ron's one-month holiday had lapsed. So the next week took his beloved wife, Disha and left home for his posting.

Daadi would not let his only grandson, Jesse leave Broadvale at any cause. Jesse felt the pain in his heart when his parents left him behind. He was consoled by his aunty Gloria and grandparents. Every morning his grandfather would ask him how well he slept or if he had a dream. The whole family would give attention if the boy had a dream. They would spend time together interpreting his dreams with a cup of morning coffee, just to make the boy happy. Gloria wrote a poem about her father and Jesse and she sent it to Richard.

WINTER DREAM

Every morning, grandpa awaits his only favourite boy

Would ask how well he slept, or if he had a dream

The loving bond between the boy and his doting grandpa.

They all engaged few minutes in interpreting dreams

'hmmm, I catch fishes 'they said 'it's money'

The boy did find some notes, coincidentally

'Grandpa, I sing a song,' they said 'it's tears'

He did cry the following days, and he remembers his dream.

'Grandpa, a dog chased me,' they said 'it's disease'

He falls ill that very week, but recovered soon

'Tom threw stones at me,' they said 'it's a fortune'

'I laugh heartily' they said 'you will be sad'

'I climb up a hill,' they said, 'you will pass in the exam'

'I saw my late mummy' they said 'it may rain'

'I died in my dream' they said 'you overeat, that's why'

'I board a flight, I fly' they said 'you will be lonely'

'I bathed'; they said 'it's good if the water is clear'

Good dream follows bad dream, and vice versa

'Mama died in my dream' with tears he narrated.

They smiled and patted their only boy in the big family

Said 'it's just a winter dream, she had heavy dinner last night.'

Jesse felt the pain of longing for his mother for the first time in his life. He was too young to know the bitter truth of life at that age. It was too soon to learn that his father loved him not more than his mother. But he promised himself that he would not disappoint his parents and always respect the decision of his father. He spent his days busy with friends and his studies. At night he spent time with his grandparents. He learnt the values of life living in the village: He was brought up with love and care. He knew the values of customs, traditions and love of nature. His parents came back home after two years with his twin step-brothers—Rolan and Milan. Disha loved Jesse as much as she loved her sons during her one-month stay at Broadvale. They again left for their new posting in Kolkata.

Once Ron came home when he got a message that his father had been bedridden for months. When he reached home his father was too weak to talk with him. Ron sat near his father and did all things which would please his father. He called for the famous doctors but they could not save his father's life. He also had to hurry back to his workplace where he had left his wife alone with the kids. The following day after his father's dead body was buried, his mother again become sick and bedridden. Now Jesse was all alone except Gloria, who would also get married anytime. His other sisters had all got married. They were busy in their own homes. He decided to let Disha stay at home and look after the family. There were many responsibilities as chief of a big village, the administration, the servants, the farms, the fields, the livestock and the big house. He left home with a heavy heart. He talked about the matter with Disha who was not willing to go back to village life in that remote place. She told Ron that she couldn't travel the long journey as she had conceived again.

CHAPTER - 15

GLORIA'S WEDDING

Gloria received a letter from Richard every month. She was expecting a letter as the new month began. A new month comes and old months go without much progress and it had become ten years then. Though her mind was young, she began to feel insecure about her life. All her friends had mothered three or four children. She no longer checked the post office for her letters. One morning, the postman came and handed her a letter with a big parcel. She quickly opened the letter. To her surprise, Richard wrote the heading "Last love letter", followed by hypnotizing lines of his poem,

YOUR DREAM IS MINE TOO

Gloria, Gloria darling, my Gloria

The name you want to hear from my mouth

Baby this is my last love letter

I should rather say it is poetry,

For I will not write anymore of my love

But will show you in action, that

We are made for each other

I know from your gestures

I see the hidden from your eyes

I know what you dream, it's innate

Just tell me the place you had dreamt

The spot where you need in your dream

I will wait till you turn up, come baby

I want to fulfil exactly how you feel

On the unnamed island on its bank

The cool breeze plays with your lively hair

Just we, only we two, in that fine evening

I too will tell how I dreamt about you

The water calmly listens to our kisses

I will make you break the silence

Hold you tightly till I fulfil

Your dream to say the golden words

From your cherry red soft lips

Whispers to my ears

I love you too.

Gloria was hypnotized so much that she instantly wrote a poem for her lover, Richard. She told her lover how secretly she loved to be beside him, how much she loved to hear from him saying her name sweetly and how much she wanted to find out his love for her.

SECRETLY

I want to be by your side secretly watching you

Listen like the spider in corner web spying on you

I want to be an air to check in, the air you breathe in

And see myself my position on how you see me

In your heart, rub all the names in history

And rewrite my name, just my name, only Gloria

Your sideways glance crushes my juicy glands

Sweetly embarrassed, swiftly a wave on my belly

I want to hear my name from your mouth only

Say my name again like the first time I heard from your mouth

I want to test how miserable you taste my absence

Watching you look around and turn around

Secretly listen, how you speak about me in secret

I want to be the wind blowing wherever you go

Stalk how you react to other's furtive girls' glances

Glad to find you bored, cold, sour with others

I just want to slip in and sleep by your side.

Gloria was overjoyed to receive the marriage party at last. The letter was written one month ago and probably Richard's family would have arrived in India by then. She opened the parcel and found a satin gown, her dream wedding set with a pair of white high heels. She at once visited the salon, trimming her hair, her nails and her eyebrows. She immediately changed her diet. Overexcited like in her teenage, she spent her days rejuvenating her skin and toning her body.

They had been in love for many years but both faced strong opposition from their families. They both stood for each other. Finally loyalty and obedience fairly paid the steadfast lovers. They proved that, in true love, customs, cultures, tradition, religion, nationality, language, height, size, age and distance were nothing. Her boyfriend came with his parents all the way from the United Kingdom to Broadvale to take his love, Gloria. Ron and Disha attended their wedding in the city Cathedral after her grand bridal blessing at Broadvale. It was one of the grandest weddings that ever happened in that time. There were flower girls dressed like the beautiful bride. There were pressmen from national and international level. Everyone who attended the wedding ceremony appreciated and blessed the couple. It was most interesting for the newly wedded couple to look at each other for the first time as husband and wife. They keep on looking at each other from time to time. Richard would lovingly whisper her name "Gloria, sweetest name, Gloria, you are the most beautiful woman in the world." Gloria wanted to hear her name from his sweet manly voice, again and again, a happy teardrop fell from her eyes, from the heart, the heart too eager to hold her love as closely as possible. How beautiful was their love marriage, it became a testimony and inspiration for many people. One of Richard's friends wrote a poem on how eagerly, the groom contentedly looked at his stunning bride. He had waited for that moment for ten years. Gloria, in all her glory, smiled to tears to hear her sweet name from the sweetest whisper that entered her heart like the waves in the ocean.

THE FIRST LOOK

With lots of love, gently unveil her face at the altar

The busy mind did look, but did not see her

A mind occupied with the ongoing ceremony

When they said, "I DO" they both had promised genuinely

The priest made the proclamation "You are now husband and wife"

As they both seated on the sofa on the platform,

Facing the Church members who witness the solemnization

He slowly, eagerly moved his head towards his right

The first side look at his beautiful wife, just married

He cares not about the audience or the Church leaders

His loving eyes on the face of his bride, Oh, what a moment!

His happy face, twenty degrees smiling, sexy eyes

The ladies out there, all envious of the bride,

Of such a sweet moment, it's worth the wait!

The bride knew it all; happily, shyly she sits like a statue

She secretly smiles inside, wishing to have a side glance

Her rosy cheeks, her lovely eyes and her silky hair

The blessings, the sweet fragrance and the romance

The most awaited moment thrills every one of her beauty

Her lovely face, wrap around by the white veil like a lily

Spectators enjoy seeing the groom so contentedly looking

Having the first look at his just married glamorous wife

For twenty-five seconds, the groom's mind is in paradise!

Gloria left home happy with all the blessings from her family. Jesse was 11 years old then. He lived with his ailing grandmother. The next year Ron came home to drop off Disha and three of her kids. Disha was once a famous artist who had no experience or interest in village women's life. She had her private nurse, attendant and babysitter. Still, she could not manage to look after the affairs. Jesse was loved, much favoured by everyone, especially his grandma. Soon after, Disha began to dislike Jesse and her mother-in-law very much. Rolan, Milan and Filan, the three brothers were all spoilt from their childhood. The four brothers grew up together in Broadvale until Jesse left home to do his further studies in the army school. Jesse stayed with his father in Himachal Pradesh.

Ron was given medical retirement after 13 years of service in the Indian Army. He was severely injured in the Indo-Pak war of 1965 while defending his motherland. Their camp was attacked by Pakistani forces at night. The enemy forces had planted bombs outside their camp. There was firing from both sides for about an hour until the enemy forces retreat from them. They planted bombs in and around the Indian Army camp. A few bombs had detonated and killed several soldiers instantly. The bomb squad employed army dogs and a bomb detector machine found one more bomb near the main entrance. While they were trying to defuse the bomb, they could not complete it in the given period. When 23 seconds were left, Ron quickly grabbed hold of the bomb, and ran outside the gate as fast as he could. He was the commander of the unit. He risked his life to save his soldiers. He took the bomb, threw it away as far and long as he could. Though he had saved many lives, he could not save his legs. His right leg was amputated, and he lost his hearing too. Ron became handicapped his whole life. The Indian Army had given him the decoration Vir Chakra to acknowledge his sacrifice, his extraordinary bravery. Historians have written golden lines about his conspicuous bravery, inspiring leadership and exemplary devotion to his duty serving his motherland, India, Capt. Ron from Broadvale, Manipur even though the war had gifted the brave man ugly keloid scars skin all over his body.

Life was difficult not only for Jesse but also for Disha, to live with her handicapped husband and bedridden mother-in-law. She was still very young to abstain from her husband. Ron felt sorry to see Disha's face. He repented that he had taken her forcibly and twisted her destiny. He requested Disha to keep on shining by engaging her life with her hobbies, exhibiting her talent in the music world. He encouraged her to revive her singing talent. When Ron's mother died, Ron announced Disha as the next ruler. Disha was given all the keys of the house, documents, seal, all the gold and diamonds. She ruled over the land sincerely for the time being. By then Jesse had also grown up and sometimes shared his ideas often interfered in public affairs to help his mother.

Disha's beauty and fame were once again revived when she played music and sang in public. She composed beautiful ballads while her sweet voice won the people's hearts. Like the waves of an ocean, her song hypnotized young and old when she sang a song that was composed by Ron many years ago. She then knew the true meaning of the lyrics which Ron had written. She realized what Ron meant to convey in his lines, *"like by the second path"* and the pain she could not share with anyone. She was then in the zigzag path, the second path where only a few trod. She realized what *"Life is not a bed of roses"* meant. The song became sweetest when she realized the connotations, the lyrical interpretation and also the hard life of the lyricist. She used to sing with tears in her eyes which moved everyone's heart. She got compliments, invitations from different bands to perform and exhibit her talent. She formed a band with her team called the "country band". She sent her sons to boarding school and started her carrier anew. It was hard for Ron as well as Disha to stay together. Sometimes Disha had to leave Ron for weeks to perform her live stage shows at different places. Though she was always accompanied by her family men, Disha could not resist the looks of her co-artist named Doon. Mr. Doon was a guitarist in the band. Disha was a songwriter as well as a singer. She also played Casio. Her live shows thrilled thousands of people. She had composed a series of albums in which she hit dozens of songs. Her lyrics touched many hearts, mostly the guitarist Mr. Doon. The two fell in love secretly wanted to quench their thirst. Mr. Doon could not stand to see the empty eyes and looks of the sweet singer, whose lyrics were so deep, meaningful and erotic. Mr. Doon knew her condition and pities her life when she sang with tears in her eyes. One day he expressed his love to Disha, but she did not reply to him. Since then, she could no longer perform her show or sing. She decided to give up singing. Disha stayed at home and devoted her life to serving Ron. But Ron knew that Disha's passion was singing from her childhood. He told her to accept invitations from her fans and show the world what she could do and become famous. She could not declare her love to Doon as he was living with his wife and children. She too had her own family and many responsibilities. Desperate Disha started taking opium and become a chain smoker. She loved Ron for no reason, cared for her children very much. She did not want her name to be tagged as unfaithful. She struggled between love and life all her years, and wrote the lines,

My passion, why have you turned a poison?

My talent, why have you become a tale?

My voice, you cannot become my fall,

My love, you have been the strength of my life

I'm not prepared for this if you chose me as your host

The guests have no right to do anything

Uninvited and unwelcome guests at my table

Make the host restless and you shameless

How I wish to grow old fast, move fast

O you mighty divine king of the day

Move fast, lest forget the look in your eyes.

O you lovely divine queen of the night

Limping and far behind the flock, I stoop

My journey to heaven, deepen my thoughts

Wish to spread out my wings and fly in pride

Younger than my age, I met you too soon,

Older than my age, I reach here too soon

Passing through the dreary desert,

When will the green meadow welcome me?

Under the countless stars where the night would be just awesome

Dancing like in the old school days with the cool breeze

Catching the golden fireflies in the lovely evenings

In the serene green valley where everyone will find solace.

CHAPTER - 16

ILLICIT RELATIONSHIP BETWEEN DISHA AND MR. DOON

Disha gave up her singing when people started mocking her relationship with Doon. Disha soon became an opium addict which shortly made her insane. Jesse came to know of his mother's condition and pitied her. He once saw his mother in a compromised position with Mr. Doon in the town. He used to keep an eye on his mother which the guilty Disha realized it in no time. Jesse wanted to help change the behaviour of his mother. He arranged to send his family elders to give her counselling. So, out of shame, Disha hated Ron and Jesse. She hated everyone and her life. She wanted to kill Ron as well as Jesse before she got exposed. She asked Ron to declare all the property and rights to her or her son Rolan. Disha left no stone unturned to get rid of Jesse. She instigated her sons that Jesse was not born in the royal house; he was an illegitimate child, not entitled to be given the birthright of Broadvale, according to custom.

Once, Gloria and her husband visited Broadvale. Gloria was ashamed of her sister-in-law and was sad to learn about her family's condition. She wanted to treat her brother Ron in London but her brother did not agree. Gloria was wondering how Disha became pregnant and had a baby daughter when her husband was as bad as paralysed, bedridden for years. Jesse told his aunty Gloria what had befallen the Broadvale family. Gloria informed her bedridden brother of the wicked plans of Disha. When Ron knew the truth, he jumped out of his death bed. He scolded Disha and Rolan saying, "All these seven years, I gave you the freedom to do your passion, had encourage you to do your hobby. I never said a word when you left home for weeks. I did not say a word nor annoyed you being together with your guitarist Mr. Doon. I know that love is not a sin as long as you keep it to yourself. Now wherefrom have you two derived the power to say Jesse is an illegitimate child? Never in this house, did women and children rule nor shall the royal sword, royal seal ever be snatched from the eldest son. All the rights and properties are in my hand."

Disha wanted a divorce from Ron. She demanded half of the property. She threatened Ron that she would leave him and that if she lefts, she would not go alone. She would take her children too. Jesse met his mother personally, told her not to go ahead with her move. He said to Disha, "Mummy, I may not be born of your blood but you are my mother and I want to worship you my whole life. My father has suffered enough. He will not live for long: I want him at least to die in peace. Rolan is my brother, I have no problem if he is the successor. I will go far away from this place, everything will be yours." Disha asked him where he would go but Jesse did not tell her anything. When she did not receive a reply, Disha said to him, "Then what are you waiting for, son of a bitch, illegitimate son of Esther, the Jew?" Jesse suddenly raised his hand to slap her. Just then Rolan and Reenarose came in and saw them. Disha cried out and said, "Oh my life! I deserved this as your stepmother. This is the reason I never want to be a stepmother. Jesse, how dare you touch me and raise your hand?" She went to Reenarose and said, "I'm not safe here, where shall I go?" Rolan got angry at his brother and left the room. Reenarose hugged Disha and calmed her down, helping her lie down on the bench in the living room. Reenarose went back to Jesse and said, "You have lost my trust, how could you do this to mummy, what do you think a woman's life is? You filthy, I hate you." Reenarose left them and went to her house broken-hearted. Jesse and Reenarose had been good friends who loved each other. Jesse went to Disha, touched her feet to show respect and begged forgiveness but the latter screamed, shouted to antagonize Rolan and Ron, "Please don't come near me, I'm your father's wife." All the servants, family members saw Jesse approaching Disha and they were shocked.

In the evening Ron called Jesse and told him to leave Broadvale without any explanation. Jesse went to Reenarose's house only to find her with Rolan. He returned home before Reenarose noticed him. He called his trusted uncle Jensta, his father's best friend of Broadvale and also his chief servant-cum-bodyguard Zamzam. Jesse narrated to them the whole story. He forewarned them not to tell his father the truth until Rolan became the successor. He went to his father's bed, silently cried at his bedside saying to him, "If you had not lost your leg, you would not have lost your love too and I would not have to move my leg away from you. I'm sorry, father." Jesse left Broadvale early in the morning leaving behind his lovely family, friends and best friend Reenarose. He travelled during the day and rested the night at whichever place he reaches. He did not have any plan or a definite destination. He did not show his face or his identity to anyone. He talked to his horse as if the latter would understand his heart. After one week of travelling: he rested near a river where there was an abandoned hut. He cried out to his heart content, shouted at the sky and prayed to God. He rested there for two days wailing without eating anything. He prayed for Broadvale, his family and his people. It was winter, the days become shorter and the nights were cold. He said to his horse, "Take me to the place where you want me to settle. From now on I will call you in the name of my best friend. Your sweet name will be Reena but without Rose." Jesse slowly mounted his horse, after drinking water from the river. The horse too slowly followed the river and at midday, they reached a village near a hillside. The villagers had gathered in the open ground. Jesse understood that they were having a wedding reception from the sounds of the big drums and trumpet. "Reena, let's fill our stomach there," he said to his horse. As Reena went to the entrance, the people welcomed the traveller with folded hands and said "Namaste." Jesse folded his hands without saying a word. They understood from his face that he was a weary traveller. They gave him drinks and sweets. Some men came and asked questions that Jesse did not answer. They were the kind-hearted Assamese, a tribe living in Assam, speaking in their language. Jesse nodded his head in reply. There was singing and dancing. The ladies wore a red blouse and a traditional two-piece like a saree of red and beige. They had large hats decorated at the borders. The menfolk wore white dresses with a turban. The bride was charming and decorated with gold ornaments from head to toe. The bridegroom was a dark, bearded and funny-looking man. The ushers of the function came and invited Jesse for dinner. As he followed them, he was taken into a hall where chefs were serving colourful varieties of dishes. They gave him a plateful of delicious food and drinks. Jesse ate them to his heart's content; he remembered his family where they used to eat and drink of their own choice prepared by the cook. He then went towards the stage where the priest and elders with the newlywed couple were seated. He took out a silver coin and gave it to the bridegroom. They accepted it by bowing down to him. Jesse then left the village and continued his journey.

After travelling for three more days his horse stopped near a waterfall in a hilly place. The place was cold and chilly. Jesse got down and fed his horse. Then he went out around the place to look for fruits. He found banana, Sohiong and Soh pyrshong. He ate and drank the cold water from the fall. He rested under a jackfruit tree, looked around the place and began to enjoy the beauty of nature. His heart became peaceful, happy to see the beautiful hills covered with mist and the waterfalls here and there in all their majesty. Soon it became dark and he rested on one of the branches of the jackfruit tree. He heard the howling of wild animals from far. Sometimes his horse neighed in fear. He became alert and could not sleep peacefully. He woke up early in the morning, headed towards the east following the river. At midday, he reached a small town where short, small people communicated in a language that he had never heard before. He approached them, showed them his silver coins. They accompanied him to the chief's house. The chief looked at him and felt pity for him. He told his men to feed Jesse. He ate, drank, bathed and rested in the chief's house. The chief had a daughter named Dinah who could speak the English language with Jesse. She talked with Jesse and translated it for her family. Jesse was given respect for his decency, wit and judgement. From his words and behaviour, they easily recognized him to be of noble birth. Dinah loved him and would do anything to make Jesse comfortable at her home.

CHAPTER - 17

JESSE AND DINAH

After a week's stay, Jesse informed the chief that he was leaving their place to continue his journey. The chief was already impressed by his attitude and manners. Jesse read his Bible before he pray every morning and evening. He prays every morning to God for his father and family. He would accompany and help the chief in everything he did. When the chief realized that Jesse had nowhere to go, he said, "You may think yourself a stranger but your one-week stay with us gives me the feeling that you are my son. You can just stay with me instead of travelling without any definite purpose. I will give you a piece of land for you if you want to stay separately from my family." Jesse was loved by all. They made a separate house near the chief's house. They stayed together with them like brothers and sisters. He taught Dinah along with her three brothers and cousin sister archery and horse riding. He also taught them music and helped them in their studies. He also helped the chief in the administration of the town. He very soon learnt their language and culture. He was tall, of good stature, and intelligent which made the Khasi girls run after him. Dinah was 19 years old while Jesse was 23. According to the Khasi tradition, the bridegroom had to leave his family and live with the bride's family. It was just the opposite for Jesse as being the eldest of the clan, to get married and stay in the wife's house was something unnatural. But he could not resist the move made by Dinah. She was jealous when any girl talked with or smiled at Jesse. She told her father to arrange the wedding as soon as possible. Jesse worked as a primary teacher in the village school. He felt lonely and sad but also wanted to know about the well-being of his family. He thought to himself either his brother or his uncle, or at least the chief servant would search for him. When they could not find him out, the rights and property would be given to Rolan by his father. But Ron had been weeping day and night longing for Jesse. He would sing and lament saying, *"Qh, had I seen him at least before he departed from me! How could he leave without my blessings? Maybe, my son has extremely become sad. He is the blessed fruit of my love with my most beloved. Is he dead or alive, will somebody look for my son?"* Disha and Rolan told Ron that however they looked for Jesse, they found no clue where he had gone. His uncle told Ron, "We searched many places but could not find him; whether he is dead or alive, we have no idea." Rolan married Reenarose to console his mother, also get the rights and property. According to Broadvale tradition when the eldest son married, if his father was happy with their marriage, he handed the property rights and paper to him. Disha arranged the wedding reception with great pomp and show. She then asked Ron if he was not happy with the marriage. Ron replied, "I am very happy with Rolan and Reenarose. It would have been better if they waited for some more years, they are too young to handle life and shoulder responsibilities; however, I will give all the rights to them if you insist, but when Jesse returns home, you should give his birthright with due respect. I know Jesse will come back someday if he is not dead. A man can never leave his family in his entire life." Rolan and Reenarose took the paper, keys and became the chief of Broadvale although there was no official announcement or celebration.

One evening, as usual, Jesse returned from school. He bathed in the open tank at the back of his room. He was lost in thoughts. His tears trickled down perennially when he reminisced on the happy days he spent with his parents and family. He wiped his tears and looked left and right. He changed his clothes and then sat on a stool basking under the winter Sun. He leaned on the wall of the tank and fell asleep. He had a dream where he was in a castle. A woman with a veil-covered face came to him with her sparkling silver anklets and jingling bangles. The lady gave him a goblet of wine. He drank the wine and it was very tasty. He slowly uncovered the face of the fair lady; he saw the face of Dinah. She took his hands and requested him to dance with her in the next room. They entered a dancing hall, where embroidered soft carpets lay with scented sandalwood. He held the hands of Dinah then they danced like a peacock and peahen; suddenly he was woken up by a voice calling," Joseph!" He opened his eyes gently when the same voice called him again "JESSE!" This time he stood up straight like a soldier on command and went straight to his room. Dinah was hiding behind the door. As he entered the room, she jumped, hugged him lovingly and said, "I know you have been hiding something from the beginning." Jesse pondered and said, "Hmm... What?? I don't hide anything from you." Dinah took out a packet of sunflower seeds and said, "Come on, let's enjoy this and talk. It's been only a while since we haven't talked but I feel like we haven't talked for months. You became too busy with your work, spare little time for your best friend." Saying so, she opened the packets carefully. They sat down on a mat and enjoyed the sunflower seeds. They talked about silly matters, sometimes laughing, sometimes fawning but Dinah looked a bit more cheerful than usual. Dinah watched him from head to toes but the man wasn't a bit nervous. Dinah asked him his real name. Jesse laughed and said, "The public question again, was fed up of explaining. Ha-ha. Better I paste it on my doorway so that I don't have to explain every now and then." He knew Dinah was not satisfied with the answer and he said again, "See, it's as simple as this. Joseph is my nickname and Jesse is my real name. Whether you say my name as Jesse or Joseph, I am the same person. Your name is Evena but we also call you Dinah, right?"

Dinah smiled at him but said nothing; her gesture made Jesse guilty of something that he could not just imagine. Dinah then told him that a man came looking for Jesse with his photograph. They told the man that they did not know who Jesse was. "I suspected you and checked your things and now, what do you say to me?" Jesse looked straight into her eyes and asked her to describe the man. Dinah said, "He was just a boy accompanied by a middle-aged man. He was big, fat of whitish complexion, square face with a spectacle, hmmm a curly hair. I can say that much." From the details, it was obvious that the man would be none other than Filan, his youngest brother who was doing his MBBS when Jesse left home. He knew that Filan would surely come for him. He was a good boy. Jesse had taken care of him when he was a little boy.

Jesse at once decided to go to Broadvale. He met Dinah's father along with the local elders and told them about his decision. Jesse knew that Dinah was not happy about his decision. She had not eaten anything for days. Jesse realized that the wilt in Dinah's freshness, a hesitant sprightliness in her vivacity was for want of love. She was like a sensitive plant that does not grow and spread in all directions but produces an indifferently-hued and dull bloom. Just as the Sun-starved plant desperately throws out its shoots and tendrils towards the light, her heart too was yearning for a modicum of sunlit love: but society, their culture and the oriental background were too much of a check for her to breakthrough. She was the eldest of her siblings and the responsibilities lay in her hand. Being the daughter of a Khasi king, she worried if Jesse would laugh off her appeal. She went to Jesse at night, knocked at his door and waited outside. Jesse opened the door and wanted to meet her outside. Dinah insisted to take her inside. Jesse held her soft hands and said, "I had seen in my dreams that you will be my wife. I will marry you when I come back. I love you. It may not be right for me to take you home at this time." She took his right hand and put it to her chest; said with tears in her eyes, "Touch my heart, feel my heart."

Just then Dinah's father entered and was taken aback. He was ashamed of what his daughter had done. Dinah cried and begged forgiveness from her father. Jesse told him that they were in love and he would take Dinah home. The next day Jesse and Dinah got married in Khasi traditional marriage style. They gave Dinah to Jesse on one condition: that their first daughter would be taken by the maternal family, to rule in place of Dinah. Jesse and Dinah began their journey to Broadvale with some of the Khasi youths following them. They travelled for 10days and reached Broadvale on the eleventh day.

CHAPTER -18

JESSE RETURNS TO BROADVALE

As they reached Broadvale after crossing the Tuivai, the blue hills of Broadvale and her lively air welcomed their long-lost prodigal son. Jesse remembered his childhood days when he used to play in the fields. He narrated to his friends how he spent his childhood days playing on the riverbank, making a sandcastle with his friends. The sight of the suspension bridge and the birds warbling on the trees evoked in Jesse, his sad regrets about leaving behind his ailing father. He said to himself, "Is my father still breathing, will he forgive and accept Dinah as my wife?" He wiped his sweat and controlled his emotions. He said to Dinah, "Broadvale might not be up to your expectations. It is not that much developed. You have to endure everything for my sake." Dinah wondered looking around the houses and roads, then said, "Where are the people, it looks as if the place is deserted. Hmm... Jesse, I am coming to bear and face anything; if they can do, I can also deal with them, I am not a weak woman."

They soon came across people returning home from the field. Here and there they saw children running around calling names and playing. They passed through the cemetery and Jesse requested them all to take rest for a while. He gets down from the chariot, hurriedly checks the graveyards and memorial stones, to make sure his father was still at home. Dinah and her men also got down. They all relaxed for some time. They all said that Broadvale was such a nice and wonderful place. Jesse told them the names of the graveyards of his family and forefathers in the royal reserve land. They drank water and had lunch, cooked black rice packed in banana leaf with roasted sesame crush with dried meat to replenish from the tiresome journey. After a couple of five minutes, they continued their journey.

One of the Khasi men asked how they went and buried their dead bodies when the cemetery was so far. Jesse explained to them and as they listened to him, they were all amazed. Jesse said, "Broadvale is a very large province. Every house has a chariot and a bullock cart. We reared horses, cows, buffaloes and Mithuns(Gayals). Every household has big fields and farms. Today is Sabbath day; so, people don't cross the royal gate. It is rather fascinating: Just imagine 400 to 500 chariots in the funeral procession just like ants on a funeral pyre. We have two gates. One is the royal gate which is the private area of the chief family. The other gate is called the military gate. They say the military gate is named after the British troops. They constructed a camp in secret in the jungle and made a wall. They made a very strong gate with bunkers. No one dares cross the military gate alone at night. We also have another gate which is about five miles from our house. Through that gate, we go to our farms. We have a coffee farm on the hill slopes, pineapple farms, chilly farms, maize farms, sandalwood farms, grape farms, lemon farms, etc. There is a beautiful lake near our coffee farm, with an amusement park nearby. One can see the floating park from the Giant Mountain. On top of the Giant Mountain, we constructed a rest house which serves as a viewpoint to see the true beauty of Broadvale."

Jesse explained to them about the important sites pointing here and there from time to time. When people saw them, they came out to welcome them. They drove the chariot faster so as not to delay their time talking with everyone. At last, the team reached Jesse's house. The people followed them and assembled in front of the royal gate. Disha, Rolan, Milan and Reenarose were informed by the servants. They all came out to opened the gate for them. Since people welcomed Jesse and his team with hugs, the family had no time to talk in private. They took bath before they were given food and drinks. Then they were all sent to the guest house. Jesse was angry and proceeded towards his room. His room was occupied by Rolan and Reenarose. Reenarose was six months pregnant, lying on the bed. Jesse then went to his father.

Ron was on his death bed, in a very critical condition. "If he can see the sunrise that will be a surprise," said the royal physician and the priest. Ron slowly opened his eyes as if he was woken up by Esther. Disha held his head and helped him rest comfortably on her lap. Ron's face played a sad smile when he saw the royal messenger standing at the doorway waiting for the command to convey a death message. Disha had prepared messengers for the neighbouring chiefs and kinsmen when Ron's condition became critical. Ron said in a feeble voice, "Send that man away; I will not die until I see Jesse." Jesse stood at his side and said "Father, you will not die; I am here. Forgive me, father." Disha told them about Jesse and Dinah. As Jesse touched his father's sunken face, tears rolled down his cheeks. Ron looked at him, touched his arms and felt his skin. He said with his jaws shaking, "Jesse, a man must be a soldier. Don't cry, my son. I should not have sent you away." Jesse replied, "No father, I had been prepared to leave before you said your words that day."

They had dinner together and made a programme for the next day to welcome Jesse. Since there were many guests and visitors, there couldn't be any private talk in the family. The next day, Jesse and Dinah were given a grand reception by all the villagers. They slaughtered for the feast a big Mithun(Gayal), two cows, three pigs, ten lambs, ten goats, fish and fowl. The whole village of Broadvale feasted together and blessed the couple. In the following days, the Khasi team who had come to accompany Dinah also left Broadvale happily. Now Disha was happy because Jesse would go back to the Khasis and there was no one she feared. Rolan vacated his room and welcomed Jesse and Dinah. However, Rolan and Reenarose could not think of living together with Jesse and Dinah. Disha ran from pillar to post to settle the matter, of who will rule in Broadvale. Some elders whom Disha convinced gave pressure that Rolan was also, no doubt, an able ruler. Dinah, who came from a different cultural background, also, who could not speak their language, would be difficult for many of them. They pointed at Dinah and quoted from the Bible saying, *"Jacob's new wife, Rachel's son, had ruled over the Israelites."* They also cited an example from Jacob and Esau, where the younger brother, Jacob was given the birthright by his father Isaac. Esau was cheated; however, Jacob supplanted his older brother but he was still blessed and God made a nation for him. They insisted Ron bless Rolan who was taking care of him every day. They told Ron that he was God to his children and there was no reason to deny Rolan after years of his chiefship. The family elders had a meeting with Ron and Rolan. Many favoured Rolan due to Disha's highhandedness. One night, while Disha was away from home, Rolan attended to his father and sat by his bedside. They talked about the developments in their village. Ron took the opportunity and told Rolan, "I hope my son, Rolan, you will not pay heed to the deceptive words of some of our family elders. I love your mother very much and don't want to interfere in her opinion. She has put so much effort and suffered for us. When I give you the birthright, I will be pleased if you take it from your elder brother if you gloriously want to rule in Broadvale. Though life is warfare, a man of God is safe, happy and blessed. Always remember what the Book of Proverbs chapter 8 verse 10 says: *Choose my instruction instead of silver, knowledge rather than choice gold.* When a man is pursuing riches in the wrong way, he would be irritated to keep on hearing the warning given to him that he has made a foolish choice. There is God and He always favours the righteous. God will send forth His sharp word until it pierces our conscience and turns our course. Still, if we kick against the warning, it would prick us, but when we obey it, we will find it profitable. Sometimes, the foolish will not change his way and at last, it leads to his destruction. Before it is too late, we should seek God and live peacefully. A peaceful life is worth better than a thousand gold coins for everyday living insecurity. Do not be side-tracked by the deceptive words of those devils and ruin your life. Broadvale family has accepted Esther as their bride though the custom was done after her death. My son, she is my first love, first wife and my soul mate; I hope you are not hurt when I praise another woman in front of you. I love your mother, Disha, as much as I love Esther. Throughout my life, no one understood my life. At least, I hope, my children will understand me. When I die, bury my body in the reserved royal land, next to Esther's grave. I want to be laid beside Esther." Rolan agreed with his father and promised to do according to his instructions. The following day Ron was made to announce his will in front of the family elders. Ron gave full authority and power to his wife, Disha. Disha reluctantly, as always was her drama, resisted in the namesake at the first instance, then announced that Rolan would rule in Broadvale. However, Rolan gave the birthright to Jesse who in turn gave all the responsibilities to Rolan. Dinah too, wanted Rolan to be crowned the next ruler officially as she was not comfortable with their language and traditions. However, the elders discussed it precisely and announced it the next morning. Uncle Jensta, an elderly man, whom Jesse had to share his thoughts with from the past, wrote the declaration and announced that Broadvale would be ruled by Jesse. Dinah's first girl child would be given to the Khasis to rule in place of her mother, Dinah.

It was not easy for Dinah to live together with Disha and Reenarose who were well acquainted with the people while she had to struggle to learn their language and way of life. Soon Dinah became pregnant. She faced difficulties from all sides as they did not love her. Even the servants were afraid of Disha and Reenarose. Jesse could not look into small matters in the kitchen, he was tied up with the village administration, settling disputes and cases. Reenarose gave birth to a son and everybody rejoiced and praised her. Her baby shower was one of the greatest baby showers ever known in Broadvale. After a few weeks, Rolan and Reenarose felt grief-stricken to find their infant dying without any illness. Reenarose was suspicious of her infant's death. She just hated Dinah for no reason. Reenarose and her mother-in-law, Disha, applied different techniques, flaunting and despising

Dinah solely to hurt her. Dinah was under the control of Disha, so she would leave Broadvale. She was mentally tortured, physically harassed and often publicly insulted by Disha for not being able to speak their language and her short stature. She had no one to share her burden or a shoulder to lean on. She did not want to tell her problems to her husband who was already burdened from his childhood. She became very thin and weak during her pregnancy.

CHAPTER - 19

WHO IS ILLEGITIMATE?

One night Jesse heard his mother crying and talking loudly; as Ron was deaf, it sounded like Disha was scolding her husband. He stood near the window quietly and listened to their conversation. He heard his mother say, "So you don't want to divide the land among your four sons. My children and I can't beg from the Khasi woman who follows no rules. She does not love the people nor do they love her. After your death, surely there will be chaos in the family. I am staying till today because of my children. It is painful for me to see you like this, having partiality among your sons. Many men wrote a wish dividing their property among their wives and children. Esther's son is born of your blood while my sons are born of your mucous." Jesse saw his mother take the hand of his father and put the thumb impression on a paper while his father seemed to be in a semi-conscious state. He also heard his mother say, "Now you can die anytime, I don't care about you anymore. Just go to your Esther. And before you go, listen, oh you deaf, know that your only daughter reigning in Broadvale is not of your blood. She's from my friend Mr. Doon." Jesse remembered and had always suspected when Disha hated him so much that she turned him out of Broadvale. He now confirmed what he had suspected for a long time, that his only sister, Maria, was Mr. Doon's illegitimate daughter. Jesse returned to his room when Disha closed her door. He went to his bed and felt very sorry for his father. He said to himself, *"So this is the reason my mother keeps Maria in the mission boarding. What a secret, what an idea, what if it gets exposed, how long can you keep the secret and hide your crime? If people come to know, what will happen to little Maria? How will my father bear the pain of such a wicked woman?"* He looked at Dinah, woke up from her sleep and said, "Let's make a commitment dear, what if I happen to be handicapped like father, will you betray me?" Dinah thought for a while and said, "What commitment? What are you trying to do at this hour? Why are you so sad tonight? Don't say such things to me at this time. Tell me only the good things. Don't even think those thoughts. I am not that weak woman. I will stand up and face life's challenges; that's how we, the Khasi women are brought up. Even if I fall, I will rise and become stronger." Jesse didn't disclose what he had intended to tell her. He kept to himself what he had seen and heard about his unfaithful mother.

The Sun festival came in March last week. Broadvale used to celebrate the Sun festival every year differently, in a unique way. They believed that their forefathers worshipped the Sun and got the blessing from it. They had celebrated every year since time immemorial. All the men in the village used to go to the river Tuivai, immerse their bodies and take bath before sunrise. They welcomed the sunrise with a clean body and clean mind, meditating and praying. The women cooked and fed their family before sunrise. After the sunrise, no one got inside the house. They kept fruits and water outside and sacrificed them to the Sun. They would eat the fruits and drink the water when it was fully warm in the Sun. They enjoyed entertainment, sang folk songs and read poems about the Sun. They would have a special dinner after the sunset. While everyone was busy outside the house meditating and praising the mighty Sun, Dinah cried in the pangs of her childbirth. No one went inside to help her, not even the servants entered the door for the whole day. There was loud music of gongs, drums played everywhere and no one heard her call. After the sunset, when the family members came into the house, they found Ron fallen from his bed, his cold body near his bed. Again, Dinah was unconscious lying in a pool of blood with her dead baby. They called the chief priest and physician. They saved Dinah's life. The priest summoned the old midwife in the village to assist him. She came and took the lifeless baby in her arms, warming it near the fireplace. She then gave her breath through the baby's mouth. She rubbed the baby's feet, palms one after another, held it in the legs and kept it upside down in the air. The baby came to life and cried out faintly. Jesse thanked them and gave her a handful of silver coins. Everyone marvelled at the midwife who had given a new life to the lifeless infant, and they wondered what the child would become, who was born on the day his grandpa left the world. Dinah thanked her, with due respect, she asked her name saying, "Aunty, everybody called you aunty, a loving public aunty, what is your name?" "Nengkholhing Lhungdim," said the old midwife to Dinah. The old midwife was requested by Jesse to christen the newborn. She held the baby in her arms, said in a loud voice, "This baby shall be called Leviticus: God gave his life the second time for some purpose, so he is a very special child. It is not I who gave life to him: God surely must have a reason for giving him life." While people were busy on the other side upon the death of Ron, Dinah was left alone with her baby. It was the tradition of Broadvale to fast until the dead body was buried. Since Ron was a famous chief, his dead body was kept for three days. They carried the dead body in a palanquin to all the important sites of Broadvale. As a sign of respect, every man from the village came out with their guns and swords in their chariot. They all dressed in Broadvale's traditional mourning dress. The men performed warrior dances in front of the palanquin all through the way. They sang valour songs as well as mourning songs. On the third day, they placed the lifeless body in a coffin. The Indian Army too came giving full respect to their Captain. As one of the few Vir Chakra awardees, the Indian Army personnel in great number followed the coffin, parading from the cemetery gate to the royal reserve land. They placed flowers on the coffin and gave gun salutes at the cemetery. After the Indian Army, the villagers too performed a gun salute ritual as part of their culture and tradition. While everyone was mourning the death of Ron, Dinah was helpless, hungry and thirsty and cried for her parents. She got up from her bed and started ordering the servants to prepare whatever she wanted them to do for her. Disha told everyone that her shameless daughter-in-law entered the kitchen, ate and drank while the dead body was still in the house. She pointed out all her flaws to her guests, and made Reenarose perform all the rites of a queen in place of Dinah. Dinah never minded, and she continued doing whatever she wanted. She learnt how to ignore things for good, she didn't pay heed to anybody's instructions. She believed her time would come to show the world the bitter truth. She could not perform any rites upon her father-in-law as she was unclean for one month. According to Broadvale family tradition, the unclean woman was not allowed to move out freely outside her room for a whole month. While Jesse was burdened with responsibilities, his wife, Dinah, made a plan to leave Broadvale to stay with her parents.

The next year, Reenarose gave birth to a healthy baby girl. Rolan's daughter was named Babee. Both Babee and Levi were looked after by the same maid. Dinah was not given a separate maid. She lived under the mercy of the royal maids who were fully controlled by Disha and Reenarose. They made Dinah's heart become hardened like a diamond. Her bitter experiences made her fierce and she became stronger day by day. She learnt their language and within a year, could express herself in public. She no longer cared if her baby shower was better than that of Reenarose or not. She no longer bothered if Disha and Reenarose criticized or praised her, she just ate what she wanted and did what she thought was right for her. She blinded herself of the vicinity but only cared about her baby and husband.

CHAPTER - 20

THE MYSTERIOUS DEATH OF MR. DOON

Disha showed the will written by Ron to the family elders. Jesse took it seriously and tried to put up the matter to family elders too, about Disha's fidelity and the roots of his sister, Maria. Jesse was not satisfied with Disha. He decided to put the matter to court and fight for justice. Dinah too wanted to teach Disha a lesson to exposed her dark side in public. They knew calligraphers would not agree with the will left by Ron as it was not Ron's handwriting. Gloria told Jesse that it was possible to prove Maria's identity by doing a DNA test that was available in London. But it was just not possible to put up the matter knowing it would not bring any good. Maria's DNA, if tested in a laboratory, would reveal the truth that she was not Ron's daughter. On the other hand, Disha and Rolan along with Reenarose announced that they would leave Broadvale if justice was not given to them. Rolan became very angry when Jesse and Dinah said that Maria was not born of Ron's blood. There was a cold war in the family that no one dared to interfere with anymore. Jesse and Dinah were given a separate kitchen. Dinah and Disha would argue over small matters which one day would surely lead to a big fire in the family. Dinah warned Disha that she would expose the identity of Maria's father. Disha was in trouble and wanted to meet Mr. Doon. Doon had been living with his wife and children in the city, unaware of what had befallen his beloved Disha. The once famous musician of his time had become a drunkard when he fell in love with Disha. Though they did not live together as husband and wife, they used to meet from time to time, both had always shared their ups and downs in life. They supported each other to fulfilled their hearts' desires once in a blue moon. The illegitimate daughter's identity was hidden as they both agreed not to marry. Mr. Doon who had lost his wife a few months ago met Disha in the same hotel they used to meet for the past 10 years. Doon insisted that they better admit their fault in public and get married. Disha denied it and said, "If we have crossed the desert land and reached the green pastures, we better build a farmhouse and rear our sheep. I have made many mistakes: I don't want to make them anymore. If we love each other truly, one of us has to go first leaving this farmhouse; otherwise, our daughter's life is not secured. Kill me, my love, it's not worth living anymore." They both went to Maria's school and met her. They hugged their daughter lovingly but did not disclose anything to her. Maria was 13 years old, innocent and cheerful. She was very happy to meet her mother after many months. She was not informed of Ron's death. Though she did not like Ron very much, she asked her mother, "How is my father, is he fine?" They said that Ron was fine, and assured her that everything would be fine. They took Maria out for sightseeing. They went shopping, visited some places for two days after which they dropped her back at the boarding. Disha returned to Broadvale, felt guilty to find Jesse and Dinah discussing with a lawyer. She became very nervous and instigated her sons Rolan and Milan that their older brother was selling some part of their land. Rolan and Milan along with family elders gave a warning to Dinah to move out from Broadvale within one month.

Heaps and heaps of snow get to build upon the Giant Mountain as winter comes with its majestic cold breeze. It was one of the coldest winters ever felt in Broadvale. Dinah requested Jesse arrange a visit to her parents as soon as possible. She did not want to talk about what she was told by Rolan and Milan. Jesse assured Dinah that they would go before Christmas. While Dinah was busy counting the days to leave Broadvale, one day Disha told her that if she did not leave Broadvale very soon, she would see the lifeless body of Jesse in a pool of blood. Dinah packed her things eagerly waited for her husband. Reenarose came to her to bid her bye as a sister-in-law. Reenarose gave Disha a beautiful copper bangle and said, "We may fight and quarrel but when the time for our parting comes, I want to say sorry for what I have done and said before." Disha hugged Reenarose and said, "Let's love like this in the days to come too, sister." As they hugged each other they heard the wail of Disha. They both went to checked what would be the reason. They saw Disha leaning against the wall in her room and wailing. One of the servants told them about the untimely demise of Mr. Doon. Disha shut the door herself. Nobody knew what she did inside her room. Jesse, Rolan and Milan did not come back home that day and Dinah was very worried. She asked for help from whomever she thought would know what happened to the brothers and how Mr. Doon died all of a sudden.

The following day the three brothers return home but did not talk to anyone. Dinah asked her husband where he had been but the latter did not tell her what she asked for. Dinah, at last, said, "If I am worthy of being your wife, tell me where you have been because I want to know seriously." Jesse said, "I don't want to tell you bad things. I want you to know only the good things. Well, listen, Mr. Doon's death was not natural: It was either suicide or murder. One of my friends said he saw Disha, Doon and Maria roaming in the city last week. I tried to meet the lawyer and now with Mr. Doon's death, she cannot go further with the case. Doon has many sons and daughters who would do anything to keep the dignity of their father. Rolan and Milan also came to the funeral. We are after one another and I could do nothing to prove that my father's death is not natural nor that of Mr. Doon's death is not natural. There is something behind the scene so I cannot leave Broadvale without digging out the secret; it's a matter, a serious matter for Broadvale. Doon's children are not convinced that their father's death was a case of suicide because the drink on his bedside table contained poison, the type of poison that makes the person slowly die while sleeping peacefully." Dinah thought for some time and said, "Then what were Rolan and Milan doing there?" Jesse stooped down and scratched his head saying, "That's what I am thinking and could not return home leaving them behind, maybe they also realize Disha's infidelity." Dinah insisted and prayed to Jesse to pay a visit to her family at Shillong, so the couple prepared to leave Broadvale the following day.

The next day, while the Broadvale family was in total confusion, Dinah's family came to visit them bringing many gifts from Shillong. Dinah and Jesse had gone out to one of their neighbouring villages to meet their friends: The guests from Shillong came as a surprise. They didn't speak or understand the language of Broadvale; though they came cheerfully with expensive gifts, they were not given a warm welcome. Those who spoke English in Broadvale helped the guests in communicating with the elders of the clan. They were not given any food or drink in the royal house. Disha and Reenarose too left the guests intentionally and went out to the town. When Jesse and Dinah returned, after visiting their friends, they were overwhelmed to see the family visiting them. They were very ashamed of the maltreatment given to them by his family. The royal families of Shillong, who were respected by the people of their land, were treated in Broadvale like a stranger or a beggar. However, Jesse and Dinah called their family elders and friends. They arranged a grand reception programme. They organized a cultural dance show followed by a grand feast. It hurt Dinah when Disha, Rolan and Reenarose did not attend her programme. Jesse and Dinah took the guests for a tour the whole week which made Disha jealous and angry. After one week of their stay at Broadvale, the Khasi guests returned home blessing Jesse and Dinah for their hospitality and the pleasant stay. Jesse dropped them up in the city. Before his return, he thought of visiting his sister Maria. When he went to the mission boarding, the sweet sister welcomed him happily. Jesse gave her many eatables and encouraged her to study very hard. He advised her not to come home unnecessarily besides also to take care of herself. He met the principal of her school and paid off her fees in advance. He loved Maria because she was sweet and innocent. He thought to himself, *"I have three brothers born of my father's blood and I should be thankful to God for giving me a sweet sister, though, from an unknown father. Oh, my sweet unlucky sister who does not know the death of your foster father as well as your biological father, do you know how much I love and care for you? May the good God bless you, so that, someday you become a light in the dark world! May you unveil the truth stone of your origin without pain and shame but become an example to others!"*

When Jesse reached home, he was wondering why, some policemen along with lady police officers gathered there, around his house. He knew that something fishy was there at the royal house. He went inside his mother's room, paused for a moment in the corridor as he felt a sharp pain in his heart because it was the first time he entered after his father's death. He saw his mother and Milan talking with a team of police. He asked them the reason and realized the case against the death of Mr. Doon by his son. The police interrogated Disha about what happened to Mr. Doon as she was his close friend and Mr. Doon had been in the band for quite a long time. Disha said loudly to everybody, "I have no idea about how Doon died. He is my close friend. We were in the same band and it was a long time back then. I have no relation with him anymore." One of the officers asked Disha what she was doing with Mr. Doon and little Maria in the city a few days before Mr. Doon died. Disha did not say anything. She acted like a mentally-ill person. She horribly just shouted at them, "I do not know what you people are talking about." She kept repeating that she knew nothing about how Mr. Doon died and wept uncontrollably at last. Rolan, as usual, got furious and said, "Why are you torturing my mother? She is having a mental problem since my father's death." He then showed them some papers proving her illness to deceive the hungry policemen. The police officer was a greedy man, beating around the bush, to convinced both the parties for his personal benefit. Rolan would do anything to defend his loving Mother, so also for family prestige whatever is the matter. While they were busy talking with the policemen, Jesse secretly opened Disha's box, took away the will that his mother claimed to have been written by his father. The next day he took the paper to his lawyer and checked out the lines written on the paper. Scientific investigation revealed that Ron had written a will indeed. But the will that was written by Ron was changed. The inks used by Ron and that of the culprit were different. Detectives discovered it by calculating the velocity and viscosity of the inks. Apart from that, calligraphers reported that the will was written by two persons.

CHAPTER - 21

THE RAPE OF MISS MARIA

Jesse started investigating and kept an eye on his mother. One day he secretly opened her cupboard, checked every nook and corner. He found a very small glass bottle that looked like perfume but smelt like wine. The very shape of the bottle was unique. He suspected it to be something related to the death of his father and Mr. Doon. He took the bottle and showed it to his friend again. After some weeks, he got the report that the drink was poison. They gave him the report that the bottle contained a very strong drink; even a single drop of it could make a person die, just like a natural death. The speciality of the poison was such that the person would die without any pain or symptoms, so people will assume it was a natural death. It could be mixed with a portion of food or any drink. Unlike other poisons, if someone drank or happened to take a drop, that person would die slowly, and easily, in a day or two, not instantly. Jesse said to himself, *"So this is the thing, the mystery behind my father's death as well as Mr. Doon. This place is not safe for my wife and children. Either I leave to save myself or expose her to save the family."* He then went to the Giant Mountain and dug a pit. He covered the bottle of poison and the paper. He dug a small pit and buried them in the earth. He returned home and was shocked to see Disha, who stood on the staircase, with loose hair in a red furious face. She knew her things had been stolen by Jesse. Disha wanted to take revenge. She could not directly accuse him of stealing her things though she knew very well that it was none else but Jesse. Jesse informed the servants to take his mother and put her to bed. Disha became wild like a mad dog ready to bite Jesse. She lost all her beauty and grace because of her wicked plans.

One day Jesse was away from home to attend an important meeting in the neighbouring village. He attended the meeting and forgot to tell his bodyguard to return home. He returned home after three days worried about his pregnant wife, Dinah. He was told by one of his friends that his house was on fire and that his pregnant wife and son were taken to the hospital. He went straight to the hospital and found Dinah in the intensive care unit. He could not talk with her, so informed his relatives who were taking care not to leave until he came back. His son was taken care by the royal maid. Jesse said, "If anything happens to Levi, you will die." He left the maid who felt rather upset about the command while she had been doing her best to defend Dinah and to save the baby. He went straight to Broadvale, shouted at his courtyard calling out to his family members. Many people already gathered there and they tried to calm down his anger. When Rolan and Disha came out and stood at the veranda, Jesse shouted and said, *"Why was my room on fire, speak up if you are a man! Why was my room on fire while the other room next to mine is safe? When Dinah and Levi are battling for life in the hospital, what are you all doing here? This is my father's house, I am the eldest of his sons; come out, you all, heartless creatures! Dinah is my better half, how dare you call her valueless, priceless? How dare you play with the lives of my beloved family when I conceal all your guilty actions?"* Rolan was speechless and he too tried to calm down Jesse.

Disha hurriedly went inside and came out with Milan after some time. Disha came out boastfully replied to Jesse, "You are an illegitimate son, you have no right in this house according to the law of Broadvale. And your woman, we said priceless woman because she has no value, no respect for elders, especially to me. If these things had been done to your real mother, Esther, you would have divorced her long ago. Don't you know what that Khasi woman did to us, she tried to kill us. She said I am an unfaithful woman, when I brought you all up, till today no one has ever said such words to me even though, as a woman, I might have been unworthy and incomplete. But I'm trying my best; I took care of your ailing father all these years sacrificing my youth even though I was forced to marry him. She said your sister Maria is illegitimate; who is she to come and point at me. Do you see the condition of your sister Maria? Go inside my room and ask her what has happened to her. And your wife, she is careless, she burns her room to fire. Who are you to shout at me?"

Jesse again retorted and said, "Till today I never raised any question or word against you, even knowing about your character. I know your relationship with Mr. Doon, about sister Maria and how my father died." Before he finished his sentence, Disha slapped his face and told everyone, "Okay, you have to prove what you have just said and if I am proved guilty, I will burn myself alive at this very place; come on, if you claim to be the eldest son of Ron, prove it, make your way to the throne. Don't you remember you were the one who convinced me to marry your father, you have promised me to obey and do everything for my happiness?" Disha fainted before she completed her words and fell at the feet of Milan. Reenarose and her servants lifted Disha and carried her inside the house. Rolan and Milan become furious, they too supported their mother. Rolan said to Jesse, "I respect you as my elder brother. But do you love us as a brother? Today I see your reality; I now believe that you will never love us if you don't love the woman who gave birth to us. And Maria, our only sister, you said that she is illegitimate. Do you love my sister Maria? Will you not even ask what her condition is now, while my only sister is battling between life and death, how can you talk about her like this? How dare you talk and point my mother in front of me? You are an illegitimate child born in the jungle. You don't deserve to rule over us. You should leave here this very night!" The hot-tempered brothers soon stopped arguing like womenfolk and fought with hands and legs. People tried to calm them down on both sides. They could not control the situation when Milan, along with some of his men started attacking Jesse with sticks and swords. Fida, Jesse's half-brother rushed in along with some of their men and drove him away from Broadvale. There was bloodshed in the royal house. Even the servants and family elders also fought among themselves. Jesse was taken away by his men to a safe place, but he was already badly wounded by his brothers. They hid him and nursed him in the jungle. They stitched the deep cuts on his body and gave him painkillers.

The next day when he opened his eyes, he found himself in a deserted house. He asked his friend, "My friend, I seem to be familiar with this deserted house even though I have never known this place." Jesse felt warm and at home in the deserted house. He enquired about his wife and son. They told him everything would be fine. They put him on anaesthesia to let him sleep. He had hallucinations as if people, with whom he thought he was familiar, were talking around him in unknown languages. He seemed to be among Spirits where he could not touch anyone. He saw some people urging him to wake up, as it was like his dream, he knew what they were doing for him but he could not identify their faces. The place was strange while everything appeared blurry. Sometimes he heard his father and mother talking near to him but when he paid attention to what they said they vanished into the thin air. Sometimes, he felt himself like a child and a woman attended to him in a baby cradle singing sweet lullabies. He cried in his dream. He was like sitting on the lap of a woman on a very long swing among the clouds. The swing made him scared, he woke up suddenly in reality at night. He found himself in the real world surrounded by his friends and relatives. He said to them, "Put me back to sleep. I want to be with them again. I want to hear that sweet lullaby of my mother and want to know those people who are around me. I hear my father's voice and the cry of a sweet baby." His uncle Jensta whispered to them, "This is your Uncle Benjamin's house, Gaitlane, where you have laughed and cried in your childhood; you have played here in your childhood and you were separated from your mother in this same house. The best moments of your childhood must be in this house. That day, I accompanied your parents and we spent some days together but your wicked Uncle Benjamin cheated on us. He took away his sister, Esther to Israel. Relax, your soul knows your roots." The priest gave them a strict warning not to put him again to deep sleep because his condition was critical. The priest told his men that his Spirit felt difficult and tired staying in a weak body controlled by strong medicine. He writhed, at times moaned, when he slept. So, his men would wake him up, tell him about Bible stories and life stories of great warriors. Jesse became stable after three days and three nights.

On the fourth day, he could walk and eat by himself. He thanked his men who risked their lives for him. He thanked his chief bodyguard Uncle Jensta, his bodyguard Zamzam, and top-secret bodyguard Fida. He asked for their advice as he had always done since his childhood. Jensta was second to his father who had always led him on the right path. They both shared all the secrets of Broadvale. Till that both trusted each other like a trusted father and son. Dinah and Levi were also ready to get discharged from the hospital. Uncle Jensta himself took the responsibility to take the mother and child from the hospital. They all met in the deserted house. Jensta, Zamzam and the other bodyguards of the village army favoured Jesse to go back and fight for his birthright while Dinah told them that she would return to her parents' house if they planned to go back to Broadvale. Dinah was traumatised to reveal what had befallen Broadvale on that fateful day when her room was on fire. However, when she was insisted on by Jesse again and again, she said, "I was spoon-feeding Levi in the morning in the veranda balcony. Disha became mad and scattered her things. She scolded the servants saying they were careless. I knew she was looking for the small bottle of poison and the paper on which our father had written the will. Just then my baby cried because of her noises. She came and scolded me saying I am a careless mother who cannot calm down her baby. I told her that Levi was not feeling well. She said many unpleasant words about me and my family which I retorted back. Oh, we are priceless," she sobbed for a while at the harsh words and remarks made at her by Disha as the priceless, the valueless woman and then continued, "Two men came soon after. They met inside her room for quite a long time. She sent away all the servants to wait for Maria at the Giant Gate. Rolan and Reenarose were away for two days, they went to the city to take Maria for her holidays. Milan too was away as usual. I became curious about them and secretly looked through a hole in the window. I heard them talking about the bottle and its power. She gave them a bundle of money. I also saw her taking out more bundles from a suitcase. They talked and argued over the price of something. I suspected her to be secretly selling some of our valuables. Just then my baby cried so I was caught red-handed. They came after me, chasing behind me…I ran straight to my room, locked the door screaming. They opened the window, poured kerosene all around in my room. They set fire to the room. I tried to douse the fire but they poured more and more oil. I went to the bathroom after I have used up all the water to douse the fire. I took Levi on my lap who was shaking with fear. We sat inside the bathroom praying to God. Luckily, the drizzling rain saved us from the fire. Soon, the servants had returned by then, and they hurried us to the hospital."

Uncle Zamzam told them that the same day their innocent sister Maria was raped. Rolan and Reenarose had gone to take her from the boarding. On their way home Rolan met one of his old friends. He sent Maria home first in a separate chariot while he and Reenarose spent some time together in the town with friends. On the way, the trusted bodyguard who was already 50 years old drove the chariot forcibly on a rugged shortcut road, planning to make the chariot, as well as the innocent girl, to meet an accident. Unfortunately, the fatherless girl whom her family had debated a lot on her biological father, fell prey to the hand of the beast. The beast was experienced in horse riding for many years. He separated the horses by cutting the rope that was tied with the back carriage. The chariot met an accident in a deserted place. Maria got hurt and became unconscious. The beastly old man tore her clothes that covered her virginity, insanely covered with his and traumatized her. He left her in the jungle and escaped. Rolan and Reenarose reached home in the afternoon to find Maria near the giant gate weeping for help. Jesse was very angry with Disha and Rolan. He vowed that he would take revenge for his sister Maria. The following day the rapist came to them to surrendered hoping that Jesse might be on his side. He sent a man to Jesse that he wanted to confess and beg forgiveness. He also sent the man to tell Jesse that, as the chief bodyguard of Rolan, he could be of valuable help to reveal to him Disha's secret and the henpecked Rolan's evil plan. Jesse called the man who came with folded hands. He begged on his knees saying, "I know, I have sinned against God and men, I am bending at your feet and begging for my life. I deserve punishment but spare my life for the sake of my innocent wife and children so that I will help you all to repay my sin." Jesse said to this man, *What is it that you can do to repay your sin? Nothing is as valuable as the dignity of a woman and an innocent girl."* Saying so, he told his men to tie his limbs with a rope and they did accordingly. They took him to the place where he had raped Maria in the jungle. They stripped him, tied his naked body to a tree. They cut his penis, hands and left him to die, saying, "Well, we did not take your life: You will die on your own."

By then, Dinah was eight months pregnant. She took her baby Levi and said to Jesse who was having a meeting with his bodyguards. "If you love your wife and child, follow my footsteps. Let's go." Jesse and his men discussed for some time. They decided to leave Broadvale and move to a new place together. They built a house for Jesse and Dinah in a place called Sunray. Jesse told them to go back to Broadvale to look after the land and its people. They embraced each other before they parted in different directions. Leaving Broadvale became the ultimate solution to have a peaceful life.

The following week, Dinah gave birth to a baby girl which they named her Shindy. After all his men left, Jesse was arrested by the police on the charge of murder. He was taken away while Dinah was away from home. When Dinah came back in the evening, she wondered where Jesse had gone out. She asked her neighbours and realized the matter. She asked for help from her new friends. She went to the town to enquire about the matter. Jesse was kept in a lockup. Dinah sold her golden necklace to a rich merchant in the town to manage her finances herself. With the help of Fida, they paid the required fee for the lawyer to bail out Jesse from lockup. Then the two went straight to Broadvale. They met Uncle Jensta, Zamzam, also some of the family elders. They asked for their help. She wanted to take some of her belongings and necessary things from her room but Disha did not even let them enter the royal house. She appealed to the chief association of the district and cried for justice. The judge demanded her to produce two witnesses if Maria was raped, also if the rapist did surrender as Jesse claimed. The next day, Jesse's bodyguard, Zamzam was killed in a cold-blooded action and the dead body was found dumped at the military gate. The dead body bore marks of strangulation on his neck and his tongue was cut. No one dared come out to stand for the witness that Maria was brutally raped by the royal bodyguard even though they had seen her being raped. Disha and her children did not like the case to proceed further. They wanted to conceal the news of her rape for fear of humiliation. They had been disgraced and criticized enough. They wanted to protect the girl who was still recuperating from the trauma. Disha did not want anybody to talk about the identity of Maria as well as the brutal murder of the rapist, who was none other than her own brother's son-in-law. On the day of judgement, when no witnesses stood up for Jesse, Dinah was desperately looking around the crowd and was speechless when none of her witnesses arrived at the spot at the appointed time. Whatever Jesse and Dinah said in the court, was countered by Disha's men, claiming that Maria was not raped. There was silence in the court; everyone was sure that according to the law, Jesse would be given a punishment of at least 10 years imprisonment and some faces, mostly of Disha's men, were eagerly waiting for the final verdict of the case. When the judge was about to declare the judgement, suddenly they heard the cry of a young girl who stood at the doorway of the hall foreboding to enter the courtroom. As she walked up to the witness box, she was shaking to her knees, trembling with fear as if she was being warned and threatened by someone. Behind her was Fida who had told the girl what she had to do in court. They both stood to give witness to the crime. She covered her head and face with a black cloth. She stood in front of the judge stooping her head, wept bitterly. She held an edge of the witness box with one hand and wiped her tears with her other hand. Everybody in the court questioned who the lady was, what she was doing in the court. The judge asked her to stop weeping. Jesse knew that the girl was none other than his lovely sister. He did not like her to get exposed and said to her, "What are you doing here, lady, this is no child's play. Go home." Maria unveiled her face slowly. She wiped her tears and said, "I am Miss Maria; I will give witness to the crime in Jesse's favour. I, myself am the rape victim; I will testify and stand for the witness of the murder accused of the royal bodyguard. Yes, I was raped; I will not remain silent anymore. One month ago, I was raped by the royal bodyguard on my way home from mission boarding. Many people including my mother had warned me, counselled me and threatened me not to disclose the incident. This is about my life, the life of an innocent damsel, who had always dreamt of the day, that someday she would be taken into marriage by her Prince, riding on a horse decorated with flowers and become the most beautiful princess for him. Now all her dreams get shattered like the sandcastle on a seashore destroyed by a violent tornado. In this world, the most precious thing that a girl can give her husband is her virginity. A father is being regarded by all as the provider while it is universal that a mother is like nature, a caregiver. Sisters are friends, a blessing from above to laugh with, share burdens with and cry on her shoulder. What is the role of a brother? What is the responsibility of a brother? Is having a brother a blessing or a curse? If your sister is raped and the rapist comes to you, what will you do? If you cannot defend her, if you do not take revenge, then what are you to your sisters? Will any girl ever trust her brother in future if he doesn't take the pain to fight for his sister? How could you punish my loving brother who takes revenge for his innocent sister?" Everyone listened to Maria's speech with their jaws dropping and there was pin-drop silence in the court hall. Everyone was shocked at the story of the young girl, they watched her in wonder, as it was for the first time in the history of the tribal village court, did any young girl ever speak in the witness box and testify herself. Even the judges were speechless and watched Maria who spoke to the audience with her hand pointing to one another, lecturing for about an hour. Jesse too, wondered how his little sister could speak out like that, breaking all the norms of the rules of a woman. He knew well that his sister was not an extrovert, who was always polite and knew her boundary. Maria no longer cried once she was provoked; she kept on explaining the life of women and how their traditions ruined, tortured women in particular. When she finished her speech, she went to Jesse saying, *"Brother, take me with you, I don't want to die in the hands of those devils."* Jesse embraced her and said, "Why did you come out of the house, don't you know what would be the consequence?" According to a cruel Broadvale tradition, if a young girl was raped, they would throw her out of the village. If a woman committed adultery, she was stoned to death. If a woman's modesty was outraged, her husband had full authority either to kill her or divorce her. The laws were harsh for women and for that reason, women of Broadvale were mostly timid, beautiful, had no short hair, had a high culture, were hardworking and soft as they stayed mostly indoors. Jesse assured Maria that he would take her with him. Dinah beckoned Maria and they hugged each other. Dinah said to Maria, "Let us move out from here as soon as possible. If we stay in Shillong, people are good, they respect women. We women rule and inherit property."

CHAPTER - 22

HEARTBROKEN MARIA

Jesse was freed from the case on the condition that he had to pay a heavy fine to the court as well as the bereaved family for taking the law into his own hands. He had to leave the village as criminals were not allowed to settle in the village according to their custom. When they came out of the judgement hall, Jesse was busy meeting his friends and family elders. Dinah and Maria along with Levi and baby Shindy came out and waited for Jesse near their chariot. Dinah consoled Maria that everything would be fine. They saw the royal chariot coming towards them. When Maria saw the royal chariot with two women sitting inside, her heart almost skipped a beat and said, "They are coming to take me, sister, I don't want to go back to Broadvale, save me." Maria got hold of Levi and moved closer to Dinah who held her on her shoulder. Disha and Reenarose stopped the chariot in front of them. They requested Maria to get in the chariot and go back to Broadvale. Maria protested and cried as she did not want to return to Broadvale. Disha forcibly held Maria's hand, pulled her away from Levi and Dinah.

When Dinah tried to talk to them, they gave her no chance to speak. Since they belonged to the royal family, nobody came out to enforce the law of the land upon Maria. Still, it was hard for Maria to step out of her house. Disha sent her back to mission boarding. But Maria's life was miserable: she suffered from the stigma and could not stand to face the consequence. She became the target of other men too as well. People came to know of her identity. When she discovered her identity, she went to Broadvale to asked her mother who her real father was. Disha was speechless for a moment. She took her chariot then made Maria seated on it. The servant asked them where he should take them. Disha sent back the servant as well as the bodyguard. She drove the chariot and took Maria to the coffee farm. She did not answer whatever Maria asked her; however, she repeated her questions. Disha held the hand of Maria and dragged her to the resthouse on the coffee farm. She asked who had told her all about that. She said, "I know, mummy, because I do not look like my brothers. I do look like you but why do you keep me away from my family? Why do I have to stay in the boarding at the tender age of eight when I am the youngest and only daughter of the family? Do you think this is fair if you were in my place? Tell me mummy, who is Mr. Doon? Is he my real father?" Disha looked at Maria, touched her face, and then hugged her. She could not tell her right that moment. She wondered how her child came to know of all these things. She again asked who had told her that she was not Ron's daughter.

At last, Maria told her, "Mummy, I don't want to live any longer. That uncle who outraged my modesty told me that I am an illegitimate daughter of Uncle Doon. Mummy, I know I will never live in peace my whole life. Where can I find peace?" Maria cried like a child and Disha hugged her saying, "You are my daughter, you are mine, myself and my blood. Do not cry, baby, it hurts your widow mother." She too could not hold her tears and both the mother and daughter cried the whole day on the coffee farm as Disha narrated the sufferings of her life. Maria was now sure that Doon was her father. In the evening, before they returned home, Maria said to her mother, "Mummy, as a woman, I will have to marry a man someday. Who will do the customary rites of my bridal blessing, who will give me blessing if I am to get married? Will my husband be a happy man? By that time, you may still be living or not, only God knows your time; will my brothers and sisters-in-law still love me?" Disha wiped her tears with her scarf and said, "What shall I do and tell you, my dear? God is there, He knows I have sinned and repented. God has forgiven me. Live in peace. Study hard and become a successful woman who doesn't depend on her man, your happiness lies in your hands, you don't need anyone's approval to be happy. Be strong and fierce like a tiger and fear none." They returned home in the evening hungry, with broken hearts. Everyone in the royal house was shocked to see them coming home with puffy eyes. Disha told them that they had visited Ron's graveyard. Maria cried for days and weeks. She went to Ron's graveyard and prayed every day. After one week of mourning, one day she told her mother when everyone was away from home, "Mother, I prayed on my father's graveyard every day. I want to make one request. Let us erect a tomb for my father and mother Esther." However, her mother politely told her that all the sufferings of her life begin with Esther, and she did not agree with her proposal.

Again, one day, Maria went to Mr. Doon's house to meet her family without Disha's knowledge. Doon's house was in the heart of the city, near a marketplace. It was a two-storeyed building with a very large campus with a servants' quarter bigger than the royal house at Broadvale. It had a tall boundary wall with a very big heavy Iron Gate. There was a watchman in uniform standing on the left side of the gate. She entered after getting permission at the entry. As she entered the house, she was welcomed by the maidservant who took her to Doon's chamber as she said that she wanted to have a look at the great musician's chamber. Doon's family members welcomed her when she said she wanted to have a look at his musical instruments and albums. Since Doon was a very famous musician, there used to be frequent visitors who were impressed with his album. Maria bought all the albums of Doon. She requested Doon's daughter-in-law, who was a very kind and jolly woman of about 30 years that she wanted to meet all the family members. They made Maria stay the night and have dinner with them. They appeared to be kind and highly cultured. When they were all seated for the dinner, Maria wiped her tears secretly. She drank water, again and again, feeling very tense and nervous sitting among her biological brothers and sisters, who were decades and decades older than her. She was happy to see the face of her three big brothers and three big sisters who lived together peacefully in that big house, under one roof. There were more than 15 children in the house. They had separate kitchens for their own family but they had a very large common living room, quite big enough to accommodate 70 people. They had big guest rooms with separate washrooms. They had more servants than the Broadvale royal family. All the sons and daughters were successful men and women. They were respectable and cool, unlike the Broadvale family who always argued over silly matters and fought for birthright. She learnt how well-cultured people lived in the city. She felt proud to be called Doon's daughter. They asked her many questions to which she responded with the same answer, *"I will tell you after dinner, I have come for some important mission."*

After dinner, when they were all seated in the living room, she started her speech while they listened to her, as they were curious to know who she was, for what mission she visited them. At first, Maria introduced herself to them, told them her story. They were all shocked to learn that she was from Broadvale. The very name of Broadvale made them annoyed to give an ear to her story as they knew their father had been ruined by the great woman, Queen of Broadvale, Disha. Maria did not know how much her mother was hated by them. Disha had not told her about the enmity between Doon's family and the Broadvale family. However, they didn't want to displease their special guest. They quietly listened to her whole story until their minds were blown away when they learnt that Maria was their sister. They all wondered how that young girl knew all those stories which were known to none of them. They also wondered wherefrom that young girl got the courage to stand in front of them to speak as if she was their mother who gave birth to them. Still, they wondered why their father would have concealed such a big secret all those years. They looked at Maria's happy face, tried to find a clue from her gestures and movement if she was their sister. However, Maria was exactly like her mother, Disha. They looked at each other for quite a long time, soon after, without discussion, they all said the same thing. All the brothers and sisters assured her that, they would always love her. They were ever ready to help her in trouble but they would not claim her from the Broadvale family. They were not ready to accept her publicly as their sister. Maria cried the whole night at her father's house. She left Doon's house early in the morning before they got up.

Before going back to Broadvale, Maria went to the city Cathedral to offer her prayers. There was no one in the Church at that time. She entered the Church, walked through the aisle and went straight to the front towards the statue of Jesus and the Virgin Mary. She knelt and folded her hands in prayer. She looked at the face of the Virgin

Mary and meditated for a few minutes. She then bowed down at the feet of Jesus and meditated, connecting with God. She opened her eyes, looked deeply at the idol of Jesus's eyes and slowly wept, her tears rolling down her pale cheeks. She felt that she was being watched from her back by someone. She quickly wiped her tears and turned her head around. There the priest stood behind her and patted her shoulder. She rose from the floor and bowed down to the priest. The priest said, "Till today no young girl has ever come here to pray. Who are you and what sin has brought you here?" Maria wiped her tears and said, "Father, I am coming to find divine solace, I have nobody in this world, I have not done anything wrong to anyone. I have been born wrong so I am asking God what I should do. Where should I go, I have no peace and no place, I am coming to share my burden." The priest then made her sit on the bench and he too took a more comfortable position. He then stood up, went towards the tabernacle and took water for Maria. He gave a cup of water to Maria. She thanked him and drank the water. The priest took the empty cup, held it in his hands, stooping his head and ready to lend his ears to her. They sat together for some time; "Daughter, how deep is the wound that brought you at the feet of Jesus? Can I be of some help to you? What are you hiding from others that you came alone at this hour? You can share anything with God, do not worry, pray till you feel your burden is gone. Speak out, this Holy place is open for everyone where we can say anything and connect with God, live unapologetically as broken and forgiven followers of Christ. You can also share your burden with me so that I will deliver it to God and lighten your burden. This is a Holy place where we carry each other's burden."

She wiped her tears, asked the priest what she should do in her life. She did not want to get married her whole life but many men were chasing her. Among the many boys who were after her, she loved one of them very much. She told the priest how her biological brothers treated her. She narrated about the Broadvale family and how they treated her. Above all, she was raped, did not have the strength to move on in life. The priest listened to her story attentively and when she stopped, he slowly turned his face to her and asked, "Well, because of all these, you want to end your precious life? I think you need to spend some time with our sisters. They will take care of you."

The priest prayed for her, advised her to spend some time with the nun sisters. He also arranged her accommodation in the convent and took her to them. The sisters welcomed her warmly. They shared their own life stories. Maria remembered what the priest had told her. She believed that there were still many people who suffered in this world more than her. She found solace when she mingled with the nun sisters. They loved her, made her stay in the nunnery revived, comfortable, worthy and pleasant. She got inspired by their lives. She once again decided to move on in life. She saw with her own eyes, the peaceful life of the nuns which was a pure blessing from the divine. She was impressed with everything that she saw them do like singing, meditation, Mass, Eucharistic adoration and rosary. She admired their devotion to God, their Bible study, their daily lives and above all their pure white dress which showed their purity in body, mind, heart and soul. She wanted to be like just them, pure and holy. She loved the lives of nuns whose lives were harmoniously ordered to preserve the continual remembrance of God, and the serene place where they worshipped together, far away undisturbed by noise and pollution. She wanted to live in peace and forget her cruel fate. She appreciated the strong bond of sisterhood among the nuns, and she believed that it would be the right place for her, where she didn't need to wait for anyone's approval or acceptance to be their sister. She asked herself, "Can I become a nun after being raped? Is the rape any fault of mine?" She thought for some time and said to herself again, "No, I am still a virgin, I did not commit adultery, and I was just being trampled. I have a clear mind and a clean body, and I will cover this clean body with the white dress, I may be unclean in the minds of mortal men but I know my mind is as clean and pure as the Angels. God understands the pain that I felt like a mortal being and He loves this pure mind. I will remain clean, faithful to God my whole life." She wanted to show the world that family was not about blood, it was about who was willing to hold your hand when you were in need. She told the priest that she too wanted to become a Catholic nun and serve humanity. However, the priests and sisters gave her counselling, advised her to go back to her family. They gave her some religious books on the lives of the nuns and told her to read them thoroughly. The priest and nuns told Maria to think deeply for some time. They told her to take advice from her mother, only then take a firm decision before becoming a nun. Before she departed, the priest again gave her some money and a Holy Bible.

CHAPTER - 23

MARIA BECOMES A CATHOLIC NUN

Maria went back to Broadvale and asked her mother if she would like to listen to her life adventures in the city. Disha hugged her and said, "Tell me some other day, my dear, I am not feeling well, leave me alone." Disha was furious to learn that Maria had been to Doon's house. She also heard that Doon's children did neither accept her as their sister nor take her into her true home and family. She felt pain, a sharp pain struck right through her heart that her only daughter was raped, and also rejected by the world when she needed a shoulder to lean on, her father's family as well as her mother's family. She was not happy about her young daughter roaming alone freely without her knowledge. When Maria returned home, no one talked to her, neither did they scold her for leaving home for two weeks nor did they ask where she had been. It was more painful for Maria when nobody asked her if she was fine or not. She looked at their gloomy faces and eyes, became pessimistic at their gaze. A sense of insecurity crept deep inside her, thinking that they all had changed and their avoidance meant to her, a great distance in relation proving she did not belong to the royal blood. All those reactions pave the way for her to start reading the books given by the priest and nuns. She read the rules and about the lives of the nuns in the nunnery. She avoided all her friends and confined herself within the four walls of her room until she had gone through all the lines of the book and digested them.

One day, she gathered all her courage and walked into her mother's chamber while she was alone. Disha had been grief-stricken when Doon's children insulted her for her illicit relationship with their father, Doon. She was down in the dumps upon Doon's family who told her to control Maria from roaming like a harlot, just like her mother, saying Maria would not be accepted into their family. Maria asked her some questions about religion and marriage, but Disha had nothing to say about religion and marriage at that moment. Maria then asked her mother what she wanted her daughter to become in life. She was not in the mood to talk with her and said, "Do whatever you want to do in life. Do not ask me, I am not worthy to give instructions or advice. You have been independent since your childhood and had been doing things behind my back. Even when I warned you strictly not to go to the village court, you had gone there and broken all the norms of the life of a royal daughter, maybe you are not of the royal blood, that's why you had been so strong, strong enough to defame me among my people. You made me defeated among my people and now I am left with nothing but to bear disgrace and despise by everyone. My story has become the talk of the village through your words and actions. You fought for yourself and helped Jesse and Dinah, whom your mother hated the most. Instead, you should give me some advice on what I should do for you." Maria became completely dejected when her mother did not understand the feelings of her daughter. She said to her mother the next day, "Mummy, I cannot stay here in Broadvale, I do not belong here. If you want me to stay here, please build a tomb for mother Esther and father Ron in the royal cemetery and call back brother Jesse. I will go to the city shortly."

Disha thought that Maria would be going to the city to resume her studies. When her holidays ended, Rolan took Maria to the boarding. Rolan was not outspoken by nature, so he did not ask anything related to what was lingering in the mind of his sister. He simply dropped her, gave her some money, advised her to study well and take care of herself. Maria could not concentrate on her studies. Again, she felt insecure when she looked at the eyes of her boarding warden and other boys. She could not trust any man. She become scared when any guy looked at her deeply. She left her boarding and went to meet her brother, Jesse. Jesse and Dinah loved her, did their best to make her comfortable with them. They understood her feelings. They also heard the news about how she was rejected by her biological siblings and Broadvale was hell for her. Jesse understood from her eyes that she felt insecure and lonely. Maria told them that she did not want to continue her studies. Jesse hugged his little sister and encouraged her, making her strong. Jesse said, "Do not be discouraged by people, be strong, my sister, I am always there for you. God must have planned something far better than what we wished for you, people will think you are wrong, but you have to make them see the right. Things will be a lot easier for us when we see God's hand in it. Rise, stand up, make your way among the crowd, we all have only one life, do what makes you happy, do not depend on a man. Marriage is beautiful but to remain unwed is far better than marrying the wrong person. Choose your way wisely, you can do many things without your man if you choose to remain single in your life. Do not be disheartened and unnecessarily bothered by what people or society will think about you, you are not born to impress them. So, do not let people bring you down. Every single day, a girl is raped. Some end their life. They cannot stand the stigma in society. The weak type of girls never fight for justice. I have seen your strength and appreciate your decisions. Many great women face the challenges and become successful." Jesse encouraged Maria to take a firm decision between her boyfriend and her career. Maria told Jesse and Dinah that she wanted to remain unwed her whole life and spend her life serving humanity. She also told them about her decision to become a nun and live with the nun sisters.

Maria's principal had given a warning to Disha that her daughter left the boarding without taking permission.

After two weeks, Disha and Reenarose came to Jesse's house and without saying anything pulled out Maria and took her back to the boarding. When Jesse tried to stop them, Disha blamed him for spoiling Maria just because she was not his real sister. Maria loved to stay with Jesse; however, she knew it would not be possible in the long run. She remembered her brother Jesse saying to herself, *"No one is willing to hold me when I need them. Family is not about blood."* She wanted to go back to Jesse but she was afraid that her decision might worsen the enmity between the families. She had no more strength to move on with life in the village when many boys were around her. She was afraid to fall in love even though she had already fallen in love with a man. She could not think of marrying a man even though the man whom she loved truly loved her too. The horrible incident which had traumatized her once would not go from her mind. It would flash in her mind whenever she thought of expressing her love. At last, she wanted to end her tiresome journey and rest in the arms of sweet Angels. She thought of jumping from the bridge but she remembered what her mother and brother Jesse had told her. She remembered what the priest told her the other day when she went to the Cathedral, "Your life belongs to God alone. You cannot simply end your life; it is a sin to commit suicide. We have to accept the things that we cannot change. Your body is the temple of God and he who defiles will be cursed." She said to herself, *"There is no rule that a woman must marry a man and bear him children. I will marry God and serve God. I must be strong enough to change the world. I must not depend on a man for my happiness and survival. I must stand on my own feet and show the world what a strong woman can do."*

Jesse always remembered Maria and was worried for her. He wanted to visit her in the Mission School. He was very busy and could not spare his time. Going to the city took two days and it was just not possible. In the meantime, he became a teacher in the village school. He did not know how time flew when one day Disha came to him and asked if he knew the where abouts of Maria. His mother asked with tears if he had any news about Maria. She told him that Maria had left the boarding one year ago and nobody knew where she had gone. Disha also told Jesse about the sudden demise of Milan's son. Jesse was upset to hear about the loss of Milan's son. Disha narrated her hard life at Broadvale with them. She told Jesse and Dinah to claim their right but they did not agree. Jesse told his mother, "I will not take even a needle from Broadvale. I am a man: I can stand on my own feet. I have fought all those years because I love my forefathers and my people. I will not come back to Broadvale." Disha pleaded to them, at least to take something so that his brothers could rule in peace. Jesse sent her back to Broadvale and assured her that they would visit during the coming quasquicentennial jubilee celebration of Broadvale.

Jesse searched for Maria in all possible ways for several months. At last, he reported to the police. After six months, police reported that Maria was in South India undergoing nun-training. He was much relieved to learn that his sister was fine and safe. Jesse and Diana visited Shillong and handed over their daughter Shindy to Dinah's parents according to their agreement. They stayed there for two months. They left Shindy after celebrating her second birthday. When they came back to Sunray village, they were very lonely. Jesse realized how a parent feels lonely when a daughter leaves home. He loved his wife much more than before and the couple consoled each other. They were soon blessed with another daughter whom they christened Melody. The year Melody was born also was a jubilee for Broadvale. Broadvale celebrated its quasquicentennial jubilee with grandeur. Disha gave her two maids and two male servants freedom as a mark of the glory of Broadvale quasquicentennial Jubilee. They erected a very big jubilee stone with great pomp and show. Names of Broadvale's royal sons and daughters were all inscribed in the genealogy book except Levi. Jesse and Dinah didn't mind any longer as they had already handed over every right over Broadvale to Rolan with a clear mind. Even the name of Maria was there. In the royal house, the faces of the new Prince and princess arrived. Rolan had six daughters. Milan begot two sons and five daughters. One of his sons died soon after birth while the other one died of flu when he was seven years old. Dr. Filan had two daughters and a son called Abbin. After the jubilee celebration, Disha and her kinsmen called Jesse to Broadvale and told him to take with them whatever he wanted. Jesse said that he would not take anything. They offered him one-fourth of their land with some money. Jesse visited his father's grave and wept bitterly. He talked to himself, *"Father, I'm sorry I have to leave Broadvale again. I am lost for words. The day my mother's tomb is built next to you in this place, I will die in peace and sleep next to you."* He then went to Broadvale, took with him his father's piano and his mother's golden ring. His brothers looked at him, dared not talk to him except Filan. Filan went to Jesse and said, "Why do you take these old things when you were offered the fortune that was equally distributed among the brothers? Why are you leaving us this way, brother? I will neither take my share nor settle in Broadvale." Jesse said to him, "I have no words to tell you, brother Filan, maybe it's already written in my destiny. When our great-grandfathers established this village, they dreamt of their descendants settling peacefully and enjoying the fruit of their labour together for generations. Instead of dividing this land into pieces, better I leave, let Rolan rule in peace and prosperity. Remember, whatever we do, our children will follow and eventually the name Broadvale, will be just history. By the grace of God, I am self-sufficient and want to live in peace." Dr. Filan too bequeathed Broadvale. He told Rolan and Milan just as Jesse had told them.

Rolan was officially made the ruler and everything was changed into his name. He was no doubt, one of the worthy sons of his father, Ron and people loved him. He gave freedom to religion in the land and many of the old traditions were changed with the change of time. He established a school and built a hospital of 300 beds. He gave warning to his men that no one could sell an inch of their land without the permission of the village authority. He appointed his trusted men to help him in different fields and the village was much more developed than earlier. The number of households also had increased from 500 to 2000. The land had its police station, post office, a government school, a government college, hospital and a hill town in the middle of the land. He developed the Giant Prayer Mountain, with 200 concrete steps up to the resthouse on the hilltop with beautiful parks. The width of each step was 16 feet with cemented five-feet borders. Broadvale became a famous place worth a visit with its scenic beauty, the beautiful blue hills and the green valley with a variety of sweet-scented flowers in the parks, its waterfalls, and the floating park with pink lotus looked like heaven on earth. Rolan had demolished the old gate and built a new village gate except for the military gate which had become an important monument, built by British troops. He also made the roads bigger and wider with blacktopping. It is said that Broadvale, like its name, has the broadest village roads of 25 feet width. He ordered to plant trees on the roadways with a small rest house every two kilometres. Broadvale had a giant leap as far as development was concerned after Milan got elected in the Legislative Assembly Election.

Maria had become a nun and worked in an orphanage in Kolkata. She devoted her life to taking care of the helpless children and beggars in the streets. She graduated in social work and also completed a diploma in Ministry. She worked wholeheartedly for the welfare and spiritual upliftment of tribal women in particular. With her initiative, the Catholic missions expanded in no time. They began to establish a home where helpless girls were given training on entrepreneurship. She never communicated with her family in Broadvale even though they care about her. Disha had also become old, wiser and gentle. She lived under the grace of her witty daughter-in-law, Reenarose and sought the favour of Rolan. Milan and his wife settled in Broadvale and became successful politicians. Milan had become the most successful among the brothers. He became a social leader who was well-known for his leadership qualities and deep knowledge. Rolan and Milan backed up each other and become successful brothers of their time. They were blessed with fame, wealth and prosperity. However, they begot no son to succeed them.

CHAPTER - 24

THE STRANGE DREAM

Jesse and Dinah along with Levi and Melody settled in Sunray village which was 20 kilometres away from Broadvale. As they had come across bitter life experiences, they realized more and more of the values of life on this earth. They were contented with whatever they had. Jesse served as the headmaster in a government school at Sunray. They gave tithe every month, gave charity to the poor and widows every year. They helped those who were needy and prayed for sick people. Everyone who knows them would say, "He is truly of royal blood, his mindset, worldview and personality speak that he is surely of noble birth. His blood is of the broad minded Broadvale's son and in his veins, runs the blood of a pious man-Benjamin. Why is he denied his birthright? His brothers will surely meet his curse." His friends loved him, respected him and people blessed him. He was a Church leader who brought justice wherever he was. Jesse was blessed with peace, love and fame.

The Broadvale brothers were all busied in their lives and did not bother one another. Jesse was happy that his brothers become more successful than him. Their very success made his life peaceful even though they never asked each other about their well-being. One day while Jesse and Dinah were busy, praying together holding each other's hand, Melody came to them and said, "Father, there is a muddy man, over there, like a ghost, and he is coming into our house. I am afraid."

Immediately the man knocked on the door and Jesse quickly went out to attend to him. The man said that he had lost his leg in an ethnic clash between the Hindus and Muslims. Upon being asked by Dinah, the man added that his enemies burnt down his house along with his pregnant wife and daughter. Dinah looked at Jesse sadly and said, "Darling." She gnashed her teeth and then went inside her room. She came out shortly with some notes. She then went to the beggar and said, "Brother, if you know what cruel fate had brought us here, you will bless us, for I truly believe that your blessing will be fruitful." She gave him money enough for a week to fill his stomach. The beggar said nothing but looked at them; he slowly bowed his head, took the money humbly and contentedly. Jesse remembered his handicapped father and called him back before he crossed the gate and said, "If you are hungry, wait a minute; I will give you some food." The beggar became nervous and said, "No sir, I am not hungry." He then looked at Melody who seemed to be tensed, he looked at Dinah saying, "I bless you sister, you will see me in your dreams."

Dinah laughed at him and went inside her room followed by Melody. Melody exclaimed, "Wow, he vanishes in the air. He is an Angel!" "Another nightmare of Melody," sceptically said Dinah. Melody looked at her father and claimed that the beggar vanished into the air. She claimed that she saw him vanish with her own eyes. Jesse ran out and searched for the beggar, looking left and right. He looked at the divergent road as long as he could. Perhaps he could not have walked away more than 50 feet by limping, but Jesse believed him to be begging at the nearby house. He did not pay much heed and returned home.

The next morning, Dinah was woken up by a strange dream. She woke up Jesse and told him that she saw the beggar in her dreams. She quickly held the hand of Melody who was sleeping beside her. She kissed her forehead and said, "Indeed the beggar was an Angel as you had said." Jesse rubbed his eyes and looked at his watch and said, "It's only half-past five." He yawned and asked Dinah to narrate her strange dream. Dinah said, "I stood on the top floor of a building, I gave birth to a son. I saw from a distance, Broadvale on fire. I heard a faint voice calling my name. I turned around but could see no one. I heard him calling my name again, I become very curious. I saw the beggar dressed in white descending from the clouds accompanied by thousands of Angels. They all bowed down to my son and moved away from me like a wave. They took away my son with them, then I heard an ambiguous thousand wailing noise echoing in all directions. I looked around and saw a white castle from a distance. The wailing seemed to come from that castle. I wondered why those Angels were wailing, and again why in that castle in particular. As I looked more enthusiastically, my son spoke to me and said, "Mummy, that castle is not built by Human Hands. It belongs to the Wailing Angels. I was woken up by their sweet musical voices."

Jesse listened to her dreams and smiled. They looked at each other. Jesse quickly hugged her and kissed her on the forehead. He then lay on his bed half sleeping with a double pillow and said, "Your dream foretells our bright future. The beggar would be a blessing, I think. We will have one more son who will be a guiding light and inspiration to society. A newborn son can be considered a blessing and good health. Angels will be a symbol of ordeals and trials that we will successfully surmount by God's grace. But I don't like you saying you saw Broadvale on fire." Dinah said, "But why would the Angels wail?" Jesse bit his thumb, and sat brooding for a while thinking, "What will befall Broadvale?" Levi who was sleeping in the next bed asked them, "What are you saying, mummy, who are the Wailing Angels?"

CHAPTER - 25

THE ONEROUS TASK OF THE ANGEL

When the sound of the bullets was heard continuously BANG… BANG…BANG… all doors were locked fast: People—young and old—ran pell-mell for their precious heads. There was chaos everywhere: Throngs were dispersing as a result. As the bullets were showered like the summer rain for several minutes, women called for their children in haste. Children too in turn called for their rescue. They ran blindly like a deer running under fear of a fierce lion's attack. Many vendors left their things as people ran over them, as if they were of no value between life and death. Everyone ran for their safety; some lay on the earth clinging to the neck of mother earth to save their lives. The incident bewildering the whole of Manipur and Broadvale in particular for the first time took place on 21st July 1999 morning around 9:45 IST; since then, Churachandpur, the largest district of Manipur had turned into a land of turmoil.

The wireless message received at the army headquarters shocked the officers. However, within minutes, sections of the Central Reserve Police Force (CRPF) arrived at the spot where the firing was going on. They took positions swift as the wind, gnashing their white teeth to face the mighty revolutionaries who were well entrenched. The CRPF personnel lost their control when their men were shot and attacked by heavy machine guns from different sides, and they began to cross the limit threatening even innocent civilians. Their brave commander was brutally fired on by the young unknown militants. To avenge the life of the brave commander, a newly commissioned officer with little experience in a real-life situation of crossfire, led the force.

The fierce encounter soon turned to firing indiscriminately volleys of bullets in all directions. They fought undoubtedly to the best of their ability and skill in the exchange of bullets with the well-trained unpaid revolutionaries.

After almost half an hour passed, the CRPF party surrounded the militants and arrested two underage revolutionaries after killing another on the spot. The rest of the militants escaped in different directions with their double profit "double arms" and ran away like rats rushing into their holes. CRPF lost seven lives including the newly-promoted commandant while their rivals were estimated to have lost three out of ten in a section, said the reporter in the daily newspaper the very next day.

Without caring for the victims, time ran on as it usually does like the running stream. Not a single man dared to rush to the spot to nurse the victims or mourn the deaths. Everyone locked their doors like rats hiding for fear of Mr. Cat, except one reporter who reached the spot with a camera, covered the scene in dismay at the pool of blood and amid the helter-skelter scattering of things all around. Many families abandoned their residences, fled to escape the usual combing operation as follow-up done by the security personnel. Where were the Church leaders, those Pharisees and Sadducees, had the Holy Spirit left them when troubles befell the land? Where were the social workers? Had the passion stopped when the real challenge calls them? No, who would dare enter that horrible scene of bloodshed and amid the operation alarm bell ringing?

The very loud yell of the innocent youth was hard to describe and unbearable for his young living Spirit. Had anyone helped him in time, he might have, perhaps, survived or at least, died with contention. He writhed and yelled calling for help from nearby. He felt thirsty. He spread out his right hand, put his palm under the pipe hole of an old hand pump, hoping someone, a kind-hearted soul would pump the water out to quench his thirst. As a result, blood spurted out from his chest and he struggled to hold back the spot to stop the blood from flowing out. He put all his efforts to press the hole but could not even locate his chest; oh, helpless young man who never was trained in that field! He lost all energy to move his limbs. He struggled with all his might as if he wished to ease the pain or perhaps left a word to whisper to dear ones. Nobody answered his feeble voice except the wind that blew in from west to east with dust following it. Only his young Spirit responded who told him to hold on, not to forsake him. His Spirit held his heart tightly and prayed to his veins and pulse, to hold on, to hold on, and never to be parted.

The innocent young man sighed when he knew his end was near. *"If only I had a brother, if only someone quenched my thirst before I go, oh God I don't want to die so young... "*Alas! He knew he would have to go to the next world worried and thirsty, while his Spirit embraced him tightly unwilling to be separated. Much blood had oozed out of the two bullet spots. His last thought blamed his best friend, Henry. He was not happy with Henry for not replying to his question when he asked, "Henry, shall we have a drink? I don't know why I'm so thirsty at this time of the day."

Henry: Your end is near, maybe; otherwise, how can you feel thirsty on this cloudy morning? Let's finish our task at the hospital. Hey, don't you think of buying a baby suit for sister Melody's baby? You want a transmitter or a receiver, come on say, man? After going to the hospital, we will go to Broadvale Park.

The bullet had separated him from Henry who took cover hiding inside a shop and the baby suit he wanted to give his sister Melody for her newborn baby. It had separated from his lovely family with the delightful world of his golden age. When they heard people screaming all of a sudden at the first gunshot, Henry jumped into the nearest shop for safety. Levi, however, looked around and saw a fat lady with her baby looking for safety. He took a few steps and helped her get inside the hardware store. As he tried to hop in too, the bullet hit his leg, his right leg and he fell to the ground. He saw a young boy near him who told him to escape in the left direction: he stood up and knocked at the door. Nobody opened the door of the shop. He saw armies and militants face-to-face just a few metres away: suddenly another bullet hit his chest. He rolled down near an old hand pump beside a road leading to the highway of Broadvale royal gate. At last, he gathered all his remaining strength and embraced his Spirit for the last and forever calling"MA!"That was all and no more pain. The Spirit gave out a piercing wail when his Holy body convulsed and breathed his last difficult breath.

The reporter heard the call "MA!" and rushed to the spot to find a young man in a pool of blood. He checked his pulse and felt sorry for him. He checked his pocket and inspected his IDcard. He then collected information for the latest hot news. The innocent youth was called Levi. He was the only son of a Spiritual leader and a pious man Jesse from Sunray village, a distance of 20 kilometres from Broadvale town. He was a very bright student and completed his graduation awaiting his result. He studied in Shillong at a prestigious college staying in his maternal uncle's house. He had come home for the holidays, to spend time with his ailing mother who was operated on recently for renal calculus. He was supposed to return to Shillong the following day. His mother had sent him to check on his sister Melody, who was expected to give birth that day. When he went to Melody's house, they sent him to Broadvale hospital. On the way to the hospital, he thought of buying a baby suit for the infant. Destiny would have made it all; oh, what fate had in store, for the young man who had dreamt of life to live to the fullest, striving hard to pursue his dreams, who cheerfully greeted friends and elders, smiled miles to everyone. Oh! The beautiful soul that soared happily under the divine Sun, vibrant in his golden age, Alas! He met his unavoidable fate there, lying in a pool of blood. His mother had always warned him not to go to Broadvale but fate made his life go and die in the land of his forefathers.

The Spirit felt very cold as soon as he was separated from the body. He longed for the pure warm blood of his Holy body and the sweet pious name he was called by the earth. He had never experienced such cold before. He looked at himself and found that he was no longer an earthling but a Shadow of white in colour, cold and slippery was his body and skin. He looked at himself, the blood mixed with the soil and exclaimed, *"No, my warm blood, please come back."* He touched the coagulated blood. He kicked at the blank thinking that he was in touch with the earth still. He began to cry like a wolf that used to howl terribly when a member of Von Carnogratz was to expire in their castle. The Spirit kicked the dusty earth and then the earth replied to him like noise from the splitting and crashing of trees in the intense cold. That rare noise was being heard only when a Saint left mother earth for his heavenly abode. The Spirit called his sweet name *"Levi, oh Leviticus,"* at the top of his voice, tossed around the dead body like a bee flying around the faded marigold, unaware of anything except the nectar! The Spirit shivered in the intense cold and cried like a calf in want of milk, running around the dead body of its mother cow!

The penetrating wail of the Spirit was so pathetic that it echoed in the whole valleys and hills from the eastern to the western horizon. No bird sang nor did the Shirui lily dance with the lovely breeze of Ukhrul, to hear that painful wail. Animals in thick jungles and vultures in deserts too, were confused and pondered what to do with that pathetic wail. The crow began to move out of that place to the thick jungle to convey to its fellow birds that a Saint had died a moment ago. Immediately the Sun became dim at a time, and to show his grief upon the Saint Spirit, the mighty Sun encircled itself with a rainbow. Out of the rainbow, the Angel Gabriel at once rushed to the spot and asked the Spirit, the reason knowingly in a soft musical voice.

Angel: What makes you cry, oh Shadow of my good man?

The Spirit was taken aback at the sight of the beam of light. He was startled for a moment. When the Angel repeated his question, the Spirit winked his eyes till he could see more clearly. He saw the Angel and quickly grabbed hold of the Angel's feet and cried out.

Shadow: Let me, oh loving Angel, let me enter, to my warm blood inside my Holy body. I pray, let me enter once again, I cannot tolerate any longer this intense cold. I don't want to let go of my blooming youth, my dear and near ones and this delightful world. I am the only son of my parents…

Angel: You are a Shadow, look at yourself. You don't have parents, brothers and sisters; you cannot enter into the lifeless body.

Shadow: No, I am Levi; let me enter into my warm body. I don't want to die young.

Angel: Oh Shadow of my good man, stop wailing. What you ask for is against the law of nature. Behold, your body is cold now, your blood has coagulated and mixed with the soil. There is no means that you will enter into this lifeless body. So, I will go far and wide to convey this message to your fellow men. To whom shall I convey first?

Shadow: I am not dead, I speak to you…mummy, come and warm me; father, come and save me!

Angel: I cannot grant your wishes I have no right to; please stop wailing. Please let me go; don't hold my feet, Shadow of my Holy man.

The Spirit wailed and held the Angel's feet tightly. The Angel changed into light and disappeared from the Shadow. He wailed all along his way for the young Shadow. He knew that the life of the deceased was worthy to be revived. Levi was a good child of a truthful man whom the Angels had seldom praised. They loved the innocent Spirit of the God-fearing young man, Levi. The Angel quickly divided himself into seven forms and all the seven forms were further divided into another seven forms. They travelled at lightning speed in all directions to inform the urgent message of the wail of the innocent young Spirit. Wherever they went, none understood their message nor could human beings smell them, see them or hear their wail. However, some recognized the presence of the wailing Angel by the unusual sound or the unhabitual noise that the Angel made when men could not understand the message. Men remembered through the legends and folktales that the noises signified that someone, his dear and near one had passed away. And the message was conveyed to them by his Spirit. Generally, human beings are not thoughtful enough to reflect and realize that secret which they blindly believe to be a ghostly act or an evil Spirit haunting them. Again, some would regard it as a warning from their Gods and Goddesses. Naughty fellows often challenge them in mass gossip. Even then the Angel would claim, "I am your Angel, conveying you the black message of my good man." When men heard the message with their ears, they would somehow believe it to be the Spirit conveying his death message to him. Their last insulting word would accuse the invisible woman BUNSHI of not wailing the last few days. They believed that Bunshi, the Goddess of mourning, should wail in advance if a Holy man was to expire from the world. Because of all these reasons, Angel Messenger said that his duty was an onerous task.

CHAPTER - 26

THE DEATH OF LEVI

By then the news had spread far and wide like wildfire. People- young and old, incuriously rushed to the spot as soon as they heard the news, that the deceased civilian was a handsome youth of whitish complexion, 6ft. tall, well-built body and lovely as the white horse, who was the only son of Jesse from Broadvale. "He is dead?" exclaimed the surprised mob. None cared to lend their ears to the seven dead CRPF personnel, who were, on the other hand, supporting their families, sacrificing their life for the country or the revolutionaries who died for the nation, without a penny, and keeping their promise as true soldiers, whom their unlucky mothers would mourn on their death, days and months later. Young and old, who knew about Jesse, left their urgent work to share the grief. They informed each other about who Levi was, who Jesse was as if their hearts were filled with the Holy Spirit. One reporter said that people loved and described Levi and his family so much that the other dead bodies seemed to be of all criminals. Another journalist compared them to the disciples of Lord Jesus Christ, whose minds were filled with the Holy Spirit on the day of Pentecost, "Such a handsome youth, the only son of his parents, son of a truthful parent." The mob disputed though it was none of their damn business, fought for their own time to exercise their tongue to say about the good deeds of Jesse, and the untimely death of the innocent young man. They would also tell each other about the secret, "The bullets are from the side of the armies." The most common question being, "Who is to be blamed for the crime? Who shall pay the ex-gratia of the deceased?" Some of the men who thought of themselves as heroes instigated the mob to go for a rally or organized a sit-in protest to inform the government of their inability to maintain law and order in the land.

When Dinah was boiling soup in the kitchen, she felt that someone took a cup behind her and drink water from the filter. She looked around and saw no one. She then heard the noise of a door flung open by someone. She went to check and believed it to be the wind because it was a cloudy windy day. Soon she saw Henry coming on a motorcycle with someone. Henry's face was dim and flushed red. When Dinah heard the red and black message of the death of her only son, the very word penetrated her tiny veins and arteries, blood ran faster than her heartbeat and she fainted after a drop of scandalized exclamation, "NO…!"Her maidservant, a young girl name Shisily, was still in the hospital attending to Melody in her delivery. Melody was married to the son of the district college principal who lived near Broadvale.

Melody gave birth to her child at the time when Levi died. Levi's younger sister, Sindy stayed at Shillong at her maternal uncle's house. Levi's father had been away from home for the past few days to attend a congregation at the state capital. He was supposed to return home that very evening. The problem was, who would arrange for the funeral, and where would the funeral take place? Who would do the necessary signature for the death certificate and post-mortem report? Milan, the sitting minister of the legislative Assembly from the Broadvale constituency, was informed by his brothers, Rolan and Filan.

Rolan and Filan went to the spot and covered the dead body with the best loincloth of Broadvale handloom, and they decided that they would bury the dead body at Broadvale royal cemetery. Disha called her sons to Broadvale and said to them, "This is purely God's plan for all the four brothers of Broadvale to reunite and forgive one another. God choses Broadvale and Angels chose Levi's life; though it is painful, this is a great sign from God that we have sinned against God by doing injustice to the eldest son of Broadvale. Levi was our son, our future and our hope. Even though you brothers are all successful in your lives, there is no future in your offspring. We are being punished for the injustice we had done to Jesse and Dinah. My sons, it is better to be late than to never do it; so, do apologize, seek his favour, take his blessings, Jesse is your second God." Disha regretted very much the treatment she meted out to Ron and Jesse. She realized her fault the day her daughter, Maria, told her about Jesse's love and sacrifice for his sister though he knew she was born of another man's blood. Maria had requested her mother, Disha, to construct a tomb for Esther, next to the grave of Ron in the royal cemetery. She had requested her to recognise Jesse as the eldest son of the Broadvale chief and accept his mother Esther as the legal wife of Ron. When her mother did not appreciate her request, Maria left home and become a Catholic nun.

The three uncles of Levi led the people and they went to the mortuary to identify the dead body. They claimed him in the name of Broadvale and did all the necessary documents. They talked with the concerned authority along with the local leaders and organizations. According to their agreement, the dead body was claimed and thousands of kind-hearted people gathered to lift the dead body of Levi. Rolan said to the public, "He is my son. He will be carried in honour in the way the ruling Prince should have but we will first go to his mother's house at Sunray." They carried the dead body in a coffin borne by Broadvale men, dressed in their traditional attire, singing valour songs all the way to his mother with thousands of people following them. Hundreds of vehicles travelled silently as if the unwilling ants were on a funeral pyre to cremate their Queen. Women and children stood all the wayside, sadly looking at the coffin and the singers.

By the way, Angels worried about how to console the wailing Spirit. They looked at one another, took off their crown and stooped their heads in defeat. Angel

Michael too, was moved by the wail of the young Spirit and he held high his golden sword signalling the Angel comforter to do his duty. The Angel comforter was granted permission to do anything except the forbidden law. The Angel comforter went to the wailing Spirit and spoke to him softly.

Angel: Oh Shadow of my Holy man, stop wailing and listen to me for a while. I know all about your desires and sufferings. I too feel sorry. Oh! It was very unfortunate and a great loss for Jesse and Dinah. It's awfully cold here. Do not ask for the forbidden law. Every Spirit of our Holy man suffered this way but they followed the Angels and entered the kingdom of no-return where they forgot about themselves. They became Angels. They are very happy and would be ready to die again for the sake of that blissful kingdom they enjoy there.

Shadow: I want nothing except my Holy body. I must meet my mother before she knows about my death. Nothing is more important than my life. I have to live for my parents.

Angel: Behold, oh Shadow of my Holy man, I cannot grant your wish but I have something better than what you had wished for.

Shadow: Yes, tell me, why does a truthful man die not of his iniquity? This is just unfair.

Angel: Sure, I will tell you, oh Shadow. When Levi was born, oh Shadow of my Holy man, we three were together until I left you to beg forgiveness from our Divine Father.

Right from his birth, Levi had to withstand his foes. You had to bear up so many tragedies during your short life: Those are your reserve punishments. If he were still alive you would have to face much more than men could ever imagine and at last, he would curse his creator. History will not repeat in this family if he lives longer.

Shadow: Oh why, what have I done wrong or my parents?

Angel: It was neither the fault of your parents nor yours. That's the very point, that his life is taken so early. It was because of your grandfathers who cursed themselves by doing the forbidden things. Oh Shadow of my Holy man, when your forefathers were blessed, they were greedy and proud. They were thirsty for the blood of their fellow human beings. They humiliated and killed many of my Holy men. They defiled the Holy land by defiling the young men and women, killing them and torturing them. The price of their bloodshed and the cry of the innocent Holy men cursed this family right from the firstborn son. You are damned to be born in the cursed land.

Spirit: My father was thrown out of Broadvale. We never inherited anything from Broadvale. I wasn't brought up in Broadvale. Why don't they start from Broadvale, I don't belong there.

Angel: You were not brought up from the fruit of Broadvale but you are the firstborn son of Broadvale chief. Your parents are too good to be human beings. They are

God-fearing and humble men. How can we judge you to suffer in our presence? Oh Shadow of my good man, God wants to keep you in an honourable place to serve your fellow human beings. Your parents will be blessed with another son and they will be consoled soon. But until we leave this world of sorrow, the blessing cannot take place. They will be blessed only when cleansed. They will be clean only when you leave them.

The Angel put wings on the Spirit who still wailed upon his own death helplessly. He looked around, saw nothing but an endless plane filled with smoke, with the three of them—he, the Angel and the dead body. He wondered how long he would endure the cold. He was in a state that he had never dreamt of in his life. The Angel was good and friendly. After putting the wings on him, the Angel said, *"If you love your family, let us proceed to the next gate. There, you shall forget all pain and sorrows. The king of ghosts in the dark world is waiting to take the Spirits left by the Angels. Angel messenger had sent a message about your dead."*

The Spirit was not willing to leave the dead body. He touched the dead body, shook his head and looked around, then he sobbed, not knowing what to do.

Angel: Angels await you at the gate to take you home to the eternal world. You can decide by yourself whether you choose to be an Angel or taken by the fairies or enter the dark world.

Shadow: What is the place called and where is the way to the next world? Where are you going to take me?

Angel: That place is called the eternal home and the stairways to eternity are made during one's lifetime. You have made a long step and we will take more from your parents.

Spirit: Can I have a last wish before we proceed to the next world

Angel: Certainly, you may have. What is your last will? I can grant it except for the forbidden law.

Shadow: I cannot think of departing. I must not leave this world. Life is beautiful and I'm precious to my parents.

Shadow speaks to himself and said, *"And … I don't wish to be among the fairies nor turned into a ghost, for people will hate me and they will also be afraid of me despite my love for them. I would then be cursed by everyone. What do I benefit from living like that?"*

The Spirit sobbed for a while then continued. He spoke irritably to conceal his discordance with the Angel.

Angel: Come on, tell me your last will, our time is limited, we are running out of time.

Shadow: Love me and let me enter with your power, I want to live for some more time.

Angel: You will feel colder and colder, and our time is almost running out. If I leave, you will be condemned to suffer this intense cold forever. You will stay like this forever without a companion, neither can you become a human nor a ghost.

Spirit: Why was I made to be born and die untimely, oh, what shall I do now?

Angel: Oh Shadow of my Holy man, it's all God's will and plan. We have to follow His prophecies. You take your final decision whether you will follow me to eternity or live in this cold zone forever alone

Shadow: Oh mummy, dear father, dear sisters and friends. God, please help me!

Angel: Aye! Look up Shadow, your people coming to lift your dead body. Get up: don't turn back or else you cannot follow me. You can stay only on the Holy blood. Once the blood is gone, you will not be able to see me.

The Spirit looked up and saw hundreds of people gathered around. He realized he had no time and said to the Angel:

Spirit: Sweet Angel, let us stay some days until my body is buried, I want to console my parents.

Angel: You will not be able to endure the cold. Your people will not be able to see you. You also cannot touch them. See, you are a Shadow while they are earthlings. Anyway, I shall accompany you as long as you can tolerate and endure the pain and cold.

The Angel lifts the Spirit and said,

Angel: From now you are granted your wish to stay here but you need to get clean in the hot zone to enter the next kingdom.

The people carried the dead body from the mortuary after the post-mortem. The Spirit followed them behind the coffin while the Angel flew above parallel to the coffin. There was sadness on every face. Oh! There was silence in the air. No tears flooded nor sighs moved a tempest; the wind was calm and the sunset was red on the western horizon. The Spirit looked lean and emaciated and shivered in the cold. Wherever he looked, he saw those pictures blur and whatever he saw couldn't be touched by his hands any longer. For a moment he was glad for being together with the people once again but then his happiness faded away the moment he realized that he was no longer a human being. As a Shadow, he must leave that wonderful place forever into the way of no-return.

Just before sunset, the people reached Sunray village. The Spirit felt that everything was odd. He remembered his happy friends appearing in his vision as the negative film in a photograph. Sunray village was indeed very quiet as if all the villagers deserted the village long ago when their enemy burnt down the village. Every creature was shocked at the sight of the coffin of a young man and animals smelt the Angels' presence. No man dared to sing or make fun or to flirt with their beloved as the news had shaken the land. People gathered at the residence of Jesse.

Sunray, the village which was hallowed by the birth of such a Holy man, once again had turned into barren land. The words and deeds of such a good son of Sunray now left that lovely place with the ashes of his sweet memories in the heart of everyone. Some people believed that he was reincarnated Saint of some centuries behind through his words and behaviour. Some of his prophecies came true to their eyes and still, some were hidden in mystery. It seemed everywhere was in darkness. Broadvale, the bustling town that was famous in the district with the sitting MLA, Minister of Tourism, a famous tourist spot, the land that Holy men and great persons hailed from, lost its charm in the eyes of the people. The state that was called the Jewel of India had turned off its brilliant light. The state that was unique in the world for the birthplace of Sangai—the Brow Antler Deer, and Shirui lily had become dim and shaken. The birds were going back home to their nests mourning for the people of Manipur. They destroyed and discarded their rich heritage and cultures. The youths of the blessed land who were once disciplined were spoilt by the worldly pleasures and ladies desired all the more. They were never contented with what they got. Their minds had become corroded. The officers had become corrupted. They opened their hearts to all sorts of evil things. The women who were once the transmission of religion, culture and traditions had lost their values in pursuit of the worldly pleasures.

Churachandpur, formerly known as the land of the second paradise for its peaceful co-existence had also turned into a land of turmoil where young and old ran for arms and black money. The more they established associations to unite the fragments, organizations to progress and fronts to march forward with the change of time, the more the society split. They killed one another, fathers killing in-laws and brothers killing their kin. There were rape cases every day that went unnoticed. There was adultery between a married man and woman every day that went unnoticed. Divorce and polygamy multiplied and the number of widows increased. Youths died of drugs and their parents were busy smuggling the drugs. They built storeys and fought the dragon inside. Women and children thus suffered a lot in the largest district of Manipur. Had not the people forgotten that they were the society, innocent lives would not have been lost. The untimely loss of precious lives made mother earth wail. She summoned the rain to warn the people. The drought came to warn them of their ruthless action on Mother Nature. So long as the rain comes to console the earth, the flood will destroy pride, drought will persist, the trees and plants will cry and the cuckoo, the bird of wealth and health will not visit the land.

As the dead body was unloaded from an ambulance, the Spirit felt everything was strange and he was curious to find out the causes. His dog that they lovingly called Tinkle, which usually wagged its tail to and fro, groaned with its eyes glistening tears. It slowly came out from the kennel; sniffing the dead body as if unwillingly. It then followed the coffin to the waiting room ready to punch at any intruder who touched his master's body. "What a nuisance!" said some men and they sent away the dog. Till then everyone talked slowly and with caution as if not to awaken a sleeping baby. The Spirit looked for his mother. When he saw his mother on her bed with some women who helped her regain her consciousness, he looked around the silent crowd. The Spirit set a silent tear in the silent moment. "MAMA," called out the Spirit. He ran and tried to touch his mother. Simultaneously, women and children could not control their tears and cried out. Dinah was suddenly awakened as if she was called by her son. She slowly moved her head. She called out aloud "Levi, dear Levi where are you?" in a torn choked voice. "Mum, here I am beside you," said the Spirit humbly. The Spirit held the hands of Dinah and said, "Mum, don't you hear me speaking to you?" The Angel felt distraught to bear the agony of parting: after departing, he took leave from the Spirit to accompany his father on his tiresome journey.

"Levi is not dead, he is sleeping, stay calm," said the womenfolk and tried to put Dinah to sleep. Despite the doctor's advice not to let Dinah see the dead body—for they thought she would die of heart failure—Dinah struggled, as a mother, pushed by her inner impulse, she stormed like thunder, resisting the doctor's injection. She took out the needle from her left hand and rushed towards the living room. She knelt and then embraced the lifeless body with all the affection collected from all corners of her heart. She buried her face for a while over the chest of her son. She then touched the withered face of Levi and touched his lips. At once the memory came to her mind, *"Mum, I will have a brother soon."* She recollected the childhood days of her son, and how he was saved from fire and water. Then she called out aloud breaking the silence of the air,

"My son, on whom I kept all my hopes, you were a treasure to me, don't you remember your words? What happened to you, say to me, my dear; wake up and tell me. Take me, my son, I will come and accompany you. Oh God, I am done, I cannot believe, what is all this? What shall I do now? Oh God, please take my life too." There was no dry eye that saw the wail of the broken mother. Though the Spirit consoled his mother, nobody heard him or saw him while he heard and saw everything like a normal human being. Unable to withstand the sight of the wailing women, the Spirit left the place. He walked steadily and looked around for a fire to warm his cold limbs. There was no way to cross the crowd. He wished he could fly and suddenly, he realized he was flying over the crowd. At first, he got a little scared, his heart sank on his first flight. He practised flying and realized that it was his entire mind that controlled his flight. He flew up to the courtyard. He knew that those places were to be left forever. He sat on the node, the strongest divergent branch of the April tree just near the gate and said, "Oh you lovely tree of April, you always bloom on my birthday. How I love to see you bloom again! Why should I leave you untouched? I have planted and nurtured you when we were both young but I have to leave you first. Take care of my family. Bloom on my birthday to please my mother. Withstand the wind and the storm to welcome home my family; always stand near the gate to welcome visitors, young and old, rich or poor." He then flew to the Gul Mohar tree near the courtyard. Some men sitting under the tree smoked and talked about current affairs. The Spirit could hear the conversations going on below his seat. He then saw his uncle in a white Gipsy van with his bodyguards followed by dozens of vehicles coming for the condolence. People turned towards the gate to look at those politicians while some of them stood up to honour them. The Spirit said to himself, *"My uncles, why do they love me so much when I am dead? Had they loved me like this when I was alive, how happy my parents would have been!"*

He left the Gul Mohar tree and flew around looking at the crowd. He saw the people giving full respect to the politicians and rich people than the Church leaders. He sat on the roof of his house and saw his father from a distance accompanied by the Angel. As soon as Jesse noticed the gathered crowd with his own eyes, he bent his neck and his hair stood straight in a wink of time. He had never seen such a large crowd gathered at his house. Children came out to look at him. Jesse was accompanied by his friends who had all attended the congregation. He could not believe that his only son would just die that day. Everyone turned towards Jesse and his friends when they saw him coming home. Some were eager to watch how he behaved: they looked at him as long as their necks would permit. The crowd made way for them as he came home like it was a dream. Jesse's face became red and his eyes were burning with anger. "Father, I am here," said the Spirit flying down from the rooftop to his father and saying, *"No, my father can neither hear nor see me. But I have to leave him shortly."* He hugged Jesse on his neck and held his right hand. The Angel held the right hand of the Spirit and the two invisible walkers walked inside the living room with Jesse. Dr. Filan walked towards Jesse and embraced him saying, "Brother, I share your grief. Please control yourself. He is sleeping in the arms of Angels. We will all meet him in heaven." Rolan and Milan got nervous to greet their brother in public. However, they felt awkward remaining unaware when many friends and relatives hugged him and cried about the misfortune in his family. Disha looked at Rolan and signalled to stand up. Rolan stood up and went to Jesse and he was followed by Milan and Disha. They hugged Jesse and brought him up to the place where the coffin was kept. Jesse slowly sat down on the chair offered by Reenarose and looked at the withered face of his lifeless son. The mourners stopped mourning and they all sang sad songs together keeping watch over the emotions of Jesse. Jesse imagined that Levi was just sleeping, would wake up and smile at his father. He saw the young face of the son who used to jump on his back to welcome his father. He remembered vividly the rhymes he used to sing to his father, *"Twinkle, twinkle little star, How I wonder what you are! Up above the* *world so high, Like a diamond in the sky…"*Those memory verses, poems, paintings and artworks that he had never expected to see from his little son, those happy moments …Oh! How happy he was when his son bagged medals and prizes which made his poor father smile and be proud. Rolan and Filan had been talking to him while he was lost in his thoughts, perturbed with the thoughts of those sweet memories. He could not believe that the dead body was of his son, Levi. He did not listen to anybody. The memories of his son's childhood life kept playing in his mind, especially the word *'PAPA'*sounded like a gong in his heart. *"My perfect son!"*he sighed. He went out of the crowd towards the restroom. On the way, he looked at the wall and paused for a while looking at the easel of Jesus Christ and the Virgin Mary. He looked up and murmured after the usual sign of the Cross which the Catholics do. He prayed to God spreading out his hand and knelt on the floor, *"Lord if I have done anything wrong in thy sight, forgive me please. Lord if it is your will, please revive the Spirit and soul of my only son. Why don't you take my life instead of this young boy?"*

CHAPTER - 27

THE INCONSOLABLE COUPLE

When Jesse came back from the restroom, he went to the lifeless body of his son. Women were wailing uncontrollably. Jesse stretched out his icy hands and touched the cold lifeless body. He uncovered the dead body to have a thorough check-up. He noticed the bullet spot on his chest. He could not bear the agony to see the wounded heart of his son. He could not bear to feel the unfathomable pain his son would have suffered before his death. Thinking of his pain-stricken son stopped the blood flow of the mighty father for a moment and he cried out like a child for the first time in his life. He had cried in many situations before and mourned throughout his life but never was his wail so painful as when he saw the flesh of his flesh, suffered and lost his life, not of his iniquity. Jesse cried like a child and mourned, *"My life, my dream, my hope, my glory and my diamond! How will I live without you, oh my God?"* The Spirit closed his eyes and turned away from his father. He stood helpless and felt apologetic to have ever seen his father cry like a child.

Rolan and Filan consoled Jesse and gently pulled him out towards his bedroom. Soon they asked the Pastor to pray with their brother for some time. At that very moment, Dinah continued the wailing, "How can you go before me, where are you going leaving us behind here? Oh, why don't we go together? It's not worth living anymore, I want to die, please take me with you, my son, you will not go alone, and I will accompany you. I don't want to live anymore." Jesse saw Dinah beating her chest as if something in her was pulling back her feminine nature not to shed tears. He knew well that Dinah was a strong woman whom he had never seen her breakdown emotionally. Though she tried to cry out to her heart's content, she could not cry out like other women. When the priests and Holy men together put their hands on Jesse and genuinely asked God to give him divine solace, suddenly Jesse experienced something divine that pierced his conscience to take care of his wife. He remembered Dinah's dream 15 years ago. He took his wife and with some friends, they dragged Dinah to her bedroom. Jesse shook Dinah and called her name slowly and hugged her. He kissed her and called her name in a torn, choked voice with tears in his eyes. Dinah opened her eyes, looked at Jesse and lay down on the bed slowly.

The Church leaders had prayers, especially for the solace of the bereaved family. The Angel and the Spirit too prayed to God to comfort Jesse and Dinah, to give them strength to move on in life. After a few hours of singing and praying, Jesse said to Dinah, "God understands the pain of losing a child. Let us compare our lives with that of father Abraham and Father Job. They are incomparable with our sufferings. God wants us for some other purpose. Men's plans and God's plans are different. We are all His creations. Levi is not ours; don't you remember when he was born, we were told that he is God's child? We have dedicated ourselves to God. The Lord gives us and He takes him back. What can we do? We should thank God that at least we had a son; we could see his happy face though only for a short while. We must be contented with what we cannot do. Everything is God's plan, so what cannot be cured should not be a curse. Many lives are lost every hour, every second and many are born every second in this world. We should not expect only good things in life: Life is not a bed of roses. We cannot challenge God just because we did no harm to anyone or did some good deeds. Life may sometimes seem very unfair, but who are we to judge a life that is not in our hands. Let us get up and talk with our men: They are waiting for our consent. Rolan and Filan have requested to bury the body at Broadvale in the royal reserve land. We can never run away from our roots. Maybe God wants us to unite with our brothers before we do good things to others. Mother Disha had promised to build a tomb next to our father. Let us go out now. We will all meet Levi in the blessed kingdom, and to enter that kingdom we should change our minds and make peace with everybody." The Church leaders took their own time to exhort and consoled the bereaved family. They were all excellent preachers who had been trained in that field to give solace to people but they felt the pain of losing a child deep down inside their hearts. The Angel too consoled the Spirit.

Jesse and Dinah were told to take dinner with their family together. They consoled themselves and took their dinner together in tears. They held their tears and swallowed hard the food. It was the first time in their life that the Broadvale family had their food together: all the four brothers and their wives along with their once-wicked mother, Disha. Everything tasted bitter and every drink became sour on their dear one's death. The food became tasteless and the water became sour in Dinah's mouth in particular. It was the first time for Dinah that she was spoon-fed by her mother-in-law Disha. Reenarose gave her water and she ate and drank as if it was all a nightmare. Her sisters-in-law as well as Disha hugged her, cried for her, gave a shoulder for her to lean on and shared their grief. They wiped her tears and help her move on in life at that difficult time. Jesse was requested to give a speech as head of the family. It was around half-past eight. The night was cloudy with the gentle breeze blowing lazily. He stood up, took his microphone and said,

"I never had imagined, even in my wildest dreams that I will stand in front of you all tonight and give this painful farewell speech to my beloved son, Levi. Dear brothers and sisters, I thank every one of you for sparing your valuable time to share my grief and sorrow. My brothers Rolan, Milan and Filan had given our brief history, how I came and settled in Sunrise leaving my family at Broadvale. My son has taught me through his way of life about my roots. We all love Levi. I hope that you all love him as much as I do. So I have decided to bury the body at Broadvale royal reserve land. Life is so ironic. It takes sadness to know happiness, absence to value presence. The dead are gone, what can we do, it's all God's plan; I need to appreciate and value the living while we are still alive. Our only sister who had struggled her own life had been working hard to reunite Broadvale. She left Broadvale saying she will return home when the family unites and lives together. Now I hear that she is in Kolkata, working in Mother Teresa Foundation as a nun. Oh, how I love my only sister!"

Jesse sobbed unable to continue his speech when he again remembered his only sister, Maria, who stayed far away from the family. She always missed the happy as well as the sad moments. Disha stood up and embraced Jesse saying, "Please forgive your mother. I promise I will build a tomb for your mother Esther beside your father's tomb. Maria will come back that day and I will make your dream come true." Milan too stood up and hugged Jesse saying, "Brother, I shall bring back our sister, we all miss her. She can't leave us like this."

The family members and the brothers embraced one another. They cried for some minutes until the people calmed them down and separated them. Love was in the air, the brothers forgave each other, at last the mother recognized her stepson. Though many wailed for the great loss in the family and society, many people took it as a turning point, a big gain for the Broadvale family to reunite after a long time. It was ironic to imagine that such royal families, who were supposed to lead their people and become an example for their people, united only after the great loss of life in the family. Jesse then continued his unfinished speech and said, "Henceforth, I will not hear thy sweet voice calling us nor see your sweet smiling face. However, people will still call me in your name as Levi's father: Until I die, I will hear your sweet name. Dear son, accept this parting as God's will and go now. This is God's plan and He always does the right thing at the right time. Do not think for us. What you have been telling me, will now be fulfilled. You will sleep with your father's fathers in the royal land at Broadvale. If anyone had done anything wrong during your short life, do forgive in your humble father's name. Forget now the good and bad things that you have learnt from mother earth. The golden ring you had from Grandma Esther will go with you. You are the eldest and only son; with you gone, there is no one worthy to keep the ring. If your Spirit hears me now, please leave us and go in peace into that realm of peace, where there is no sorrow and pain. Do not even turn back, my dear."

The Spirit held the feet of Jesse and cried. He then went and sat on the lap of Dinah and kissed her on her cheeks.

Spirit: "Father, goodbye, I had no reason to stay anymore but I love you. I love you all. I cannot bear this cold and pain any longer. I have to go."

The Spirit kissed, then embraced his father Jesse who had never scolded nor shown his angry face to his son. The Angel said to the Spirit, "Oh Shadow of my good man, you are blessed to be the son of such a good father whom the Angels praise and love. Be brave and kind like your father and put everything to God." The Angel asked the Spirit if he wished to see any other person. The Spirit told him that he wanted to see his soul mate Sophia once before they proceeded to the next gate. The funeral ceremony had begun and people sang sad songs sweetly. They made the funeral programme according to their Christian religious rites and rituals.

The Angel and the Spirit flew to Sophia's house which was about half a mile from Jesse's house. Sophia was the third daughter of a Pastor who was a good friend of Jesse. She was 17 years old. She had long hair that reached up to her knees and people branded her Rapunzel. Her shiny hair and sparkling eyes rightly matched her fair skin. Her beauty was such that her sparkling eyes would light up the darkness. Her manner was such that she was being admired by the young and the old. She was a jolly type of girl but not outwardly so at the first impression. She was good at painting, drawing, writing poems and dancing. Sophia and Levi had been in love secretly without telling each other. Sophia's brother, Henry was Levi's best friend.

Levi would spend his holiday at Henry's house and befriended Sophia. Sophia too loved him dearly. They knew and understood each other from their eyes and their hearts knew each other's feelings. They got in each other's minds, knew exactly what and why the other was thinking. They inspired each other and cared for each other maturely. They were comfortable with each other and would act together like idiots. Since both the families were very close, there was no restriction for them to meet anytime.

The Angel and the Spirit reached Sophia's room in a second. They saw her sitting on a chair looking at the photos she had clicked with Levi. She did not cry but her soul cried from inside which made her dull, pale and gloomy. She had not brushed her hair or taken a bath. She had not taken food or talked to anyone. Everyone had gone to Jesse's house and she was alone with her elder sister. Her sister knew her mood, so left her alone in the room. She opened her autograph and read those lines written by Levi again and again. She opened her diary, read the poem that her soul mate had written and dedicated to her. She read the poem again and again.

Rose! If art thou love,

Rose from thy dreams.

Why do you have thorns?

Life! If thou art not rose

Why do you bloom?

In the dream of the great June

Doth art thou an immortal being

Why can't thee fade

Like the petal of thy rose

Fading amid the fog

Of a New Year's Eve.

Bathe I a thousand baths

Like rays of the saffron beam

Ere crossing the younger horizon

It's the beam of repentance rays

Shedding lights in a changing world

Whose change of phase will unchain

The captive loss of an island

To shine in the expanse of a peninsula

Where I shall discover you more

O, love! Am I dreaming? Yet I do hear the roosters' crow

The sad songs and the Church Bell."

Another poem:

I am born with the instinct of man

The basic instinct like all normal men

I learn about the earth and heavenly things

But never how to love you, my dear

You are already in me before I know you.

Destiny made me sojourn this sunray

Just to meet my morning star

Life s beautiful with you, empty without you

It's a mystery for I know what is in your mind

When I am far away from you

The winds whisper and dreams speak of you

I can sketch your beauty and pain your mood

It's all in the mind, in the heart, in the soul

I am the best sculptor of your beauty

I am the best artist of your smile

You can't get a piece of better music or the best poet

I see the beauty of nature through you

I know the blessing upon me through you

We are one soul in two hearts and four hands

My breath and heartbeats only for you, my love

Let's dance in the rain and laugh in the Sun

Through thick and thin, through.........

You will stand by me just like I do

I want to unveil and give you love bites

We don't need approval when you are burning

There is no shame and ego when you are touch

In the divine fire of love, my love.

Sophia read some of the favourite poems that Levi had dedicated to her. She had never written even a single line of poetry but her love had made her a poet at that moment. She closed her eyes for a moment, then beautiful poetic words came up and flooded her mind. Sophia took her pen and wrote a poem about her love for her soul mate.

Soul mate

Never before do I feel empty in my life

You had been my strength and joy

I want to be on top of the world this time

I need that laughter and get naughty with you

Bring out the child in us and laugh together

Carry away with that folly funny talks

Oh! What a sad news, am I dreaming?

From chemistry to mystery, where are you?

Wish I'd become deaf before I heard

You died with pain, thirsty and helpless

I can imagine, oh, what you have gone through

Coz you are my soul, heart and love

This world is cruel and thirsty for blood

If I were to buy your life back, my love

I would give my heart and give you life

You are more important than me for some reasons

My love, can you take me with you there?

I want to hold your hand and accompany

We had been friends for the days to come

Hundreds of years ago my soul had known you

Even to the land of the dead

I want to come than live a dead life

Alone and lonely like this empty evening

I miss you, dear, please take me with you."

CHAPTER - 28

LEVI'S GIRLFRIEND, SOPHIA

Sophia recalled the bygone days when both of them enjoyed looking at each other without talking, oh, those childhood days when they played together and ran wild ways. She remembered the day Levi carried her on his back when she got bitten by a dog. She wanted to go to Broadvale to join the burial service but the next day was her exam, and her parents would not let her go. Tired of recollecting the never-ending love affairs, she glanced at her wrist and the shorter hand struck 1. She looked at her watch and loved that moment once again when Levi gave her the watch as Valentine's Day gift. She realized that it was the last gift from her soul mate. She valued it more and more so she took it off her wrist. She kissed it, put it back in the gift box. She opened her locker and saw her album. She opened her photo album, looked at them, her eyes following all the lines and shapes of her beloved. She didn't have anything to do to kill her time and wondered how she would spend the rest of her life.

A piece of soft music came into her mind. She then went to her brother Henry's room. She took his tape recorder and headphone. She selected the songs from the pile of cassettes. Her eyes stuck to the album that Levi used to sing and listen to. She took a rather old album of the 1980s English hard rock band. She had never listened to them but just loved it because it was Levi's favourite. Since then, she became a music lover, a critic, a poet and a songwriter.

The Angel left the Spirit to Sophia. He went to Jesse's house and listened to Dinah's speech. Dinah wiped her tears and said, "Every day I used to say 'God is good all the time'. When God gives me what I take as good things, I praise God and rejoice. I have no right to question why; yes, I have no right to question God. I have to be contented with what God had given me. Everything is given by him and He always thinks the best for me. So, I will say again, God is God all the time." She cried and people held their tears and they all said, "Yes, God is good all the time." She then continued her speech, "Despite such a tragedy befalling upon my family, I am thankful to dear friends, brothers and sisters, who condoled us, who helped us in kind, cash and deed and who prayed for us. I express my deepest love and thank you all for giving us your precious time and the love you shower upon Levi and his family. I wish, let this tragedy never befall any of your family and dear ones. As a human being and as a mother, I cannot take this and accept it.

As we all know Levi was a sincere and obedient boy. He was always cheerful and hardworking. He was intelligent, God-fearing and a peace-loving child. When he was born, I remember, on the day of the Sun festival, I was all alone and did not hear him cry. I was unconscious, completely helpless. Around one and a half hours after my delivery, an old nurse helped us. God restored his life through the old midwife. When he was one year old, my room was on fire, still he was saved by God. When he was seven years old, he again got drowned in water. I was washing clothes near a pond. I did not know how he got drowned in the water. My friend and I searched the pond, soon found him under the water. I prayed to God to restore his life. God always used to answer my prayers.

Even though Levi was a little boy, he loved peace with everyone. At school, he got beaten by his friends for not obeying them to join their gang. They forced him to smoke and drink. He became very sad for his friends. I always told him to ignore them. When he became a big boy, he would question me why I did not want him to go to Broadvale. I explained all the reasons and also warned him not to go to Broadvale. But he was not convinced and would blame me for separating him from his family at Broadvale. He would ask me if I will never forgive them. He used to tell me that he would reunite the Broadvale family and fulfil his father's vision to build a tomb for Grandma Esther in the royal tomb.

What a sweet boy he was! He always got up early in the morning and regularly went to Church. After his daily prayer, he would take bath and study his books. I could never convince him to celebrate his birthday after ten years. He told me to give something in return to his Sunday school teachers instead of spending it on his birthday celebration. So, every year, I used to send gifts to his Sunday school teachers on his birthday. He would mention now and then, the names of his uncles especially Milan when he won in the elections and the lives of his cousins who live in luxury. I didn't want him to grow up envying the luxurious lives of others, so I sent him to Shillong with my parents. Even this morning he asked me if he could go to Broadvale and meet his friend. He mentioned his uncle Milan, saying people praise him for his good deeds in the media. He mentioned his cousin brother Abbin, saying he's a flirt and a spoilt, drunkard boy. He said that he wanted to see Broadvale once before he returned to Shillong. I told him to meet his sister Melody as she was expected to give birth today. Broadvale is in his veins, Broadvale is in his blood, and Broadvale is in his heart and mind. So, God chose Broadvale for his last breath, not that fire or the water that tried to claim his life. So, in the name of my son, I have changed my mind and announce tonight that I forgive everyone in the name of God. I am sorry that sometimes as a parent we fail to understand their passion and the love that our children have. I am sorry, my child."

There was silence, complete silence amid the thousands in the crowd. Everyone felt the pain of a mother. They were shocked to learn about the relations of the Broadvale family. The silence was broken up by Dinah herself when she said the concluding lines of her speech, and they all wiped their tears:

"Levi, my child, please forgive me. I will follow your principle to live in peace with everyone. We will lay your lifeless body in the royal tomb tomorrow and you shall sleep by your Grandma Esther's side. The name Levi shall never pass away from my heart till my last breath. Oh God, I need your Holy Spirit, give me strength, I know you understand the pain of losing a child."

Dinah embraced the cold lifeless body, cried and called her parents while some of the men in charge of it did their duty to lay the dead body inside the coffin to be sealed forever and rest in peace under the sweet care of mother earth. The Spirit had come back from his soul mate Sophia and heard his mother wail. He looked at his dead body. The Angel held him in his hand and said,"Levi, go now, rest in peace. Do return to the earth that gave birth to you."The Spirit said,"I am Shadow. I have to leave them now. I cannot tolerate this cold."The Spirit kissed his parents, touched his uncles and aunties, friends and relatives and left the place. The people felt something in the air surrounding them. The air became suddenly warm and blew at them violently for a minute. Dogs whined and growled, cats cried and sudden clucking of hen terrified women and children. People tirelessly waited for the sunrise in Sunray village. Many great men and leaders from different organizations took their own time for condolence messages the whole night.

The funeral ceremony ended with a speech from the chief of Sunray village. The next morning, they all proceeded towards Broadvale where the royal family mournfully welcomed their martyr and was buried in the royal tomb of Broadvale.

The Angel and the Spirit sat among the clouds and looked at the damn Spirits. The Spirit saw that there were countless other Spirits on the earth who also wailed for their warm body and blood. Some dead bodies were buried, some cremated while some were left to decay like animals. The Spirit loved and prayed for the wailing Spirits. He saw the Spirit of children, innocent men, murderers, accidents and many more different kinds. He sighed, *"If only men on earth could see those sufferings of their Spirits!"* He learnt about the barrier between Spirits and humans. He also noticed that men walk to move forward or backwards while Shadows and Angels do not walk. The Angel told the Spirit to clean him in the divine fire for two days. He touched the eyes of the Spirit and left him. The Spirit opened his eyes and felt no longer cold. He was alone in a world that became hotter and hotter and he wailed again. He had to endure the fire to cleanse him for staying too long outside his blood. He slowly became weak, hungry and thirsty and wailed for the Angel to take him out. There was none, he was all alone.

The Angel went around visiting the dear ones of the spirit of Levi. He saw the women wailing at Broadvale while seven men gun saluting, a tradition as a sign of respect for their royal son. Thousands of men gathered in Broadvale, all hearts burdened with the sad thoughts of their land and people. The day 22nd July was a lovely day for many people. Yet it turned into a dark gloomy day of mourning for some people. Levi's friends and teachers at his college who were shocked at the news announced by the principal, observed two-minute silence in honour of the departed soul. His school at Sunray too observed two-minute silence in honour of their brilliant alumnus who had been the topper in the school from his childhood. His family and friends at Shillong missed him very much. His grandparents in Shillong mourned the loss. They left home for Broadvale to console Dinah and Jesse. People loved him so much that they said to one another, that the Angels too would wail upon the demise of such a good boy from a good parent. His friend, Henry wrote a poem about him which read it out to Levi's family and the guests, the next day at the burial ceremony.

Sad are the songs we sing

Ah strange a thing

Fasten thee to the valley gloom

Ne'er to bloom

Until comes the last trump

Then seraphim's hum

To the shore of land unseen

Thou drifted apace

While thee youth cheerily hath been

Miles of smiles face

Thee in haste swiftly shift

By nature's will

To one any eternal joy or grief

Where time stands still

Go tears and heart to lament

For our dear departed

Tears we send to where thee went

To tryst with fate:

Mournful are the hearts that pours

Tales of ere days

Under the divine Sun where youth soars

And rend wild ways

Rose in the garden of friendship!

But not until noon

An hour came: adieu from our lips

For parted we soon

Reposed, quietly reposed

In the deep realm of peace

A yard of grasses and mosses

Everything worldly missed!

Sad are the songs we sing

Painful is the boon that sting

Ah! For the moon, the stars above

Dim and shaken

Deep hearts called thee long love!

Fresh awaken

O mighty divine!

Life and death in thy breast

Lull this friend of the earth,

Gently rest in thy arms

Console the hearts of dear ones.

Fill the vacant of loss with divine solace.

Rolan promised Jesse and Dinah that he would build a tomb for Ron, Esther and Levi such that the tomb would attract even tourists so that people would tell the story of Broadvale far and wide. However, Jesse and Dinah did not take the offer of their birthright even though they had forgiven them. When Milan asked about their wish, they told them that they wanted to visit the Holy land of Jerusalem before they died. They also told them that they would devote their lives to missionary work.

CHAPTER - 29

THE MESSAGE OF WAILING ANGELS

After two days the Angel went back to the Spirit and saw him wailing in the fire. The Angel wiped the silvery tears of the Spirit and said, "Oh Saint, if you show your face to your loved ones, you will render their life to suffer. Behold, men should not see the face of unearthly beings, else they will die young. I will not be able to accompany you to the next gate if you are unclean again." The Angel consoled the Spirit and continued, "Oh Saint, Shadow of my good man, before Levi was born, we had planned and prepared everything. He was destined to live a hundred years, bear all the cruel sufferings and pains because of the curse on his forefathers; you and the body, we are born of the blood of Broadvale's eldest son Jesse. When I heard the name of the body soon after his birth, I left you with the body to prepare the world according to his deeds. We desired that he die young because he was too precious, like our diamond, to struggle life with the reserve punishment. Jesse and Dinah are good parents, both born of good parents. This humble man must be given a reward instead of punishment because of his forefathers. Oh, those cruel forefathers of Ron, they humiliated and killed our Holy men, defiled the temple, burnt the Holy Book to ashes. Those cruel creatures raped women and children and killed the innocents. They ate and drank and worshipped idols.

We want to put you in an honourable place. Let us not delay our time. When we reach the new world, you will be a Saint and Angel: There is no hunger, no more thirst or suffering. You will be just like me. You have served our purpose well, now it's time for you to take rest in peace."

The Angel lulled the Spirit and sang a very sweet song. The Spirit felt tired, hungry and thirsty. But he asked the Angel what would happen if he slept. The Angel said, "You will sleep and forget everything, the pain, the solitude, the hot, the cold, the memories, the hunger and thirst, your family, your dear ones, everything." The Spirit asked again, "And then what will happen to me?"

The Angel said, "The moment you open your eyes you will be among the Saints."

The Spirit becomes more and more curious. He said, "I am worried about my family; if I can tell them how much I suffer! If I can tell them about life after death!"

The Angel said, "Why don't we proceed to the next gate, you have endured enough cold and fire, more than enough. Now you are tired, hungry and thirsty, I cannot let you suffer anymore."

The Spirit said, "Where are my cruel forefathers on behalf of whom I got the punishment?"

The Angel: Shadow of my goodman, your cruel forefather's sin made Angels wail. The cry and curse of our Holy men made them unclaimed Spirits. They may be born in another part of the world as an animal or human and suffer. We don't bother those cruel heartless men or their Spirits. We bother for the Saints like you, who can still endure pain to know more about the heavenly things. You are a Saint.

Spirit: But, oh Angel, I never heard anyone calling me Saint, I am not worthy to be a Saint, am I?

Angel: Oh Shadow of my Holy man, Saint, here it doesn't particularly refer to the earthly Saints who wear a white dress to cover their body and their hearts are wicked and dirty. It rather means a man born of a righteous man, a man whose heart is not polluted by the worldly pleasures, a heart that is filled with righteousness and had a connection with God but lost their life because of someone else's sin and curse.

Spirit: I love the earth: I love my people and want to have a look for some more time. If I can do something for men, I will come happily to the next gate.

Angel: There is no place for us on this earth. This world is full of sins and the earth is unclean with the blood of cruel men. We should not step on the unclean place nor touch them.

Spirit: I want to visit the Holy places before I leave, I will endure all the pain.

The Angel and the Spirit flew away from one Holy place to another place, the places where Holy bodies were buried or lived. Angels watching the Holy places were happy about their visit. They also visited the Holy place where Levi's blood was mixed with the soil. The Angel had proclaimed that a part of their land would be a Holy place for pilgrimage for the other Angels who guarded each Holy land. They also visited other Holy places where men worshipped their own Gods with all their hearts. They visited mountains and seas, the Spirit saw earthling Saints in deep meditation. They served the Saints for some time in different ways. They stood on the highest point of the world and looked at the wonderful nature for the last time as Shadow. They started climbing a stairway to heaven. The Spirit looked back and saw the miseries of the world. He was not happy because he could not help them in any way. As he climbed the stair, he heard the wail of some people. He becomes curious as to where he was heading. He walked faster despite his hunger, again heard the wail more clearly. As he proceeded nearer, he heard the wail, a numberless wail, a finite wail of some creatures, because he knew no men ever wailed that wail. He imagined that such a wail would be more painful than the cry of a motherless newborn baby, it was more horrible than the howling of wolves in the jungle. The Spirit at once enquired about what the wail was. The Angel did not respond to him. The Spirit stopped climbing the stair and demanded the Angel to tell him about the wail of those unseen people. The Angel sighed, then began to wail just like them. The Spirit became very anxious and restless on his way to the next world. He repeatedly told him to stop wailing instead explain what was going on. The Angel wiped his tears, then put the Spirit on his lap. He then sang a very sad song which made the Spirit even sadder. He told the Spirit to close his eyes to be able to understand the language of the Angels and interpret the meaning of the song. The Spirit slowly closed his eyes, began listening to the songs with his heart all open for it. Soon he could comprehend what the Angel meant in his sad song.

Angel: Oh Shadow! There was a time when the atmosphere was clean, trees were green, water clear as the sky and men were innocent. They praised their creator, sought the blessing of nature through love and care. The earth was a Holy place for the Angels. We lived together in peace. But what happened to our men of this generation, who don't value the beauty of nature. Men learn the forbidden law and go against the rule of nature. They steal the treasure box of power from the Angels, not for their goodwill but to destroy nature. They forget that they are part of nature, that they are the society. They used the power to challenge the creator, and forget about the Angels. They worship what comes to their mind and defile worship places. They ruin their hearts with greed, lust and wealth.

Despite God's love for them, men forget that being ignorant is a great blessing. God promised not to destroy the human race for He loves His children very much. Men climb the ladder of progress, they become more and more wicked, greedy, unclean while jealousy crept into their minds. They created many differences among themselves, in the name of that, they killed one another. They humiliated our Holy man and killed them. They torture our good men and defile Holy places. Oh, how many unborn Spirits have suffered due to their lust, how many young Spirits suffered due to their wicked mind? If only they can see the Spirits of those soldiers who lost their lives on the battlefields. We value their lives. Their blood is precious. Those innocent people who are killed in the name of their God or their nation, the world is filled with the cries of those helpless Spirits who want to live and enjoy their lives. They suffer in the intense cold longing for their warm blood. Mortal men pollute their blood with the pleasures, fooled themselves through the power of drugs and defile my temple with the herbs we bless for their healing. They trod on the path of destruction. They celebrate their lives by drinking the wine of our lower creatures. They worship God to hold high their heads with no true peace. They embrace evil and shunned righteousness.

We preach to them in all possible ways, they see it in their own eyes, they hear it in their ears but their hearts are not open for us. It is incomprehensible for men to realize our message when their minds are preoccupied with their physical needs and their hearts are filled with worldly pleasures. Angels, who are preparing for their next world, found nothing worthy of praise. We do not want to record all the evil acts men had done upon themselves. Unable to bear the agony, those sweet Angels throw away their golden robes and diamond jewels. Men are bound to suffer and inherit the next world with the reserve punishment. We cannot bear the agony to see them suffer in the bottomless pit. These sweet Angels, who watch the life of each man, pray to our creator, together wailing for the goodwill of men. It is their wailing, oh Shadow of my Goodman, doesn't it echo from horizon to horizon? They are **The Wailing Angels**.

Spirit: Angel, why did not I hear of such a pathetic wail when I was a human being? Why are men not able to hear such wailing?

Angel: Human beings: Their hearts are hardened, fully attracted to worldly pleasures and greediness. They had to think for their survival. They think for wealth and fame too much that there is no vacant path for the Wailing Angels to enter and dwell inside mortal men. They dominate the love of God not trying to cultivate it among themselves. If they hear even a little bit, they will inherit the blessed land, a heaven on earth. But oh Shadow of my Goodman, if men meditate without any worldly desires seek the truth, stand for ages like the tree, they will be able to hear and understand the wail.

Spirit: If I could have a rebirth, will I be able to hear their wailing?

Angel: If you are granted the rebirth, your blank mind will be trained to receive the worldly pleasures, you would be taught from your childhood how to become like others in the pursuit of knowledge, wealth and fame like your fellow human beings. There are laws in the society, rules in your family, promises between you and your conscience that will wipe away the wail of the Wailing Angels giving no chance to penetrate your heart. You will not know anything about what you hear and see now. Even if you try to seek the truth and God, your people will disown you, your fellow beings will keep you out of society. They won't believe in you. I will tell you the story of one of my fellow Angels. He was the man for whom the other Angels wailed upon his tragedy during his lifetime. That Angel, when he was a human, was one of the sons of a powerful king. The king had seven wives all from the royal family except the last wife who was the daughter of the king's chief servant. The last wife was the first to give birth to a son. Later the other wives also gave birth to sons. His brothers hatched a plan to grab hold of the kingdom and his birthright. They had tortured him from his childhood but could not just kill him. The man who never raised his hand against anyone was considered meek and timid, unworthy to be a ruler. When their king died, they hatched a plan to eliminate the whole family. When he was away for the Holy pilgrimage, they killed his mother, wife and daughter. He was tortured and threatened by his brothers. He left the palace and meditated in the deep jungle to seek God. The Angels tested his faith and said:

Angel: Oh mortal man, why do you seek God when you have nothing?

Mortal man: I have always sought God from my childhood. God is my refuge, God is my strength, God is the beginning and the end. God is more important than my family and people.

Angel: If you seek God first you have to make peace with men. Peace is the key to finding God.

Mortal man: I have no enemy; they all love me. They just want material things and power. I have given them.

Angel: Go and preach to your family to be Godly. Then only you will be given the key to the golden path and I shall dwell in your heart.

Mortal man: They will not believe me.

The mortal man went back to his people. People were afraid of his dirty, long hair. He wore no clothes to cover his body. He staggered in the streets preaching to them to love one another and live in peace. At first, people ran away from him. After some days, the people held him and decided to stone him to death. They stoned him, beat him black and blue. The Angels could not stand to see him suffer and so they shielded him. That mortal man felt no pain. He shouted at the mob saying, "Stop that barbaric act; you all are throwing the stones at the

Angels." Still, they thought him to be an insane. They left him half-dead on the spot. The next day they threw him into a river. The Angels in the water took care of him and he was taken to an island. There he meditated and lived with the Angels. Behold, oh Shadow of my good man, that mortal man attained salvation when he sacrificed his life for the cause of God. Once our true mortal man sacrificed his life, all the tortures and sufferings in the eye of humans were borne by the Angels. Their body was the body of the Angel too. Their blood was Holy and precious. Anyone who tortured a Saint was taken as blasphemous.

The Spirit realized that human beings would hear the wailing of the Angels when their Spirit separated from their blood. The Spirit lamented for human beings and wished he could do something to tell them such an important hidden message. He wanted to have a rebirth. So asked the Angel again if he could grant his wish.

Angel: I am happy to see your perseverance. You are truly a Saint. You have endured intense cold, fire and hunger and thirst. Don't you want to leave this place and rest in peace among the Saints? Why do you bother for those wicked men? Why do you love the world so much? We have sent many Spirits before you with this mission but once they are human beings, their minds are polluted from their childhood for material pursuit; there is no room for the Angels to dwell. Let's proceed to the next world.

Spirit: Tell me the way to have my wish and bless me to do the mission. I am ready to suffer to any extent to have my wish. But make sure that I am on the mission and Angels to pave the way to accomplish my mission.

Angel: Close your eyes and talk with the Wailing Angels if you are ready to suffer the test.

The Spirit closed his eyes, meditated calling the Wailing Angels, the Angels to talk to him from his heart of hearts. He heard the wailing from different directions but he kept calm and called the Wailing Angels unceasingly. He never opened his eyes. The Spirit called, prayed to them, praying thousands and thousands of times. The wailing became very loud which after some time it gradually stopped. The Angels asked him questions to test his faith.

Wailing Angels: Shadow of my strong man, tell me, are you ready to stand in the fire for 77 days? Are you ready to suffer an intense cold for another 77 days? Are you ready to suffer the pain of the highest degree for 77 days? Are you ready to bear hunger and thirst for 77 days after that?

Are you ready to separate from your mother from your childhood? Can you control your thirst for love for the most beautiful woman your eyes will ever see? Can you resist your hand from wine and intoxicants when you are thirsty to the highest degree?

The Wailing Angels tested the faith of the Spirit and they were happy that at least one Spirit out of countless numbers could pass the test. After all the tests were done, the Spirit heard the clapping of a thousand hands. The Angel told him to open his eyes. The Spirit saw the golden path that was laid in front of him. He asked him to tread on the path to choosing his life of rebirth. The Spirit trod immediate on the first path. The Angel praised him for the prompt action and said, "I am happy that you are too eager to take your next journey on earth, your decision obviously tells that you don't choose to test the other different lives though you are given the choice." The Angel and the Spirit followed the first golden path. The Spirit was so happy that he forgot his hunger and thirst. The Angel told the Spirit the secrets of heaven, the things hidden for a mortal man. The Spirit rejoiced all along the golden path. They reached a gate where he was not allowed to enter. The Angel showed the garden of heaven and the Saints. The Spirit looked at them from a distance. They stood at the gate and saw delicious foods served on big tables, a table that had no edge. He saw the Saints and Angels enjoying and singing. They were happily eating, dancing like innocent children. The Spirit asked the Angel: When many Angels were wailing, how could these Angels sing and dance?

Angel: They are Saints. They will enjoy it as long as they like and that's just the beginning. There are still places, unexplored places for you, forbidden to be known right now. They are Angels too. If you don't choose to go back to earth, you too will enjoy it there and rejoice with them.

Spirit: Can I eat and drink to my heart's content before I am back to the earth as I am very hungry?

Angel: You can have it if you wish, oh Shadow of my good man: Angels will come and take us to another world. Just close your eyes again.

The Spirit closed his eyes, then opened them again when he was told to. He found himself seated on the most comfortable chair ever in his life or after. There were hundreds of delicious foods served in front of him. There were fruits, juices and the best bread he ever had. He looked around and saw hundreds of Angels dining together with him. The aroma of the food and the sweet fragrance of flowers filling the place made the food more appetizing. The Angel comforter told him to eat to his heart's content. The Spirit looked at the food then cried out saying, "I cannot eat this food, I have to go back fast to accomplish my mission." The Spirit could not have the food when he was thinking about mortal men and the Wailing Angels. The Angels fed the Spirit milk and honey. The Angel also fed the Spirit bread and gave him grape wine. The Spirit wiped his tears to have food so tasty after months of the pangs of hunger and thirst. The Angel comforter sang a melodious song and fed the Spirit to his heart's content. The sweet song and music were so lively that the Angels told the Spirit to sing and dance as he liked. The Spirit lamented for human beings and said, "When your heart is happy, you can sing and dance. I am worried about what will happen when I am back on the earth; will my people believe me?"

The Angels were pleased to hear his words. They praised the Spirit, they all said that he must be sent back to earth to live in comfort in the most respected family so that people would believe his words. The Angel comforter looked down at the earth and said:

"Oh my beloved human, why do you let these thousand sweet Angels wail all these ages? Why have you turned the world dark from the bright light? Why have you turned the rivers and mighty oceans deep red just to quench your single thirst? Why don't you love one another as we love you all? Why are you enjoying life without thinking about your life after death? How long can you stand on your own feet? Wherefrom do you derive such wisdom if God had not bestowed it upon you? Do you think you can perform miracles; tell me, can you block the path of thunder and change the direction of lightning? Can you mould man in your image and breathe the divine air? Can you discover the language of your heart? Can you tell what language the Angels use? You can count the countable, why cannot you count the infinite? Who made those infinite things? Can you tell me how I accompany your Spirits in the womb? Can you tell me how many hairs we numbered in your head alone? Can you tell me at what time your bodies grow? Can you measure how big the wonderful stars are? Can you tell me what happens to your Spirit when you sleep? Can you tell me where your dreams come from? Can you catch and hold Shadows? Can you tell me the way to heaven? Can you tell me who takes care of your babies inside the womb? Can you say to whom the baby smiles? Can you tell how the earth spins without support?

O, damn, man! Don't you hear this wailing, didn't it echo from horizon to horizon? Why do you create differences among yourself and kill one another? How dare you raise your hands against our Holy man? Don't you know that they are Angels on earth? How dare you claim yourself superior and suppress the weak, don't you know you are hurting their Angels? How could you quote the words from sacred books with your hearts defiled by jealousy, greed, pride and hatred? O, hypocrites! Do not pray to show others that you can do it. Do not pray to show off your knowledge and sugarcoat. Do not pray to move others' hearts by weeping and speaking loudly. Why don't you have a true connection with God by your words and deeds? Why do you worship God for position and gain worldly power? The benefits that you draw in the name of God, your nepotism, the Angels count your greedy thoughts, fake smiles, lies, destructive authority, injustice and all sorts of evils you derived through such power, the Angels count your steps, remember. Oh my beloved human, do you know that the water in the vast ocean is incomparable to the tears of the Wailing Angels? You will repent the moment you step into the cold dark world. Purify your hearts and make peace with your enemies, your father's enemy and your mother's enemy too. If you do not follow the laws of your religion, how will you find peace? If religion does not mean you love one another, how will you find God? The heaviest part of your body is the place all evils start; so, fill it with love. Do good things, do not revenge an insult, never revenge blood for blood, an eye for an eye. Do not let your heart hurt nor hurt others' heart; it is a sacred place in the body where God dwells."

CHAPTER - 30

THE REINCARNATED SPIRIT

The Angel lulled the Spirit until he put him to deep sleep. The Angel held out his hand and touched the Spirit from head to toe. He then muttered in the Angels' language, prophesying over the second life which the Spirit was destined to meet.

"You shall be the man who will be the divine light of life. You shall be called the blessed man for you inherit both the treasure of the earth and heaven. You shall be the man who will preach the wail of the Wailing Angels. You shall be the divine Prince of Peace. You shall be the Holy man whose hands will mould a thousand dismayed hearts. You shall travel millions and millions of miles across the seas and oceans in the hearts of laymen as well as nobles. Your image shall be erected, for men will love you and respect you. Men will worship your Holy words and the words will dwell in their hearts: Your words will be immortal. You will find salvation in the deep woods. You will live your life far away from human dwellings.

Your words shall travel across the ocean and mountains. Your statue shall be erected by your followers. People will admire your wisdom, your words shall be written down in the history of mankind. You will be a living legend, a legend and immortal. You will beget a son who will succeed on your father's throne. But the day will come when your statue shall be destroyed, that will make your words travel faster and spread farther more. You will be praised for ages and ages to come, by peace lovers. You will be the wonder for such a nation who raises their hands against you. You shall be written down in the history as the immortal Prince of Peace.

I shall remember you and bless your disciples. They shall sacrifice their families to take your instructions as a duty. They will abstain from wine and unclean foods. They will abstain from lust and adultery. They will live far away from human habitation. They shall seek God in the serene deep dark woods and follow non-violence. I shall remember you and feed them with the divine bread. Among your devotees, a woman shall weep before your statue. I will remember you and answer her prayers. That woman shall conceive a child and I and you shall be in her womb. You shall be reborn again and again to accomplish the unfulfilled task in your previous births. You shall also see with your own eyes, the statue of yourself destroyed and collapse. You shall put the pieces of the destroyed image and remould the shape, shape it bigger, stronger and taller. You shall be called the true Soldier of God. The world will love you and respect you. You shall devote your life caring for the fatherless, nursing for the motherless, sacrificing for the parentless. You shall be called the Mother of all Nations. You will be loved by all children. You will be called mother by the motherless. You shall live long but unwed. You shall teach your people to love and care in action. You shall be written down in history and become immortal in millions of hearts. You shall have numberless disciples who will all follow in your footsteps. They will be unwed abstaining from all sorts of worldly pleasure and materialism. Their eyes shall give confidence, their dress shall show their sanctity, and their mouth shall be like a honeycomb. Their hands shall hold the sword of peace and justice. We will remember you and dwell in their hearts. Whoever raises hands on those beautiful souls shall meet with the worst curse of the Wailing Angels. Cruel and barbaric men will become like a beast, their evil eyes will plan to quench their thirst and defile my temple mercilessly. I shall revenge on those evil minds that outrage the modesty of my sincere soldiers.

The time will come after your second rebirth when men will suffer on earth. They will see mysteries from heaven. They will suffer hunger and thirst. They will fight and kill one another to survive. There will be epidemics, diseases and disasters. They will fight with the rain and the Sun. They will fight with the birds and animals. They will fight with air and water. They will fight for their progress. There will be no more respect for the old, no more love for the young. Men will marry and eat and drink without love. They will kill the newborn as well as the unborn without mercy. They will play with marriage. Men will marry the beauty of women while women will marry the wealth of men. There will be no more love, no more respect for our soldiers. My soldiers will be tortured, my Holy places demolished. That time I will send you, oh my trusted Saint, but you shall rule those cruel men with your power and order. I will bestow you with supernatural power to destroy the cruel men. You shall rule with authority as emperor on the earth, and spare none who disobey your orders."

After prophesying, the Angel put a mark on the body of the Spirit: that mark which humans called a mole but unusually bigger with hairs covering it as a birthmark of reincarnation. The Angel shouted at the top of his voice which struck the sense of a baby inside the womb of the blessed Queen. The screech of the Angel turned the Spirit to regain consciousness and found himself once again comfortably warmed in blood. The Angel counted the Moon and the Sun to complete the stage of moulding his Spirit. Being eager to see light and sometimes feeling congested, the innocent Spirit struggled, kicked and moved as if playing excitedly with the Angel. During those moments, the Angel and the Spirit would hear the scream, seldom a soft cry of a young lady whose voice was very sweet. How they wished to see the face of the blessed woman and hear her sweet voice! They heard the sweet voice of the blessed woman singing a melodious song praising God, reading the Holy books and solving puzzles for the development of her baby's brain. She recited hymns, poetry and sang daily. She played music, meditated daily for the well-being of the unborn baby. Her maidservants gave her all the good foods and drinks to nourish her body. They were all excited, eager to see their first baby. The Angel caressed the Spirit, hugged him tightly as the day for their parting drew nearer. The day for their separation came at last, for the Angel to see the new faces of his family and the vast blue sky. The Angel heard the scream, the wail of a young woman. Very soon he again heard the exclamations, spoken around him, "Our next king!" "Wow, the Angel Prince!" "Yes, a handsome son of the mighty ruler!" The Angel smiled, was ecstatic compared to the previous exclamation, "Come on, don't give up, push harder, the baby's head is out of the door." He knew that he was now a human being. How he wished to trod on the divine mother earth and meet his fellow Angels! Soon after, he heard the commandments as if a commanding voice of which one can imagine about his long whiskers, broad shoulder and the mark of the highest rank on his head. The voice commanded,

"Every house of this kingdom shall light a lamp to welcome the baby Prince who will be the light of not only this kingdom but to the whole world. Give alms to the poor and widows, and arrange a feast to celebrate my fatherhood." The Angel being anxious to see the new faces, opened his eyes. First, the Angel saw the roof of the royal palace beautifully carved by the great architects, pictures of multi-colour decorations on the wall. He looks around, saw the happy faces of beautiful ladies dressed in embroidered satin and with lace veils on their heads. As they come to see the baby, he was pleased to hear their graceful footsteps with their bangles jingling as they giggly danced in joy. He loved the soft human touch; he felt the soft human kiss and was happy to suck the breastmilk of the blessed woman. On the third day, when the baby's umbilical cord healed, the birth of the royal Prince was celebrated with great pomp and show. As the day for his naming dawn, with the royal rituals, the royal ladies bathed him in milk and massaged him with virgin olive oil. They cut his nails and wrapped him in white cotton clothes. The royal priest and his followers along with the royal family, sang and danced praising God. After all the rituals were done, the eldest of the family, his grandpa, christened him by saying, "Our son is a blessing from the Almighty. We have fought battles and won over our enemies. We have fallen and risen again. We have lost many lives yet we won the victory. In all these situations the Almighty is with us. I want this grandson of mine to live in peace, never face the hardships and struggles of life. I want him to enjoy life to the fullest in this royal palace. His name shall be called ROYALBLISS which means Prince of Peace."

CHAPTER - 31

THE RETURN OF SR. MARIA

As soon as the Angel heard the name of the baby, he came out from the body leaving behind the Spirit. The Spirit cried for days and nights feeling empty and lonely. The Angel heard the wail of the baby and was hurt very much. The Angel said, "I cannot come back, oh Spirit, I cannot defile the temple and be named the Evil Angel. I must look after you from outside your body. You are a human and I am Angel. You shall be human as long as you stay in the blood. I am always near you, a place restricted to be unfolded in the minds of humans, so you can never see me. You will feel my presence the moment you seek me with love and truth, in a clean mind and clean body. I need to take a Holy bath to clean myself for mingling with humans. I will now go for my Holy pilgrimage and come back to you shortly." Before he went to the Holy bath, he wanted to spend some more time visiting the Holy places, after which he would soar high up the sky to that unnamed kingdom, to that hidden realm of peace, where the Angels would ask him if he was clean. The Angel would tell them, "I undertook a pilgrimage to the Holy places and had a Holy bath in the Sacred Trinity River." The Angels would then give him the Golden robe and Diamond jewel, then anoint him with the Holy oil for accomplishing his task. The Angel remembered the Spirit who once wailed in the intense cold for his warm blood. So decided to start his Holy pilgrimage from Levi's blood and body. He went to the spot where the blood was mixed with the soil. Grasses had grown all over the place. He then went to the place where his body was laid. As he went to Broadvale royal reserve land, he was pleased to see the magnificent tomb of Levi next to the tombs of Ron and Esther. The tomb was not big but it was polished with gold. He saw dozens of young men and women decorating the place, arranging seats as if it was the day of the dedication of the tomb. He heard two people talking about the tomb saying, "These tombs are the best I have ever seen in my life. It is built by Disha, Rolan and Milan. Each of the tombs is 30x40 square feet and the height is 30 ft each. Inside the tomb is the statue of each dead person, which looks exactly like them. I was taken aback the first time I saw the statues surrounded by a mirror mirage where you can see the statue from 12 different angles. The statues are carved with white marble by a foreign sculptor. The common garden outside is ten thousand square feet." He watched five young men fitting the microphones and commenting on the beauty of the tomb. At the exit gate of the cemetery, the Angel saw pretty girls arranging sweets, food and drinks for thousands of people. Then the Angel saw dozens of vehicles coming towards the tomb. He saw the Broadvale royal family coming to unveil the tomb. The Angel was pleased to see Dinah once again revived. God had blessed her with twin sons who looked exactly like Levi. The Angel wanted to touch the sweet babies but then he would be unclean if he did so. He just watched the people, especially Jesse and Dinah. Then he saw hundreds of vehicles coming towards the tomb. Thousands of people had gathered in the cemetery in no time. They started the programme with an invocation from the Priest. The Archbishop of the Province dedicated the three tombs followed by short speeches from elders of the Broadvale royal family. Disha said in her speech, "I am blessed to have a lovely family and good people. I was high handed and jealousy had once crept into my mind. I had scattered the family, especially the loving siblings far and wide. My daughter Maria requested me to build a tomb for Ron and Esther. She left Broadvale and became a nun. She said that she will not come back to Broadvale until I build the tomb for the soul mate couple, Ron and Esther. I hope she will come home now, my Maria, my only daughter. For many years I had been thinking of doing this good thing but I couldn't convince my stubborn heart. But this sweet son of Broadvale, Levi came to me that morning, before he died. He talked to me like an Angel. He touched my feet and called me lovingly **'Grandma'**. I took him to Rolan and Reenarose. He gave his respects and greeted them **'Uncle'** and **'Aunty'**. He told us that he wanted to lead a happy life with his uncles and cousins. This son of

Broadvale moved my heart. But after a few hours, I heard that he had died from gunshots, by stray bullets. Dear children, let us forget the past and count our blessings from God."

Jesse gave a rather long speech telling his life story, also about Levi's life history. The Angel listened to him attentively and was contented at his concluding lines when he said, "As a father, it was hard for me to accept the death of my only son. I didn't want any wealth or fame or any more love. I was exhausted with life. I joined the Holy trip to Jerusalem with Dinah. We went there and met Uncle Benjamin too. The moment I dipped my body in the Holy water, I experienced a miracle, a divine solace, and I have peace of mind. God spoke to me in the waters and said, 'Take your wife now and make love, for I have greater blessings for you that you might never imagine.' I came out of the water and felt that I have become younger, stronger, and healthier and was thinking of myself as if I was never a married man. Dinah too came out of the water. She was like an Angel. I had never seen such beauty in Dinah before. I say this because it's a miracle, a solace from above. We prayed together to claim the blessing. When I saw the twin babies, I was taken aback and wondered how these twins look exactly like their deceased elder brother Levi. Indeed, God is great. God truly understands the pain of losing a child. I count my blessings and indeed I feel that am not even worthy to be a servant of God my whole life if I were to repay what God had done to me and my family." Before

Jesse finished his speech, they heard a strange sound. The sound came nearer, louder and people got tense. Soon they looked up at the sky and saw a helicopter. The helicopter stopped a mile away from the royal tomb. Five ladies all dressed in white from head to foot came out of the helicopter. People looked forward to them as to who might be those ladies coming by helicopter. Disha, Rolan and Reenarose stood up, then all of a sudden Disha shouted, "It's sister Maria, Maria is back, my baby is coming home." Milan's Security guards went to pick up them in the bulletproof Gipsy. Soon, Maria too arrived at the spot and turned a day of mourning into a happy day. The once charming innocent girl was now an austerely beautiful nun, a rape victim who struggled to spend her golden life in the nunnery traumatized by the evil eyes of men. The illegitimate daughter unclaimed by her brothers had now risen, grown up into a mother figure, full of respect and power in her words. Her followers called her 'sister' while children called her 'mother' for the love and care she showered on them and her dedication to humanity. They hugged one after another with tears in their eyes yet a sweet smile on their lips. Jesse hugged Maria and said, "I am proud of you, Maria; today you are the sister of all men and children. God bless you." Maria saw her brother from her biological father Mr. Doon who was standing near her too shy to talk to her. Maria knew them and replied to Jesse while her eyes focused at her other biological brothers. She said, "Thank you, brother Jesse, for everything. You are my true brother. Family is not about blood; it is about who is willing to hold your hand when you need it most." She then went and sat near Dinah. Dinah smiled at her and asked her a favour to bless the babies. Maria took the twin babies and asked, "What are their names, sister Dinah?" Dinah answered, "The elder one is named Broad and the younger one is Vale. They are the future of Broadvale." Maria took the elder baby, Broad and kissed his chubby cheeks. She then said, "He is a blessing to our family, his name is Broad Bliss and Vale's other name will be Vale Peace; he will keep peace in Broadvale." The families reunited after two years of Levi's death and after 25 years of Levi's birth.

THE END